THE
LAST
LAP

THE
LAST
LAP

CHRISTY HAYES

The Last Lap
By Christy Hayes
Text Copyright © Christy Hayes
All Right Reserved

Paperback ISBN 978-1-62572-028-3

Book Cover Design by The Killion Group, Inc.
Proofread by PBProofreads
Formatting by

emtippettsbookdesigns.com

Other Romance & Women's Fiction Titles by
CHRISTY HAYES

Golden Rule Outfitters Series:

Mending the Line, Book 1

Guiding the Fall, Book 2

Taming the Moguls, Book 3

Connected to GRO Series:

Dodge the Bullet

Shoe Strings

Kiss & Tell Series: Clean New Adult Romance

Stalling for Time, Book 1

The End Run, Book 2

Kiss & Makeup, Novella 3

Maybe it's You, Book 4

Formula for a Perfect Life, Book 5

Fancy Meeting You Here, Book 6

Connected Romance:

Heart of Glass

The Sweetheart Hoax

Single Title:

Angle of Incidence

Misconception

The Accidental Encore

Short Story:

Good Luck, Bad Timing & When Harry Met Sally

Non-Fiction:

The Power of Faith When Tragedy Strikes, A Father-Son Memoir
by Chris and Terry Norton

Other Romance & Women's Fiction Titles by
CHRISTY HAYES

One

Megan Holloway could sell a fifty-cent snow globe to a traveling fool, but she couldn't sell a peanut butter and jelly sandwich to her twelve-year-old niece.

"I'm not eating it." Lily placed her hands onto slender hips with a pleading look in her blue-gray eyes. "Everybody buys their lunch, Aunt Meg. Only babies eat peanut butter and jelly."

And only silly spendthrifts threw money away on mystery meat and soggy sides. Megan Holloway was a lot of things. Frugal, sure. These days she had to cut corners. A hot head, occasionally. Her red hair served as a warning and a testament to her short-fuse temper. Stubborn, when push came to shove. Lately, with Lily's mama dead and raising Lily all alone, there'd been nothing but shove. But spendthrift, not in her lifetime.

"We've been through this, Lily. We can't afford any extra expenses right now. If you bought lunch every day, that's seventeen dollars and fifty cents per week. For that price, I could buy enough bread, peanut butter, and jelly to feed everyone in your class."

The expression on Lily's face said she knew she was fighting a losing battle, but she wasn't ready to give up. "I'm not taking that to school."

"I wish things were different." Meg softened her voice but continued to make the sandwich. Wanting what they couldn't afford was a waste of time. "But it's PB&J or it's nothing."

"Then it's nothing."

Meg knew what it was like to want to be like everyone else. But they weren't like everyone else. They never had been. If Lily wouldn't listen to reason, Meg had to try a different tack. "That's up to you, but you're going to have a hard time passing your science test on an empty stomach."

Like all preteens testing the waters, Lily could be snarky, smarmy, and as salty as the south Florida humidity wafting by on the ocean breeze, but the smarty pants still cared about her grades. Megan thanked God for small favors. At this point, small favors were all she could afford.

"You eat it." Lily lifted her nose, as determined as her mother to get the last word.

Megan had twenty-eight years of experience fighting the last word battle. "Honey, what do you think I eat for lunch every day? Filet mignon?"

"I don't even know what that is, but it sounds better than baby food on stale bread."

Thanks to Amanda, Meg remembered how much baby food cost. Meg remembered how she and her sister worked their fingers to the bone to pay for mashed carrots and puréed pears. Lily was too young to remember all the scrimping and saving they'd done to raise her. She was too young to realize with her mama gone, Meg was struggling to keep a roof over their heads and food in their bellies.

"I don't have time to argue." Meg smashed the pieces of bread together and tucked them into a baggie. "Go brush your teeth and find your shoes before the bus comes."

Lily huffed, flicking her blonde hair over her shoulder before prancing down the hallway to her new bedroom.

Amanda's death left a gaping hole in their lives. The smaller apartment was one of many changes they'd made since Amanda died. Parenting Lily alone was the hardest, but so was tightening the purse strings of an already snug purse and working ten-hour days to fill her sister's missing shoes. Something had to give and give soon, or Meg was going to lose control of her niece, her mind, and her business—and not necessarily in that order.

Lily could no longer deny her mother was gone, but she seemed to have stalled in the anger stage—and Meg was her favorite target. Meg did her best to take it—the sass and the attitude—as her penance for not doing more to stop her sister from being so foolish.

Lily looked so much like her mother. Budding like a flower ready to burst, her beauty hidden inside the folds of lanky legs and wide-set features. Before long, Lily would have more than science tests and school lunch to worry about. Before long, Meg would need a whole new skillset to keep the boys at bay.

Amanda learned the hard way what attention from boys could bring. Pregnant at eighteen by her good-for-nothing boyfriend who took off before Lily was born, Amanda had paid the price for her carelessness. She paid the price in spades.

Meg had thought her big sister a fool. By the time her belly grew so big she couldn't hide the bump, she was out of options and out of luck. And then Lily was born, and they were too busy to think of anything at all. Survival became the name of the game.

After more than a decade of scraping by, they found their footing and were eking out a life. Until another good-looking, good-for-nothing guy caught Amanda's eye and she paid the ultimate price for her horrible taste in men. Determined to do right by Lily, Meg fought tooth and nail to provide for her niece while working too many hours trying to keep their gift store afloat.

She placed the sandwich, some carrot sticks, and a snack treat into a brown paper bag and put the bag inside Lily's backpack. Like it or not, Lily was having peanut butter and jelly—and so was Meg.

Lily stomped into the kitchen, reaching for her backpack as she marched toward the door.

Meg considered letting her go without another word, but since losing Amanda, Meg would never let another loved one walk away again mad. "You forgetting something?"

"I told you I'm not taking that sandwich."

Meg walked to the door, held her arms out for a hug. She watched emotions flash over Lily's face—irritation, exasperation, grief, and acceptance—before she slumped her shoulders and stepped into Meg's embrace.

"I love you." Meg inhaled the sickly-sweet scent of Lily's cherry shampoo and placed a kiss on her head.

"Love you too," Lily mumbled into Meg's shoulder. Lily pulled back without making eye contact, unlocked the apartment's two deadbolts, and stepped into the morning heat.

Meg stood in the doorway, the air like hot breath in her face, and watched her niece walk down the stairs and across the parking lot to the front of the complex where the bus picked her up and dropped her off. Being able to see Lily board the bus was one of the reasons Meg chose this dumpy apartment. They used to drive Lily to school, Meg or Amanda, depending on who took the first shift at the shop. But they lived farther away from the school now and Meg couldn't afford the extra gas money the short trip cost.

When the bus arrived, Meg watched Lily board through the heat wavering from the scorching asphalt, freeing Meg to start her day. She needed to get to the shop, sit down in front of the computer, and try to make heads or tails of the books.

Amanda had been the numbers girl. She'd kept the books and paid the taxes and logged the merchandise. Meg was the creative one who staged the stock, made fanciful displays in the big bay window, and came up with advertising and promotion strategies.

Together, Amanda and Meg had made A Day's Wait shine. Now that Meg found herself alone, the gift store their parents started thirty years ago was on the brink of ruin.

Math made Meg edgy and nervous. If her eleventh grade algebra teacher knew she was responsible for keeping A Day's Wait in the black, she'd have bet against her every day of the week. Truth was, Meg would've bet against herself too. But all bets were off when there was no one around to handle the finances except a nervous Meg and a point of service program that left her head spinning.

Meg loaded her car and headed off to work with a pit of dread in her belly. It had been four months since Amanda died. Four agonizing months since everything Meg cared about in the world landed squarely on her shoulders—her niece and the family business. Helping raise her sister's daughter and co-owning a business had never felt so daunting when Amanda was alive, when they could muddle through together.

But alone and lonelier than she'd ever been in her life, Meg was barely keeping her head above water. All the fun and creativity working at A Day's Wait had fostered became a gaping yawn of obligations that felt like a cinder block anchored to her feet. But she couldn't give in to the nagging doubts that haunted her around every corner. She wouldn't.

Two

Bryan Westfall looked out at the high school baseball field and tried to focus on the game without the weight of his burdens crushing the experience. These were his kids—his students—and they deserved his time and attention. Attention that had been elsewhere for the past four months.

Baseball was their sport—his and Corey's—one of the few things the brothers had in common. Sitting in the bleachers surrounded by parents, he closed his eyes and inhaled the unmistakable scent of his youth. Fresh cut grass. Tangy, red Georgia clay. The dank, slightly moldy smell of the dugout. Meat sizzling on a too-greasy grill. The earthy-sweet scent of leather.

The sounds hit him next. The pop of the ball against a glove. The tinny whop of a hit off an aluminum bat. The rhythmic tat tat tat of players walking in cleats on concrete. The cheers from those nearby. *Be a hitter. Let's go, kid. Two outs. Play's at first.*

Bryan couldn't remember the last time he'd sat down and done anything for enjoyment in the last few months. Sports, TV, books—nothing held his attention for long before he'd have to get up and occupy his body so his mind couldn't wander to places better left alone.

He felt someone's gaze on his face, turned sideways and caught Rachel Ashe staring. He lifted his chin in acknowledgment. She flashed a fleeting smile and glanced away. As two of the six teachers honored by the seniors, they were forced to interact before the game. He liked the shy English teacher with her gymnast's body and pretty blonde ringlets, but whatever had been brewing between them hit a dead end when he'd gotten the news about Corey.

Dead end. Ha. Talk about irony.

He spotted a man with his dad's distinctive gait walking toward the field from the parking lot. The gnawing feeling in his gut could have been from the hot dog he ate earlier or the idea of facing the disappointment in his father's grief-stricken face.

Four months wasn't anywhere close enough for either of them to get over Cory's death. Especially when only one of them was trying.

Bryan stood, edged past the other spectators seated on his row, and met his dad on the path behind the home team dugout. "Hey, Dad." He leaned in, gave his dad a hug. "What are you doing here?"

"You put that tracking thing on my phone." His voice sounded gravely and tired. "It works both ways."

Bryan needed to remember that. "You could have called."

Ed Westfall jerked a shoulder. "Sometimes you don't answer."

Guilt was like a layer of skin, tough as leather, scarred and weathered over time. Bryan's wasn't hardened enough to keep the stinging buzz of shame from his face. "It's the end of the school year. I've been busy."

"Not too busy to watch baseball."

He shouldn't have to explain. He was a thirty-year-old man, for goodness' sake. But he knew the accusation in his dad's voice came from a deep well of grief and envy at Bryan's return to normal life. "It's senior night. One of the kids chose me as their favorite teacher." Pathetic, really, that he could influence a bunch of seventeen- and eighteen-year-olds and not his own flesh and blood. "We were honored before the game. It didn't seem right to leave."

His dad rubbed the silver stubble on his chin—the silver stubble that hadn't been there four months ago. His dad had aged ten years in a few months. "Well, that's something."

Bryan jerked a thumb over his shoulder. "You wanna sit and watch for a while? It's a good game. We're up by two in the sixth."

His dad's gaze drifted to the field, his eyes squinting as if in pain, and took stock of his surroundings. "I don't know. A lot of memories on the baseball diamond."

"Good memories." Corey and his foolhardy behavior had tarnished everything, but he couldn't change the memories. The good or the bad. "I was worried before I got here, but it's been nice to remember the good."

"Remembering the good doesn't erase the bad."

"No, it doesn't. But it eases the sting."

His dad looked him dead in the eye. Bryan's stomach bottomed.

"Right now, the only thing that'll ease the sting is wrapping up his estate. Your mama and I are paid up at Corey's through the end of June. We can't afford—mentally or physically—to go into July. We need you to go clean out his place."

"I am, Dad. I will." He'd put it off, thinking it would be easier with time. He'd been wrong. Putting off the inevitable only heightened his grief and kept him up at night wondering what he'd find. "As soon as school is out, I'm going down to Florida first thing."

"I'd go with you if I could but your mama ..."

He left the rest unsaid. They both knew Cindy Westfall couldn't handle another blow or Ed's departure. Ever since they'd found out about Cory's death, husband and wife hadn't been apart for more than a few hours. "I know. I'll take care of it, Dad."

Ed looked back at the field, to the bleachers. "I guess a couple of innings won't kill me."

A knot loosened in Bryan's chest. He squeezed his dad's shoulder and led him back to the bleachers where they settled a few rows up from where Bryan originally sat.

"Which one of the kids chose you as his favorite?"

Bryan pointed to the outfield. "Kevin Tossler, center field. Good kid. He's going to Georgia Tech in the fall."

Ed gave Bryan the side eye. "Tech, huh? Must be smart."

"He is. He's the kind of student who makes me remember why I got into teaching in the first place."

"It wasn't the money."

Bryan's chuckle felt rusty in his throat. "That's for sure."

The pitcher threw a nasty curve ball for strike number three and the teams switched positions on the field. The guy doing play-by-play announced half-price burgers and dogs at the concession stand.

"You want something to eat?" Bryan asked. "Some candy or a drink?"

"No, I'm good." Ed sat quietly for a while, rubbing his palms against his decades-old jeans. "I thought you were crazy when you left your job at the bank to become a teacher."

"You weren't the only one." He'd lost touch with most of his coworkers, and changing careers was the beginning of the end for another of his ill-fated relationships. He was beginning to wonder if he'd ever find the one. So was his mother. Every time he saw her, she made some dig about never having grandchildren. Thanks to Corey, it was up to him now.

"You like it?" Ed asked.

"Teaching?" Bryan inclined his head, sighed. "It's not easy."

"That's not a ringing endorsement."

It was hard to put into words the highs and lows of a high school math teacher. For his dad who was making an effort by watching the game, he'd try. "At the end of the day, I like using what I know to help others who might take what they know and change the world. The ones who care make it worth putting up with the long hours, the lousy pay, and the less than enthusiastic students."

Ed's gaze was on the field, but his eyes were a million miles away. "You always cared about school. We could never get your brother to do more than the bare minimum. All he cared about was having a good time."

And watching Corey goof off and the ensuing arguments at home were what pushed Bryan to succeed. Corey was smart—smarter than Bryan by half—but his refusal to apply himself caused near daily arguments that turned their once happy home into a battlefield.

"He didn't know how to study."

Ed looked at him, a question in his eyes.

"I see it all the time. Kids—smart kids like Corey—who never learned to study because they never had to. When things get tough, they give up instead of digging in and doing the work."

Ed's exhale may as well have been a groan. "I guess that's what happened in the end. He just gave up trying."

Maybe, Bryan wanted to say. Maybe not. They may never know why Corey wandered into the riptide and never came up.

He was afraid, after his trip to Florida, he'd know exactly why. Knowing is what scared him the most.

Three

Meg parked at the back of A Day's Wait on Key West's famed Duval Street and unlocked the door, disheartened by the display window that should have been changed out weeks ago. She didn't have the time nor the energy to rearrange the exhibit—not while learning the ins and outs of the point of service system that had been the focus of Amanda's job.

Tourist season was edging past full swing. Meg had stretched herself thin enough to hire a part-time salesgirl who came in after school and worked until close so Meg could get Lily off the bus and get her fed before coming back to the shop to shut it down. It was an expense she could little afford, but unless she learned to clone herself—or better yet her dead sister—during the busy spring cruise line season, paying a part-time employee had been a necessary evil.

With the end of the school year in sight and the arrival of the

Atlantic hurricane season, the part-time help would have to go so she could afford to send Lily to the assorted camps that would keep her busy while Meg worked. Meg dreaded working the shop alone and taking full responsibility for A Day's Wait's success or failure. The line between the two had never seemed so thin.

Eva Grannell waved from the front of her flower shop next door as she watered the potted plants at her entrance. Since her parents' retirement and relocation to Orlando, Eva had been like a mother to Meg and Amanda. "How ya doing, Meg?"

"Hanging in there." Meg eyed the red geraniums and the other colorful flowers she couldn't name spilling out of large turquoise pots. "Those are nice."

"I went with a fanciful theme for the start of summer." Eva glanced at A Day's Wait's window. "If you need to spend some time on the display, I can send Kaitlyn over. We're caught up on orders."

Of course she couldn't refuse the offer; she had spent so much time on the books instead of the display. She'd been saying for weeks she was going to change out the items and never gotten around to it. She might never get the chance. "Are you sure you don't mind?"

"Not at all. If we get busy, I'll need her back, but she's all yours for now."

"Thanks, Eva. I owe you one."

Eva turned the spigot off and dropped her arms, her head lilting to her shoulder like a flower in the heat. "Oh, honey. It's the least I can do."

Meg gave her a closed-lip smile she hoped conveyed gratitude and not the melancholy she felt at the pity coming off Eva in waves. Yes, Amanda was dead. Yes, Meg was devastated and struggling and hanging on by a thread. Knowing others could tell—even a

14

substitute mom like Eva—made Meg determined to tough it out with a smile on her face.

As much as she could.

Kaitlyn arrived within minutes, allowing Meg to undress the window mannequins still sporting thin sweatshirts, jackets, and closed-toed shoes. A Day's Wait used to be known for their fabulous window displays. Every month Meg created new and inventive designs—beach balls hung from string in varying lengths, succulents, leaves, umbrellas all artfully arranged to match the mood of the season and Meg's whimsy. Every display, no matter the season, paid homage to the island's most famous resident and store namesake—Ernest Hemingway.

The current display with stuffed cats hiding between fern fronds hadn't changed in going on five months. The locals knew what happened to Amanda. The tourists and paying customers—the only ones who counted toward the bottom line—just saw a quirky but outdated display.

Meg flung the items into a large, wheeled laundry bucket. Like an artist with a blank canvas, she needed the space sparse so she could focus her mind and think. She stared at the foam flooring and white cork walls, her mind as empty as her bank account. She stood back, cocked her head this way and that. Nothing. Walked outside to stare at the space from the sidewalk. Nada.

With no time to spare and her creative well dry, Meg did something she hated to do—she went back to the office and opened her laptop to search for inspiration. Everything looked unoriginal and unbecoming to a casual island gift store on Florida's southernmost point. It always made her smile to think of her free-spirited parents opening a gift shop in the most flamboyant city in the country and raising two daughters there—one the polar opposite of freewheeling.

Meg rubbed the ache in her belly as recognition dawned. Without her parents, without Amanda, it wasn't just the books that would suffer. Her family's store, their lifeblood and only source of income, would drown in the abyss if Meg didn't get out of her funk and rediscover some of the joy her job once offered.

Making fun window displays to draw customers inside used to matter. Making small talk with tourists used to matter. Making a living doing what she loved used to matter. When all the things she used to love no longer mattered, Meg didn't know what to do.

Kaitlyn poked her head in the back, a sheepish look on her face. "Eva just called. She needs me at the shop."

Meg waved her on. It wasn't much use to have Kaitlyn in the store when Meg sat paralyzed by indecision. "Thanks for coming over."

"I can try to pop back in a little bit. We've got a couple of orders that just called. I'll check back when we're done."

"Don't get in a bad spot with Eva. I appreciate you being here now."

"It's no imposition. She loves you, Meg. She misses Amanda. We all do."

Hearing her sister's name out loud was like a flare gun shot to her stomach. Meg missed Amanda with a fierceness that clawed up her belly and strangled the breath from her throat. She missed her so much her fingernails ached. But under all the sorrow was a thick sheet of icy anger freezing her to the core. No matter how hard she tried, Meg couldn't let go of the bitterness she felt at times like these when even her favorite things in life felt overwhelming.

She wondered if she would ever be able to miss her sister and not feel chafed by resentment at Amanda's reckless impulsiveness.

"I appreciate your help."

Kailyn nodded and disappeared around the corner, the door chime jangling in her wake. Meg had stock to sell, stock to order, and customers to charm. Nothing good would come of her sitting in the office wasting time, wishing things were different.

She picked some colorful pinwheels of varying sizes and a couple of kites, some turf, a few frisbees, some life-size blow-up rafts and a cloud shower curtain for a backdrop. She picked out two of the trendiest bathing suits so she could dress the naked mannequins. The idea was simple, and mindless, and any hack could do it, but it would feel good to mark one thing off her list.

Customers wandered in and out as she tacked the materials to the window bay. She'd stop, welcome them to the store, and let them know to ask if they needed assistance. When Amanda was alive, they would tag team the customers. Size them up and wordlessly determine which sister was best suited to make the sale.

They'd grown up watching their parents do the same. Some skills, unlike math and accounting, could be learned through observation. Her parents were a one-two punch, the schmoozer and the deal maker. Known and loved by the Key West community, Steve and Celia Holloway built a legacy of hometown success.

A legacy Meg and Amanda tried their best to continue after their parents' retirement to Orlando and their mom's early Alzheimer diagnosis. A legacy sitting on Meg's shoulders that currently felt like an albatross around her neck.

Once she'd finished with the window, she went outside and stood back, giving the display a critical gaze, trying to see it as a customer would. A little fun, a little generic, it would have to do for now. Now was all she could handle. Now was all she was promised. She went back inside, grateful for the blast of air conditioning, determined to make some headway with the books.

Four

Bryan heard the knock, abandoned his half-filled suitcase, and went to see who'd come by. He found his best friend on the doorstep wearing his usual corporate attire. At eleven o'clock on a Tuesday, why wasn't Dustin at work?

"Hey, man." Bryan stepped back to let him in. "What's the occasion?"

Dustin shrugged and walked past into the apartment. "I was in the neighborhood. Thought I'd come by and see you."

"This neighborhood?" Dustin worked in downtown Atlanta and lived in the high-rent part of the city. Bryan's suburban community was far outside Dustin's daily bubble.

"I had an appointment out this way." He looked around, spotted the suitcase through the open door on the bed and nailed Bryan with an appraising glare. "You going on vacation?"

"Something like that."

"Let me guess. The Florida Keys?"

Dustin knew Bryan better than anyone—including his complicated relationship with Corey. Growing up two houses down, they'd shared endless games, countless secrets, and even a first crush. Bryan dated Dustin's wife in middle school. Dustin locked her down in high school and they'd never looked back.

Dustin had been Bryan's first call when his dad told him about Corey. He'd been there through everything—the funeral, the paperwork, the messy emotions. He'd encouraged Bryan to go to Florida right away and not put it off. "Just take the time and get it over with. Putting it off is only going to drag this out."

But Bryan didn't listen. He used school and his parents fragile mental state as an excuse. As if waiting would make it easier and lesson Bryan's anger at his older brother. As if a miracle would happen and Corey's stuff would just disappear, freeing Bryan from having to do a deep dive into the unknown of Corey's life.

"Key West is on the agenda."

"'Bout time."

"Say what you mean, Dusty." Bryan deliberately taunted his friend with his long-ago nickname and dropped last night's takeout box into the trash, shucking his hands onto his hips. "You mean past time."

Dustin wasn't fazed by Bryan's nasty tone. They were brothers, he and Dustin, and brothers spoke the hard truth.

"One and the same."

Bryan snorted. "No, one of us was right when he told me to get it over with."

Dustin's face broke into a grin, reminding Bryan how long it had been since he'd seen his friend smile. "Are you saying I'm right?"

"Maybe, but I'm not saying it again." Bryan walked into his bedroom and resumed folding clothes to put into the suitcase. "What do you think I need besides swim trunks, shorts, and t-shirts? I can't think of anything else."

"Sunscreen. A nice pair of khakis, that fancy hair gel you use to tame the beast."

"Anything else?"

"That should cover it. Maybe a copy of the death certificate in case someone questions why you're rooting around Corey's place."

"Already packed it."

Dustin ran his fingers over Bryan's neatly folded shirts. "Look at you, still neat as a pin. Tegan should have married you."

And there it was. The reason it had been so long since he'd seen Dustin smile. With all the hubbub since Corey, he'd forgotten or willfully ignored the news that Tegan and Dustin were having problems. "I'm sorry, man. Y'all still …?" He let it linger, unable to name or even fathom the dynamic duo on shaky ground.

"We're seeing a *counselor*." Dustin spat the word as if counselor were a metaphor for a psychic.

"That's good, right? That might help."

"For three hundred dollars an hour, I don't need someone asking me why I'm not happy. Maybe I'm not happy because my wife keeps insisting I'm not happy."

Bryan watched his friend prowl around the small bedroom like a lion on a circus train, his eyes unfocused, his expression grim. Bryan kept his tone neutral so as not to poke at his prickly friend. "*Are* you happy?"

Dustin looked like he couldn't decide if he was ticked off or confused by Bryan's question. "Who knows? Is anybody happy? Are *you* happy?"

With his family in shambles and any hope of a relationship dashed, happiness didn't even seem like an option. "I'm not the best person to ask."

"Exactly." Dustin tossed his hands in the air. "No one's happy." He looked at Bryan, a smile forming on his downturned lips. "I can come with you. Help you sort through Corey's stuff."

Bryan cleared his throat, put on his teacher's hat, the hat he wore at parent conferences when student and teacher didn't see eye to eye. "I don't think that's a good idea."

"It's a great idea. You need help and I need to get away for a few days."

Getting away sounded like running away. And Bryan wasn't about to be his accomplice. "I don't know how long I'll be gone now that school is out for the summer. Corey's rent is paid up through the end of the month. I was going to go down, look through his things, see if I could puzzle through what happened those last few months when we lost touch."

"You don't want to do that alone. I've got some vacation stored up. I'm not swamped at work right now. I could swing a few weeks."

A few weeks? With his marriage stalling like his old Saab Turbo? "Dude, how do you think Tegan will react if you disappear for a few weeks? You think that'll be good for your marriage?"

"Some time away might be just what we need."

How dumb could Dustin be? Tegan was the best thing that ever happened to him, and he'd be a fool to let her slip through his fingers—which she would do if he took off without her. "Why don't you take some time away together—you and Tegan—and work on your marriage?"

Dustin only scowled at Bryan as if he'd suggested working on his taxes.

"Go somewhere nice—the beach or the mountains. Somewhere the two of you can be alone and reconnect. Running away with me won't solve your problems."

"Do you seriously think Tegan is going to take time off work?"

"You'll never know unless you ask. Besides, I need to do this by myself."

Going through Corey's stuff sat like a moldy lead biscuit in Bryan's gut, violating and vile. Bryan dreaded the task more than curriculum night and PTA meetings and parent conferences all put together. But opening Corey's place—his life—to someone outside the family, even someone as close to family as Dustin—felt like a titanic breach of trust. "He was my brother. My big brother. And I let him down."

And letting Corey down meant Corey had taken someone else down with him.

"He let himself down. I was there, Bryan. I saw him skirt through life and pin whatever trouble he got into on you or someone else he could blame. You were an easy target."

"I was blood. I should have been there for him."

"You were. Repeatedly. You know as well as I do you couldn't save him. He had to save himself."

Bryan wondered if Dustin heard himself—heard the parallels to his marriage. He doubted he did. "Doesn't matter much now. We're both going to man up and do the right thing. I'm going to go to Florida, and you're going to stay here and fix your marriage. We'll both be better off in the end."

He only prayed that was true for both of them.

Bryan followed the GPS to the address of Corey's apartment,

pulling his truck to the curb and squinting through the alley leading to the one-bedroom cottage his brother had called home for the last year of his life. Smothered by uncertainty, Bryan sat frozen in the blazing heat even though his bladder screamed for relief, and his legs ached from the thirteen hours in the car.

This was it. Corey's last residence. Corey's life. Corey's secrets waiting to be uncovered.

What would he find behind the door at the end of the brick walkway flanked by drooping palm fronds and neon elephant ear leaves? Corey's landlord had called his parents after the police did a cursory search of the apartment after Corey's death. He'd let them pay, month by month, until Bryan could come and clean out the space. He'd been more than generous, all things considered.

Bryan had a little less than a month to pack up and remove Corey's belongings from the tiny space. He didn't need a month to do the physical packing. He'd take the month—if necessary—to puzzle out what drove his brother and a beautiful woman to a different Florida beach and into the dangerous riptide.

Bryan had his suspicions. The drinking that never seemed to stop no matter how much Bryan tried and failed to intervene. Corey's daredevil nature. His need to impress and be the center of attention.

Corey was a good-looking guy who drew the ladies like a feed trough drew cattle. Even his lack of ambition and empty bank account never derailed him from doing well with the opposite sex. Bryan both admired and was befuddled by Corey's appeal.

And who was Amanda Holloway? Was she Corey's girlfriend or another target he'd charmed into his orbit? How long had they been together and how deep did their connection run? What, Byran wondered, would he find when he followed her trail?

The scant details from the police still bothered him. Corey and Amanda had shared a room together in a dive motel off the east coast of mainland Florida where the rip currents were known to strike and strike hard. They'd checked in on a Monday, died on a Wednesday. No room service. No disturbance calls. No drugs in the room. Nothing but a harmless few days away.

Except they'd died. Drowned. Both of them.

An eyewitness said Corey went into the water first, beckoning Amanda to follow. She waded out and joined him and they floated far into the distance, disappearing into the current. Neither resurfaced. Both bodies were found a few miles down the beach after a vacationer saw them from the shore and called the police.

Armed with that information only, it was up to Bryan to figure out Corey's last months and report back to his grieving parents. He picked up the phone from his console and texted his dad. **"I'm here. I'll let you know if I find anything."

His only response was a thumbs up emoji.

Bryan hated emojis. Corey used them all the time. Whenever Bryan would try to call, he'd get Corey's voicemail and had to resort to texting. *How ya doing? Just checking in. What's new?* All texts were met with short and cryptic responses. *Good*, or *living the dream*, or the freakishly annoying thumbs up emoji.

That one hand symbol seemed to convey an entire conversation. "I'm fine," it said. "Stop worrying," it expressed. "I know you don't care but are asking to make yourself feel better," it screamed. Bryan wasn't sure whether to feel annoyed or grateful Corey's answers never demanded further communication.

Bryan was busy. Unlike Corey who never held down a paying job for long, Bryan had obligations to fulfill, people he couldn't let down. His students. His school. His parents.

But he couldn't hide in the car forever, not with the price of gas inching skyward and the clock ticking on his agenda. The landlord said he'd leave the key under the mat. That's exactly where Bryan found it, hot to the touch in the 90-degree weather that felt more like a sauna than a heat wave.

The smell hit him first. The stale, musty air was like an olfactory punch. Bryan stepped inside, closed the door, and went straight to the high windows along the wall in the galley kitchen. He yanked the cord to lift the blinds and unlocked the windows, shoving the wooden frames up. He repeated the process on the two windows in the tiny living room and let the heat and fresh air stream inside.

He glanced around. The place was neat but lived in, a little impersonal, but not messy like Bryan was expecting after sharing space with Corey for almost twenty years. The gray fabric couch looked well-used, as did the scuffed coffee table that held the TV remote and a couple of local takeout menus.

After locating the bathroom at the base of the stairs (not as neat—thanks, Corey), Bryan relieved his bladder and washed his hands, drying them on a hand towel hanging from a nearby hook. Bryan lifted the towel to his face, inhaled, and felt both relief and disappointment that the only smell was laundry detergent.

Would Bryan recognize Corey's scent? Would he want to?

A knock on the door scattered his thoughts, had him scrambling to replace the towel and get out of the bathroom. He found a woman on his doorstep, her head poking inside the door.

"Hello?" the woman called. Her face morphed into concern when she spotted Bryan. "Who are you?"

Bryan's heart rate settled. With her streaked gray hair and flowered house dress, Bryan figured the woman had to be in her seventies. She clearly was not a threat. But he wasn't about to be put on the defensive in his own brother's apartment. "Who are you?"

Her hand slipped from the doorknob, and she straightened to five foot nothing. "I'm Betty Sue English. I live in the house next door. What are you doing in Corey's apartment?"

"You know Corey?"

"I *knew* Corey. He died."

Why, after all this time, did hearing that out loud feel like a slash against his heart? "I'm Bryan Westfall, Corey's brother."

She studied his face before letting her gaze wander down his body and back up. "You favor. You're not as pretty, not as tortured, but still handsome."

"Tortured?"

"You're his flesh and blood. What would you call it?"

Whenever Bryan thought of Corey, tortured wasn't what came to mind. Spoiled. Entitled. Lazy. Tortured meant his brother wasn't as good at hiding his demons as he used to be. Either that or Betty Sue was more than just a nosy neighbor.

"I suppose I'd call him troubled."

"Troubled, tortured." She rolled her wrist between them. "One and the same."

Not really. One implied Corey had issues, the other implied those issues were forced upon him. Corey and Bryan shared a pleasant childhood. Whatever Betty Sue thought haunted Corey happened after he left home, but Bryan wasn't going to argue semantics with Corey's neighbor—not when she could help him piece together the last few weeks of his life.

"Perhaps," he said.

"What's your plan, Bryan Westfall? You packing up his stuff?"

"That's my plan." Eventually.

Betty Sue nodded, a crevice between her brows that was

deeper than the other lines on her sun-weathered face. "Well, keep it down. Your brother was a respectful neighbor. I expect you to be the same."

"Sounds like you and Corey were friends."

"He was a good neighbor. Like I said, he had his issues, but he was quiet and nice."

"Did Corey have any friends who came by? Any girlfriends that you know of?"

Betty Sue squinted at Bryan. "You mean Amanda, the girl who died with him?"

Prickles of awareness shimmied along Bryan's scalp. "Did you know her?"

"Not particularly. She was local. Ran a tchotchke store over on Duval with her sister."

"Tchotchke?"

"You know, trinkets and t-shirts and the like."

"Was she …" How did he ask if she was a good girl? A nice girl who didn't frequent men's apartments and go off with them for binge-drinking days on end. "His girlfriend?"

"Can't say she was or she wasn't. Came around a few times. They seemed to enjoy each other."

From the smirk on her face, Bryan pinned the nosy neighbor badge on Betty Sue. "How long would you say they dated?"

"I'm not saying they dated. What they did wasn't any of my business, but I saw her sniffing around a couple of weeks before they died."

"Two weeks?"

"Maybe more, maybe less. I wasn't his keeper."

And she wasn't obligated to answer his questions. From the look on her face, Bryan knew any more inquiries and she'd clam up all together. "I'll try and keep it down while I'm here."

She looked around, looked at Bryan. "You do that." She turned to leave.

Bryan exhaled and looked around the unfamiliar space. What would he find lurking in the drawers or hiding under the mattress? And how did the mysterious Amanda Holloway factor into Corey's life?

Five

Meg fixed the display of koozies after a group of teenaged girls left the store, leaving the display in shambles. She restacked the koozies in the basket and untangled the necklaces they'd entwined, renewing her love-hate relationship with the cruise industry.

Yes, almost a million cruise line passengers frequented the island every year, adding substantial tourist dollars to the city and a lot of foot traffic to her store. But the day shoppers were often flippant with the merchandise, touching everything, moving it around the store, trying on clothes in the dressing room with the care of a teenager in her best friend's closet.

A Day's Wait was not a closet, thank heavens, but couldn't they be a little respectful of the stock?

Lily came out from the back of the store where she'd been playing computer games at Amanda's desk. Meg's desk was too cluttered to even attempt to use it as a workspace. "I'm bored," Lily announced.

"You can help me if you're bored. I need those boxes along the back wall unpacked."

She crinkled her nose and sagged her shoulders. "Do I have to?"

Lily was twelve. Labor laws alone meant she didn't have to. Family or not, the girl deserved to spend a Saturday having fun. "No. But I'm stuck here until we close."

"Can I call a friend?"

"Sure." Spending time with friends helped Lily forget for a while. "Who?"

Lily ran her hand along a row of hangers with brightly colored sarongs. "How about Gina?"

Meg pursed her lips to keep the disdain from her voice. She was pretty sure Gina Sizemore's older brother sold pot and other drugs out of their ramshackle trailer. Even if he didn't, his pack of friends were the last people Meg wanted Lily to be around, especially since Gina's mom wasn't sober enough to know or care what Gina did with her time. "She'd have to come here."

"Why?" Lily's voice pitched before settling into snark. "And do what? Unpack boxes?"

"You can go get ice cream and walk around for a little bit as long as you take your phone and check in with me every fifteen minutes."

"That's so lame. Why can't I go to her house?"

Meg wished Amanda were here. She'd always been the one to smooth over the stickier parts of parenting. Meg would advise Amanda and her sister had gotten good at persuading Lily to see her point of view. Meg never acquired that skill because the sisters' good cop/bad cop routine worked like a charm. Without Amanda there to play good cop, Meg just came across as mean. "Because I said so."

Lilly huffed. "That's not fair. Mom would let me go."

The pouted sentiment stung like a dagger to her heart. The painful truth was that she would have. Amanda had had a hard time setting boundaries for Lily. She found it easier to give in and not cause a scene. Fortunately for Lily, Meg had always been there, butting her nose in and setting Amanda straight. With Amanda gone, there was no one to soften the blow.

"Okay." Meg stopped fussing with the bathing suits. "I'll give it to you straight like I did with your mom. Garret Sizemore uses drugs and hangs out with a rough crowd. He's not the kind of person I want you hanging around."

"I don't want to hang around Garret." Lily's defiant tone turned timid. "Gina doesn't do drugs. She doesn't even like her brother."

"Then why would either of you want to hang around their house when you know he's there with that pack of trouble he calls friends?"

Lily rolled her eyes, picking at the skin around her thumbnail. Just like Amanda. But when she continued to pace around the store deep in thought, Meg knew her straight talk had been the right approach.

"What about Cammie?" Lily asked.

Meg knew Cammie and her parents enough to encourage the girls to play. An afternoon around Cammie Lester wouldn't scar Lily for life. "Cammie is fine, but I can't take you to her house."

Lily wrinkled her lips into a pout and swooshed them side to side as she pondered her dilemma. "Can I ask them to pick me up?"

"No, but you can tell them you're at the store. If Cammie wants to play, she'll know her parents have to come get you or drop Cammie here for the day."

"And if she wants to come here, we have to get ice cream and walk around?"

Meg would have loved to take the afternoon off and take the girls to the beach or a movie. But until she got a handle on the finances, days off would have to wait. "It's that or unpack the boxes."

Lily's sigh ruffled the hair hanging along the edges of her face. "Let me call her." She disappeared into the back.

Resigned, deflated, Meg continued straightening the stock. Now that school was out, it wasn't fair to Lily that she had to spend her summer at the store. It wasn't fair to Lily's friends' parents to have to carry Meg's load. Life, she learned every hour of every day, wasn't meant to be fair.

She gave herself a mental scolding. Meg was a glass half-empty kind of girl. Amanda and her glass-full personality had smoothed Meg's downer tendencies. Without the light, the dark threatened to eclipse the good in their lives. She couldn't—she wouldn't—extinguish Amanda's light. Amanda may have been naïve and had a hard time setting limits on her daughter, but Meg missed her like she missed a limb. The world didn't feel as kind or right without her sister.

Meg had Lily. They had a roof over their heads. Food in their bellies. A life some would envy. "We got what we got," her mom used to say when Meg was little and complained about something she wanted but didn't have. "We got love, we got life, we got each other. Learn to be happy with what you got, and you'll never feel sad, Meggy girl."

She should have her mom's wisdom tattooed on her arm or

etched in a bracelet so she could see it every day, remind herself of the good. As far as Meg could tell, her mom hadn't even registered Amanda's death. Maybe that was for the best.

The bell chimed and a man walked in, pulling Meg out of her gloom. It wasn't unusual for men to come into the shop. They had enough generic items like sunscreen and beach towels and lip balm to encourage both sexes to shop.

"Welcome to A Day's Wait." Meg finished arranging the rack of bathing suit cover-ups and stepped to the side to get a better look. The guy was tall—over six feet of broad-shouldered ranginess— with frizzy brown hair and dark, serious eyes. He'd stopped just inside the door as if he'd forgotten what he'd come in for. "Can I help you find something?"

His arms were tanned up to his t-shirt, but his legs looked as though they hadn't seen the sun in a while. When he cast his eyes in her direction, the ground beneath Meg's feet shifted, like tectonic plates loosening below the surface of the earth. Her nerves went on high alert and the muscles around her shoulders tightened. She didn't know the guy. She didn't recognize him at all. But something about him seemed familiar—and not in a good way.

"Ahhh," the guy stammered, his voice a deep timber of uncertainty. "I'm looking for—"

Lily skipped out of the back, her hair swinging like kite strings in the wind. "She's coming to get me! I'm so excited I don't have to hang around here all day long."

Meg turned back to the customer, watched his expression drop as he stared at Lily, watched him blanch before her eyes. The nervous feeling in her belly doubled and doubled again as he stood staring as if in a daze.

Lily, who knew better than to talk to Meg when she was dealing with a customer, stood fidgeting under his scrutiny.

"I'm sorry for my niece's interruption. What can I help you find?"

"Uh … I … never mind." His attempted smile fell as flat as the coastline, and he bolted out the door.

Meg's greeting smile faded with the jangling of the bells.

"Sorry," Lily said. "I didn't know you had a customer."

"Did you recognize that man?"

"No." Lily shrugged the way her mom used to, loose limbed and limber. "Did you?"

Meg shook her head. The last few months had been a blur, but she wouldn't have forgotten the man who'd fled the store like his butt was on fire. Not because he didn't have a very nice butt—because he did—but there was something about him that raised her hackles. "The Lesters are coming to get you?"

"Cammie has to finish her chores and then they'll be here."

"She volunteered? You didn't ask?"

"I promise, Aunt Meg. She offered."

The bells jangled and a gaggle of girls entered the store.

Meg shook herself back to the business at hand. "Welcome to A Day's Wait. Can I help you find something?"

Six

Bryan stepped into the oppressive heat and walked briskly down the sidewalk cold and clammy as a corpse. Amanda Holloway had a daughter. A daughter who could have been her twin by the grainy picture he recalled from Amanda's obituary.

Why didn't Bryan know about the girl? He'd read her obituary—hadn't he? How had her existence slipped through the cracks only to smack Bryan in the face when he'd foolishly, impulsively gone into Amanda's store? Now he knew, and now he couldn't forget the angelic face that would haunt him like the ghost of her dead mother.

Had Corey known Amanda had a daughter? Had he cared? Choking on the thick air and the questions swirling through his mind, Bryan stumbled into a corner bar that sat like an oasis shaded under thick palm trees. He nearly bumped into the sandwich board announcing the day's drink specials and made a beeline for the outdoor bar.

Bryan rested his elbows on the glossy surface and ran his fingers through his hair.

The bartender approached, a friendly smile on his face. "What can I get you?"

Bryan wasn't much of a drinker, and he certainly didn't make a habit of drinking during the day. But desperate times called for desperate measures. "I'll have a Jameson, neat."

The bartender poured the amber liquid into a tumbler and placed it in front of Bryan. He picked it up with an unsteady hand and took a generous sip. The whiskey singed as it went down, burning a hole in his already flaming gut.

Bryan circled the glass around the bar top and reflected on the morning. He'd made some headway on Corey's cottage, starting in the kitchen where he was least likely to discover anything untoward. Other than some moldy bread and stale cereal, things were pretty much as he'd expected. He'd moved the boxes to the den, but got sidelined by hunger as the caffeine buzz that had fueled his morning disappeared.

Bryan never intended to probe Amanda or her family or her place of business so soon. He'd planned to go through all of Corey's stuff, see what if anything he found, and then segue to the life and times of Amanda Holloway.

He had parked along a side street near a four-star sandwich shop he'd found on a review app and followed the directions on his phone. He'd just crossed an intersection when he came face to face with A Day's Wait. He'd stood in the blazing heat, dripping sweat and lightheaded from hunger, staring at two bikini-clad mannequins in a window display, wondering at the tickle crawling up the back of his neck.

When he'd realized he stood steps away from Amanda's store,

he'd debated what to do. Whether it was impulse or insanity that had him pushing open the door and stepping inside, he'd never know, but right now, heady from the alcohol coating his empty stomach, it really didn't matter.

Deciding not to test fate, he'd popped in, looked around, and planned to get out as fast as possible—no harm, no foul. Until the redheaded stunner had stepped into view and stopped him in his tracks.

Other than her coloring, she looked a lot like her sister. Same slender build. Same piercing green eyes. Same arresting face. For a moment, all he could do was stare and appreciate her on a purely base level. He forgot where he was and what he was doing and got lost in all that glossy auburn hair.

Until the young girl had bounded into the shop from somewhere in the back and jolted his heart like a defibrillator.

The bartender reappeared, jostling Bryan back to the present. "Can I get you another?"

Bryan glanced at his empty glass, didn't remember finishing the drink. "Sure." He shoved the glass in his direction. "Thanks."

"No problem." He refilled the glass, gave it back to Bryan. "You in town for business or pleasure?"

Bryan cocked his head. "You assume everyone's a tourist?"

The bartender jutted his chin at Bryan's arms. "Your sunburn. Dead giveaway."

Bryan glanced at his arms, lifted the sleeve of his t-shirt. Sure enough, his bicep was pink against white. "I guess I am."

"So, which is it?" he asked. "Business or pleasure?"

"Neither." Bryan looked at the guy, really looked. He had close-cut hair and a wiry build. Tattoos that must have started near his shoulder extended beyond the sleeve of his shirt and wound down to his wrist—something medieval and undecipherable. "My brother lived here."

"Oh yeah? A local?"

"For the past year. Almost."

The guy nodded. "I'm Tim, by the way. No business or pleasure means family obligations."

Bryan zipped his gaze to Tim's.

"I get it, man. Family's a little bit of both." Tim possessed a bartender's greatest gift—that of entertainer, server, and shrink, all in one. Bryan bartended through college, but his skills were as rusty as some of the boats he'd spotted in the harbor.

"I'm Bryan. Bryan Westfall." He lifted his hand to shake.

Tim narrowed his eyes as he gripped Bryan's hand. "Westfall, huh? You're Corey's brother."

It wasn't a question, and his tone gave nothing away. "You knew Corey?"

"Not really." He reached for a rag, wiped the gleaming surface. "He came in a few times. Typical transplant."

"What do you mean?"

"A lot of guys come to the Keys to get away or disappear or just live off the grid. Wasting away, as the song goes."

Tim and Jimmy Buffet had nailed Corey's life. He'd wasted it away doing what Bryan dreaded to discover. "So, you did know Corey."

"Look, he was a friendly enough guy." Tim tossed the rag into a sink, his shoulders bunching beneath the black t-shirt with a rock band logo. "He was quick with a smile, a little scant on his past, like a lot in the area. I'm not judging."

Bryan took a fortifying sip, let the warm glow of a buzz boost his next question. "You knew Amanda?"

"Everybody knew Amanda." There was no mistaking his tone now. Whatever Tim thought or didn't think of Corey, he had strong feelings about Amanda. "She was a good girl. Born and raised here. She's mourned and missed."

And there it sat like a two-ton turd. The truth in neon color. Corey was mourned, but was he missed? The old Corey, sure. When they were kids, Bryan idolized his older brother. But drifter Corey? Irresponsible Corey? Petulant Corey? Not so much. Reality sloshed like the whiskey in his empty stomach.

"They were together when they died. Were they a couple?"

Tim held up a finger and waded down the bar to a threesome who'd just arrived. Bryan sat staring at his drink. Any more whiskey on an empty stomach and he'd be fully drunk. Even as it stood, he couldn't drive. He sniffed, realized the steamy air was tinged with burnt grease, and figured the bar had a kitchen. It was past time he found out.

Tim made the new customers' drinks, punched a few keys of the computer, and returned to stand in front of Bryan, resuming their conversation as if he hadn't left. "I don't know how to describe what your brother was to Amanda, but, like you said, they were together when they died. Kinda speaks for itself."

Bryan nodded, although he didn't agree. Whatever Corey and Amanda were to each other may have spoken for itself, but it seemed spoken in a language Bryan didn't understand.

"Can I get you another?" Tim asked.

Bryan pushed the empty glass away. "No, but I'll take whatever you recommend for lunch."

"Can't beat the hogfish sandwich."

"Sold. And a water, please."

Tim knocked once on the bar. "Coming right up."

Alone with his thoughts and a puzzle that left him reeling, Bryan thought of the young girl with white-blonde hair and the singsong voice who no longer had a mother, thanks to Corey or, maybe, despite him. The distinction, Bryan knew, was all that mattered now.

Seven

Meg startled when her phone vibrated from its perch on her desk. She'd been staring at the numbers on the screen, thinking about her earlier encounter with the stranger in the store. She reached for phone and swiped to answer the call. "Hey, Dad."

"How's my Meggy girl?" His voice, that familiar soothing tone, sounded weary and worn.

"I'm doing okay. How's Mom?"

Weary and worn dropped to wretched. "She's slipping away. Faster than I expected. It's … hard to watch."

"Does she … has she said anything about Amanda?"

"I don't think she understands. I talk about her, about all of you, but she can't seem to grasp that Amanda's gone. It's probably for the best, but …"

The unsaid screamed in Meg's head. The woman he loved more than life itself was dying before his eyes. Everything they built together forgotten—her children and grandchild included. Not knowing Amanda was gone may have been a kind of relief for her mom, but it left her dad to grieve alone. If her father hadn't been her hero before, he'd have leapt to the head of the line by his devotion to his wife and the example he set.

"I wish I were there for you. For Mom."

"You can't be, honey. We both understand."

He may have understood, but Meg felt the loss acutely. Her mother, so different from her youngest and yet so alike in their creative endeavors, needed her family to be strong. Meg mustered a non-committal noise.

"I wish I could be there for you too. But your mom needs me, and Lily needs the familiar. If you were to take her away from all she's ever known, it would break her."

It wasn't an attack—of that she felt sure—but it still stung to hear and to feel in the marrow of her bones. Meg had already changed so much—their home, their routine. Daily she struggled with the idea of closing the store and moving to Orlando where Meg could get a regular job and help support her mom and dad. Daily, she second guessed her decision to stay. "I don't know, Dad. So much has changed already."

"She's stronger than you think. Amanda lives inside her. I see it in the pictures. I hear it in her voice when we talk on the phone." He chuckled, sadly and full of remorse. "Your mom and I were upset and disappointed when Amanda got pregnant. She was so young, so ill prepared to be a mother. Now, with all that's happened, I'm so grateful for our Lily-pad. More grateful still that she has you."

I'm hanging on by a thread, Dad. I'm doing the best I can, and it never feels like enough. The words clogged in her throat, begging for release. The truth, as soon as it broke free, would add another layer of regret to her already burdened father.

"I'm not sure Lily would agree." Their relationship was so fragile. For all intents and purposes, Meg was the only parent Lily had left. Neither knew what to think of or how to process that still unbelievable fact. "But we have each other. For now, that's enough."

"It's everything, Meggy. That doesn't mean she won't fight you. She's coming up on the teenage years where she'll fight you on everything. You're enough. You've always been there for her. She knows you love her. Above all else, the love will get you through."

Meg swallowed the tears that begged to be shed. She had to be strong for her father. For her mom. For Lily. She couldn't show weakness, even though she'd have crawled through the deepest depths of hell for one moment to spend in his big, open arms. "I know."

"I love you, Meggy. I'll call you in a day or two."

"I love you too, Daddy."

Calling him daddy showed her weakness. They both knew it. He mercifully let it slide.

Meg set the phone down and laid her head on the desk, shedding the tears she could no longer control. She missed her parents. She would have made a deal with the devil to have them back—healthy and whole—and to have their daily support.

Meg heard the knock, popped her head up, and hastily wiped the tears from her face before getting up to unlock the back door of the office. Eva stood on the porch with a dish in her hands.

"What's that?" Meg stepped back to let Eva pass.

"Veggie lasagna, made fresh from Barb's garden." She set the dish on Amanda's desk and studied Meg with kind eyes.

"Eva …"

"I know, I know, we shouldn't have fussed. But you know Barb."

Barb was Eva's sister. They were business partners and

roommates since the death of Barb's husband many years ago. The two of them had pampered Amanda, Meg, and Lily for years—before her parents retired and after. Since Amanda's death, they hovered like a couple of robins protecting the nest. "I don't want you two going to any trouble."

"It's no trouble. Besides, she had extra zucchini that was going to go bad." She looked around the office. "You making headway on the books?"

"I'm getting there." She'd never tell Eva the depth of her worry or her inexperience.

"You know, in addition to her fabulous cooking skills, Barb is also a magician with the books. If you need help, all you have to do is ask."

She did need help—and Eva and Barb helped all the time. They fed her and Lily, checked on them, and was Meg's first call when she needed a hand. But if she accepted Barb's help, the woman would inevitably tell Meg's dad who carried a big enough burden with his firstborn gone and his wife slipping away day by day.

"I'm figuring it out. You don't need to worry. I'm getting the hang of things. I'm better off doing the work myself. If I let someone do it, I'll never learn."

"I never said she'd do it for you, but she can answer your questions or check your math. Better to catch mistakes now instead of later when the bills are due, or taxes are owed."

Meg wouldn't—she couldn't—take the chance of Barb burdening her father. "I appreciate the offer. If I need help, I'll call Barb." She placed her palm to her chest like she was about to recite the pledge of allegiance. "I promise."

Appeased, at least for the moment, Eva leaned on the desk, a smile stretching across her wrinkled face. "I saw Lily get picked up by Cammie Lester. She looked like her old self—giddy and squealing like a kid. It did my heart good."

"I know." Guilt and helplessness wound around Meg's ribs like twin vines, squeezing painfully as they took root. While stalled in survival mode, there was little Meg could do to make Lily happy. "She needs to feel like a kid again."

"She will." Eva straightened and stepped to Meg, patting her on the shoulder before turning to leave. "Give it time."

Everyone said to give it time. Four months had passed, and the pain was still so raw. Meg spent her whole life as a part of a duet. With Amanda gone, she felt rudderless, floundering in the spotlight of a solo act. Her sidekick, her mentor, had walked off the stage without warning.

Before Eva could slip through the door, Meg called her name.

Eva turned, her brows lifting skyward. "Yes?"

"Did you see a guy come into my store today? Around lunchtime. Tall with dark hair and dark eyes."

Eva pursed her lips. "Can't say I did. Why? Was he bothering you?"

"No, nothing like that. He just … there was something about him …" She couldn't explain her reaction to the guy. Part familiarity, part dread. She'd done her best to tuck him and his odd reaction away during the day, but he hadn't receded from her thoughts. The way he stood staring at her so seriously, as if he couldn't remember why he'd even come in. And when he saw Lily … "Never mind."

"Was he cute?"

Meg sputtered, shaking her head. "I don't know. That's not what I meant."

"What did you mean?"

"I'm not sure. He came in, I asked him if he needed help, and when Lily came out from the back he just stared at her and then took off like he'd seen a ghost."

Eva stepped away from the door, placed her hand on the desk. "Do you think Lily's in danger?"

"I don't think so. He seemed almost scared of her." She shook her head, wished she hadn't asked. "Like I said, it was weird."

"Honey, if he comes back and makes you uncomfortable, you let me know and I'll be right over. We have to look out for each other."

"I appreciate it, Eva. And I appreciate the lasagna. Tell Barb thank you for me."

"I will. She said three-fifty for an hour." She turned to leave and then turned back, a mischievous gleam in her sparkling blue eyes. "When was the last time you went out on a date?"

The question landed like an alien from outer space. "What?"

"A date. You remember what that is?"

"Eva, we live in a fishbowl. Tourists come and go, and the locals are like family. Who am I supposed to date?"

"Not all tourists come and go."

A shaggy-haired, no-good guitar player flashed to mind. "No, some of them stay to string you along and then hit the road when you get attached." Meg needed to get a grip on her lips. The last thing she wanted was to rehash her disastrous relationship with Zander.

"Not everyone is like that musician who broke your heart."

"You're right. Some men smooth talk you into going away and get you killed. I guess I should consider myself lucky."

Eva tsked, her face scrunching like she'd bitten into a sour apple. "You can't judge all men by the bottom of the barrel. And you're too young to live like a hermit. You're a beautiful young woman with a lot to offer. I think you need to make some time for yourself."

Between the store and Lily, she'd never had much time. Since Amanda's death, she could barely fit a shower into her life, much less a man. "Unless you know how to add hours to the day, I'm not sure how I'd make time for anything right now."

"Ask for help," Eva said, her expression as serious as she'd ever seen it. "We love Lily like our own. Spending time with her is a precious gift. Have we ever said no?"

Meg's sigh sounded as cranky as she felt. "No."

"Consider this an open offer. Whenever you need a break, just ask. We're here for you, Meg. We're here for both of you."

It was an offer they'd made before and one she had no intention of abusing. Besides, dating required an interested man, and men— other than the mystery man—were the last thing on her mind.

Meg opened the store on a muggy Wednesday morning. With no cruise ships on the schedule for the day, she looked forward to a lighter crowd and some much-needed time for back-office work. They had blown through a lot of the stock throughout the busy weekend, and she'd spent the last few days unpacking, pricing, and getting merchandise out onto the floor in between customers.

Keeping up with their inventory seasons ahead of when the merchandise needed to be ordered, while keeping the floor stocked was hard.

She'd just set up the cash drawer when the door bells jingled, alerting her to a customer. Meg's ready smile bloomed when she recognized the owner of nearby Westies Bar & Grill. "Hey, Tim. How's it going?"

Tim ran a hand over the short haircut he'd worn since his stint in the military. "It's going good. How ya doing, Meg?"

"I can't complain." Oh, but she could. She really, really could. "What brings you in?"

He waved a stack of yellow papers in his hand. "Would you mind if I hung one of these flyers in your window? In the corner, like usual, so I don't block your display."

"Of course. What's the occasion?"

"I just made a last-minute booking for a big band next week. I'm trying to get the word out since I promised them a packed house."

"You always have a packed house with live music."

"Usually, yeah. But this is short notice."

She found the tape from the behind the counter and tossed him the roll. "I'll let you do the honors."

He nodded and disappeared inside the display.

Meg selected a playlist for the day, something reggae and fun she hoped would lighten her mood, and straightened up behind the counter, making a list of things to do. Tim set the tape on the surface, flashing the sleeve of his intricate tattoo.

"Appreciate your help."

"It's no problem." The business owners on the street had a long history of working together that made them all friends. "How's business?"

"I can't complain." He mimicked her earlier response and glanced around the shop in no hurry to leave. "How bout you, Meg? The store looks good."

She looked around, tried to see it from his perspective. Nothing much had changed in the front of the store with Amanda gone. All the changes were behind closed doors and only those who knew their family dynamics would worry and wonder. "Thanks. I'm doing the best I can. It's an adjustment without Amanda. I never really appreciated how much she took on."

"You were partners. Her death was a devastating blow—in every area of your life."

So much for putting on a good front. "Yeah, it was." And if he led her any further along the pity trail, she'd never get any work done. "I'm getting by. Eva and Barb have been a big help."

Tim chuckled. "Those two mother hens have nurtured us all, at one point or another."

"Thank heavens."

"Amen to that."

When he made no move to leave, Meg smiled at him with a question in her eyes.

"Listen, I'm not sure if you want to know this, but a guy came by the bar last week. Corey Westfall's brother. He asked about Amanda."

Just the mention of his name—the name she never uttered—had Meg's muscles tightening and pressure building behind her eyes. "His brother?"

"Name's Bryan. Nice enough guy. Seemed harmless, but I wanted you to know."

She flashed back to the guy who'd popped into the store last week as a two-alarm fire scorched her belly. "What did he look like?" Her voice, choked by anger and resentment, came out whisper soft.

"Ahh ..." Tim stared over her shoulder. "Wavy brown hair, brown eyes, medium build, maybe six-one or six-two. Sunburnt, so I pegged him as a tourist." He looked at her. "Are you okay?"

"I'm fine." She was anything but, after Tim described the man who'd dashed in and out of her store. No wonder he'd bolted after getting a look at Lily. She looked just like Amanda. "Did he say anything?" She shook her head, tried to clear the cobwebs. "Why is he here?"

"He asked if I knew Amanda. If she and Corey were a couple. Other than that, he didn't say much. Ate lunch and left. Look." He touched her hand where she gripped the pen in a white-knuckle grasp. "I didn't mean to stress you out."

"You didn't."

He gave her a disbelieving stare.

"I'm glad you told me. Will you do me a favor, please, and let me know if you see him again?"

"Of course. I'm sorry I upset you."

"You didn't upset me, Tim. I'm just surprised. I never imagined his family would try to get in touch."

"I didn't tell him anything he couldn't have read in the paper. They were together when they died. What they were doing or what they meant to each other was none of my business. I told him the same."

She nodded, tried to hold onto her mask of indifference. She knew it was an epic failure by the sympathy on his face. "I appreciate your letting me know."

He rapped a knuckle on the surface. "You take care, Meg. Thanks for the window space."

"Anytime."

She watched him leave as a thousand scenarios zipped through her head. The barnacle had a brother. She'd never given a second thought to the man who'd died with Amanda, whatever family he left behind, or what they might be going through. All she could think about—all she could process in the months since her sister's death—was Lily and their lives without Amanda.

If his brother was here and asking questions about Amanda, it wasn't outside the realm of possibility he might try and talk to Lily. The fire in Meg's belly ignited a fuse that raced along Meg's nerves. She would never allow anyone to approach Lily and ask questions about her dead mother. Never.

She looked down, realized she'd crumpled her to-do list in her fist. It was just as well. With Tim's bombshell reverberating in shock waves, she had a new task that overtook anything on her list. She couldn't take the chance the barnacle's brother would approach Lily. She wouldn't.

Meg pulled her phone from her back pocket and Googled his name. Bypassing the dozen or more articles and news stories about his and Amanda's tragic deaths, she found an online obituary. Listed as remaining kin were his parents, Edward and Cynthia Westfall, and a brother, Bryan, all from Atlanta, Georgia.

Another Google search led her to Bryan's scant social media presence. She pulled up a link. A bucket of sand doused the fire in her belly and sent her stomach swirling in a free-fall. Bryan Westfall was the man who'd come into her store and quickly fled after spotting Lily.

The store and her list forgotten, Meg started making calls. If Bryan Westfall was in town and asking questions, she would give him all the answers he deserved. She just had to find him first.

Eight

Bryan taped a box and reached for a Sharpie to label it as a giveaway, wiping the sweat from his brow. No matter how low he set the air conditioning, it did nothing but circulate hot air. No wonder the landlord had been so nice. He'd collected a rent check without having to fix the air, the barely functioning refrigerator, or hire an exterminator.

In the week and a half he'd been in Key West, Bryan had made slow progress. So far, everything he'd packed was going to charity. What did he or his parents need with mismatched dishes, a ragtag collection of pots and pans, and a handful of mystery paperbacks?

He'd gone through the kitchen and living room examining everything—flipping through books, looking at every slip of paper, boxing up everything but the essentials Bryan needed for the weeks he'd remain. A couple of coffee mugs, the coffee machine, a handful of silverware, and some cups.

All that remained were the bedroom, bathroom, and closet where the bulk of Corey's belongings were stored. So far, he'd found nothing to indicate how Corey had spent his last few months. Receipts for takeout restaurants, yep. Proofs of purchase from the local liquor store, of course. Other than a couple of paystubs from a rental shack at the beach Bryan had checked out over the weekend, he couldn't figure out how Corey paid for rent and groceries from his part-time gig renting jet skis and teaching tourists to wind surf.

Nothing about his brother's life made sense.

Bryan had settled into a routine of getting up early to start sorting and packing before mid-day when the heat became unbearable. Around noon he'd drive around the island and stop for lunch at the kind of places he thought Corey would frequent. More likely than not, he'd find a bartender who either knew or knew of Corey.

Bryan heard the same story over and over. Nice guy. Good with the ladies. Liked to drink and play pool. He didn't get in bar fights. He always paid his tab. Knowing Corey's pattern eased Bryan's conscience, but it left more questions than answers.

After a tasty lunch—the food on the island was fantastic—Bryan would head home and resume sorting through Corey's things for as long as he could stand the heat. He'd take breaks to cool off in the shower, occasionally going to the ocean when he needed to clear his head.

The last time Bryan and Corey had been in touch, Corey was working on some deal in Key West, some get-rich-quick scheme Corey was convinced would solve all his problems. Most of Corey's schemes caused more problems than they solved, but since Bryan had cut him off financially, Corey had stopped divulging the details of his shady investments.

Until Corey died, ignorance had suited Bryan just fine. Now that ignorance sat like a trap door beneath his feet. One wrong step, and Corey's seedy world would swallow him whole and spit him out into the hollow depths of the unknown. Bryan kept waiting for someone to knock on the door and demand payment for some past-due loan.

Three bangs on the door jarred Bryan from his thoughts and had images of a beefy henchman waiting on the other side slapping a baseball bat into his open palm. Bryan stood, his knees popping, and walked soundlessly to the door. He listened, heard nothing, and without a peep hole or a side window, he had no choice but to open the door and face his fate.

He inched the door open a crack and his heart jammed into his throat. Instead of a beefy henchman, a willowy redhead stood fuming on his doorstep. He swung the door open wide and gawked at Amanda Holloway's sister, tapping her sandaled foot on the mat.

"Stay away from us." Her velvet voice quivered with rage. "Do you understand me?"

"Uh …" Bryan couldn't organize his thoughts into anything resembling words. Seeing her in the store had been like punch to the gut. Standing inches away on his doorstep where he could count the freckles across her nose and smell the perfume on her skin left him senseless. The woman didn't need a baseball bat. She wielded a punch with her presence.

"You've got nothing to say?"

He extended his hand. "I'm Bryan Westfall. It's nice to officially meet you."

"Nice?" She gave his hand a death stare and her tone pitched higher. "You think this is a social call?"

Bryan dropped his hand. "I don't have a clue what this is."

"This is a warning." She aimed a finger in his face. "Do not come near me, my niece, or our store, ever again. I don't know what you're doing here, but you're not going to weasel your way into our lives like your brother did. He did enough damage, thank you, very much."

Whatever evidence Bryan had been searching for landed squarely at his feet with her threat. Corey's presence in this woman's life had changed it for the worse. "Listen …"

"Meg."

"I'm sorry for your loss, Meg."

His simple statement and quiet tone stopped her cold. She straightened her stance and folded her arms across her V-necked white t-shirt, an apostrophe forming between her brows. "What do you want from us? Why are you here?"

Bryan stepped back. "Why don't you come in and I'll explain."

The crevice between her brows deepened and she shook her head. "I don't think so."

Of course she didn't trust him. He was a stranger. His brother had slithered into her sister's life and torn it to shreds. Meg was the living, breathing, reminder of what happened when people let Corey and his devil-may-care outlook into their orbit. "I'm cleaning out Corey's apartment. Trying to piece together his last few months."

"You're his brother." It wasn't so much a statement as an accusation.

"You and your sister were close?"

The sadness in her eyes said as much as her choked agreement. Grief sat just below the surface. One tiny shift was all it took to uncover her pain. "Very close."

"Corey and I …" How could he explain their complicated

relationship? He couldn't, not without a history lesson she didn't care to hear. "We had a falling out."

She snorted. "Of course you did." She stared past him into the apartment filled with boxes labeled for charity. "That must make this pretty easy for you, huh? Boxing up his stuff, giving it away as if he never existed. You're probably relieved he's gone. No more fighting, no more messy feelings about your flesh and blood."

Shame heated the skin of his neck, giving his voice a dangerous edge. "Nothing about this is easy."

"My sister and I lived and worked together." She raised her chin in the air, determined to drive her point home. "We raised her daughter together. Nothing about losing her was easy on any of us. I'm sorry for your loss, Bryan, but you can look for answers elsewhere. We've been through enough. The last thing we need is another slick-talking Westfall poking around where he doesn't belong."

Would she feel better or worse to know they shared the same impression of Corey? He decided not to find out. "I'm sorry. I didn't mean to trouble you."

"It's too late for that. Just hear me loud and clear—leave us alone. Pack your stuff and go back where you came from. Whatever Corey was up to before he died doesn't change the outcome. He's dead and he dragged Amanda down with him. If you care at all about those of us left behind, you'll go and never come back."

She turned to leave, and a panicked surge of impatience had him stepping toward her, had him saying something he should have thought through. "I know you feel—"

She turned back so quickly her hair tangled in her teeth. She pulled the strands free and speared him with an angry scowl. "You don't have clue how I feel."

He didn't, not really, but neither did she. "I lost my brother, too."

She closed her mouth and stared at him, the heat coloring her cheeks dimmed.

"Maybe we weren't close. Maybe I couldn't have changed the outcome, but you're not the only one grieving. He may be the villain, but he was my brother. He was a man—a flawed man—with a family who cared. I'm not here to get you all worked up, but I need answers. My family needs answers."

She watched him with wary, grass-green eyes. "Your answers don't involve us."

"Your sister knew him better than anyone."

She shook her head and the red strands caught fire in the sunlight. "That's not saying a lot."

He had no other option but to beg. "Please, Meg. I don't know where else to turn."

She stared at him, grasping the strap of the leather bag slung over her shoulder in a chokehold. "Then I guess you're out of luck." She pivoted and strode away, eating up ground with her long, slender legs.

Bryan watched the sway of her miniskirt as she stormed off, then closed the door and turned to face Corey's apartment. He rubbed the ache in his gut. He may have needed answers, but finding them just got a whole lot harder.

Nine

Meg got back in her car, turned the ignition, and gripped the steering wheel, her heart thumping like a kettle drum in her chest. She juked the air and let the coolness spray across her face, hot from anger and humidity. Bryan Westfall and his brother were nothing but trouble. Bryan's presence, his questions, would lead him nowhere but back home where he belonged.

Hopefully, sooner rather than later.

The barnacle had been a good-looking leech who caught the eye of her naïve sister. The moment he'd started sniffing around Amanda, Meg knew he was up to no good. Bryan may have been smarter, calmer, and more nuanced in his approach, but Meg wasn't easily fooled. She didn't fall at the feet of every handsome man who turned on the charm. Not anymore.

Whatever he was looking for, whatever he hoped to find out about his brother, didn't involve Meg or Lily—or even Amanda.

She prayed he'd heed her warning, pack his brother's things, and go home.

When her heart rate settled, she checked her mirrors and pulled away from the street, her hands still shaking from the encounter. Meg wouldn't let herself think about his face, the pain etched across his forehead when he'd said they'd had a falling out. His rocky relationship with his brother was none of her business. She didn't want or need any information about the man who'd led Amanda to her deathbed taking up space in her head. What good would it do to feel sorry for him—to feel anything for him other than contempt?

Meg parked behind the store and, instead of going inside, took a deep breath and knocked on the flower shop door. Barb appeared, holding floral tape and wearing a smile. "Hey," she said. "That didn't take long."

"Nope. Thanks for watching Lily."

At the mention of her name, Lily turned her head and narrowed her eyes. "I don't want to go home yet. Barb is showing me how to wrap flowers for a button-air."

Barb laughed, her ruddy cheeks crinkling. "A boutonniere." She looked at Meg. "We were just getting started."

Meg watched Lily at the counter, her fingers fumbling with the stems. When was the last time Lily had had fun doing anything at the store?

"Please, Aunt Meg," Lily begged. "Barb said I could help."

Meg raised her brows at Barb. "You sure you don't mind?"

"I don't mind at all. I can use her help." She wiggled her fingers. "These old digits aren't as agile as they used to be."

"Okay." Meg inclined her head to the left. "I'll be next door. Let me know when you're done."

With the adrenaline rush gone, Meg slumped, exhausted, into the chair at Amanda's desk. She jostled the mouse to bring the computer to life and took a deep breath, tried to clear her head before recording the day's sales. As the program chugged to life, Meg's mind wandered back to Bryan Westfall.

He looked like his brother. Same dark, flyaway hair, same broad stature, same all-American good looks. But the resemblance ended there. Bryan's brother had oozed charm like sweat from his pores. Every woman was a mark, every encounter a chance to impress. The barnacle had been all talk and swagger. Bryan's expression held more sympathy than temper. He wasn't the type of guy to use his looks and fancy words to manipulate.

Guilt needled its way under her skin, worming up her spine to lodge a defensive attack on her heart. *I lost my brother too.* Like a shout across a mountain range, his simple statement echoed in her head. His dispassionate tone wasn't meant to shame. He'd stood there and met her fire with a cool calmness she had to admire—and envy.

Bryan Westfall had accepted his brother's death. Their estrangement meant the details of the barnacle's life were a mystery, but Bryan didn't radiate the frantic, shamefaced energy Meg bathed in every day. Bryan knew he couldn't change the past. Logically, Meg knew she couldn't either, but that didn't stop her from dragging guilt into every facet of her life. Guilt colored everything in a hazy film of shame. No matter how hard she scrubbed, she couldn't wash herself clean.

Lily's giggle carried through the open door. Meg squeezed her eyes tight and savored the sound. She had to let go of her anger and find some peace, accept reality, and move on with grace. Meg's mother modeled grateful living, her sister had lived a thankful life, and her dad faced every day with a grateful heart, even as his wife slipped away in front of his eyes. In the face of all that grace, why couldn't Meg dig deep and find the peace that her family held in spades?

After recording the figures from the day and updating the program, Meg shut the computer down and gathered her things. She found Lily and Barb, heads bent conspiratorially, working together with a mound of white roses.

"You ready to go?"

Lily jerked her head in Meg's direction, a frown tugging on her lips. "Do we have to?"

"Afraid so. I've got to stop by the store if we want to have any food for dinner."

"You've been a big help," Barb said to Lily, patting her on the shoulder. "It's time to call it a night."

"But we haven't finished," Lily protested.

"There's always tomorrow. Go home and relax. Whenever you want to help, you just say the word."

Lily placed her work in progress on the table and examined her hands. "This is hard on the fingers."

"They toughen up after a while." Barb opened her arms and enfolded Lily in a hug. "You sure are a blessing, sweet girl. You've earned some down time."

"That was fun. I like working with the flowers."

"You're a natural."

Lily lifted her brows at Meg. "Did you hear that? I'm a natural."

"I heard." Meg nodded her head at the sink and Lily stepped over to wash her hands. "And I'm not surprised. You're good at a lot of things."

"Like what?" Lily asked.

"Like helping people, making your bed, school."

Lily dried her hands on a towel and wrinkled her nose at Meg. "That stuff doesn't count."

Barb took the towel from Lily's hands, a placating smile on her face. "That stuff counts a lot. Helping people, doing your part at home and at school is important. You're a smart, beautiful girl with a caring heart and a bright future."

"When did you know you wanted to be a florist?" Lily cocked her head and waited for Barb's answer. Her inquisitive mind never ceased to amaze Meg.

Barb chuckled and led Lily to the door. "That is a conversation for another day. Go help your aunt and come back soon."

"I will. Thanks, Barb."

Meg mouthed thank you over Lily's head.

"You're welcome. Both of you."

Meg unlocked the car doors and tossed her bags in the back. When she settled behind the steering wheel, she looked at Lily. "You thinking about becoming a florist?"

Lily jerked a shoulder. "I don't know. It seems fun, working with flowers. It smells good in there and it's nice to create something cheerful."

Meg thought of her art, the tubes of paint and stacks of blank canvases she'd neglected for too long. "Yes, it is." Meg started the engine and heard the familiar teeth-grinding whine from beneath the hood. At some point, she had to get her car serviced. She pulled out of the lot, her shoulders relaxing as Lily sang along to the song on the radio, something poppy and fun. "What are you in the mood for? Spaghetti or sloppy joes?"

"Spaghetti, please. Can we get meatballs?"

Meg winked at Lily. "What's spaghetti without meatballs?"

"Boring."

"Exactly." She pulled into a parking space at the discount grocery and cut the engine. "How about you go get the meatballs and while you're in the freezer section, pick us out some ice cream for dessert."

"Really?"

The surprise in Lily's voice made Meg's heart squeeze. "I'm feeling crazy tonight." And determined to live by grace.

"Yay! Thank you, Aunt Meg."

"You worked hard. You deserve a little treat."

They walked into the store. "Can I get chocolate?"

"You can get whatever flavor you want."

Lily gave her a side-eyed glance. "Where did you go when you left me with Barb?"

"Why?"

"Because you're being a lot nicer than usual."

The squeeze became a squish. "I love you, Lily. I'm sorry I've been so grumpy."

"It's okay. I know you've got a lot going on."

A twelve-year-old shouldn't think about the responsibilities of adults. "That's no excuse to be in a bad mood all the time. I promise I'll try and be nicer."

Lily's smile was like a gift for Meg's soul. "Me too."

Meg passed Lily a grocery cart and pointed to the back of the store. "Meatballs and ice cream. Meet me at the register."

Lily smiled and took off at a sprint.

Meg watched her go, emotion clogging her throat. She had a lot to feel grateful for.

Ten

Bryan's encounter with the beautiful Meg Holloway left him restless. Frustrated by his impulsive entry into her store and her angry reaction to his presence on the island, he'd charged ahead with the upstairs loft. Working through lunch and the choking heat, he'd spent two days packing most of the bathroom and a good bit of the bedroom without finding any evidence of Corey's affairs.

Exhausted, defeated, he flung himself onto the couch and called home.

His dad answered after two rings. "Hello?"

"Hey, Dad."

"How's it going down there? Haven't heard much since you arrived."

"I've been taking my time going through Corey's stuff to make sure I don't miss anything."

Ed paused and sniffed as if wary of what Bryan had to report.

"What have you found?"

"Not much other than a few photos." Bryan found them in the bedside table along with assorted scraps of paper and a handful of matchbooks from area bars. Corey looked drunk, his eyes in slits, a Silly Putty grin splitting his face, his arms around strangers in similar stages of intoxication. "I packed up most of his stuff to go to charity—the kitchen, the linens, a few paperbacks."

"That's probably for the best."

"We never talked about his furniture."

Ed sighed heavily. Bryan pictured him rubbing his temple. "Don't have much need for any furniture, unless you do."

"I don't, and it's honestly not that great. Looks like secondhand stuff."

"I guess charity for the furniture too." His voice sounded as flat as a deflated raft.

Bryan felt the force of his dad's despair land squarely on his strung-tight back. "I'll be done in a day or so, but I'm not sure about coming home right away."

"There's about a week left on the lease. Are you thinking of staying longer?"

"I'm off all summer." He needed more time. The one thing he felt sure of after Meg's confrontation was there was more there than met the eye. "Did you know the girl who died with Corey had a daughter?"

Bryan's stomach freeze-dried in the pause that stretched.

His dad cleared his throat. "I did."

"Why didn't you tell me?"

"It was right there in the obituary." The edge in his dad's tone was sharp enough to cut. "Figured you saw."

"I didn't."

"It doesn't change things, son. We're not responsible for her."

"I know we're not responsible—for the daughter or the aunt—but it feels ... like a weight against my chest."

"It's got nothing to do with feelings. You don't know them, Bryan. They can't hold you responsible."

"I know." But knowing and accepting were two different things. "I met the sister—the aunt. She's angry. I have to try and make things right with her before I can even think about coming home."

"Make things right how?" Ed swallowed the temper rising in his voice. "You read the police report. It was an accident. Corey didn't drag that girl out into the water, and neither did you."

"I know, Dad. I know." But accidents had consequences—people left behind, adrift in a sea of grief and worry and stress. Wounded, fragile, beautiful people. It wasn't easy to feel blameless in the face of all that hurt. "I'm staying through the week, and maybe beyond. I'm just letting you know it may be a while before I get home."

"Son, listen to me." Ed sounded like one of Bryan's kids trying to talk his grade higher at the end of the semester. "You've got a generous heart. That's what makes you a good teacher. You like helping people and that's admirable. But this is madness. Those people are strangers dealing with their own grief. We got enough to deal with ourselves."

He couldn't explain or defend his position, so Bryan took the coward's route and changed the subject. "How's Mom?"

"She's getting by." His dad inhaled a shaky breath, loosening the tightness in Bryan's shoulders. Ed couldn't get worked up about the Holloway family when he was consumed by grief and worry for his wife. "Some ladies from the church are with her now. It helps to have people around. Helps her forget."

Bryan wished he could forget. Unlike his mom, he didn't have people around to distract him from his thoughts. The only people around reminded him of Corey and all the mistakes Bryan made when dealing with his brother. "Give her my love. I'll call in a couple of days."

"I love you, son."

"Love you too, Dad." But Bryan wouldn't leave with things so unsettled. He wasn't responsible for Amanda's death, but he couldn't get the image of angry, wounded Meg and her innocent niece out of his head. Until he could, he wasn't going anywhere.

The posters were all over town. A band Bryan had never heard of was playing at Westies, the first place he'd stumbled into after foolishly entering Meg's store. The bartender at Westies was nice, the food was good, and Bryan needed a night out of his own head and Corey's apartment more than he needed his next breath.

Dressed in khaki shorts and a quick-dry shirt, Bryan headed to the bar, making sure to give A Day's Wait a wide birth when parking and walking to the venue. No need to force another confrontation when all he wanted—all he needed—was a night to forget and recharge.

The place was packed. Bryan felt lucky to find a single stool at the end of the bar running the length of the back wall. He waved off the cigarette smoke from three seats away and waited for Tim, wearing another rock band t-shirt and a haggard expression, to work his way down.

Bryan watched the band set up their equipment piece by piece. Tim finally inched closer, a flustered look on his face. "Bryan, right? What can I get you?"

"I'll take the IPA on draft."

Tim stepped over to the pulls and filled a plastic cup.

"You shorthanded?" Bryan called over the noise of wall-to-wall people.

"I'm drowning. Biggest band of the season and one of my bartenders called in sick."

Bryan scanned the crowd. They were packed from the stage to the bar and lined up outside the entrance. "I used to tend bar in college. Let me know if you need a hand."

Tim set the beer in front of Bryan, his expression a mixture of skepticism and hope. "Are you serious?"

"I mean, it's been a while, but I can handle the basics."

Tim paused before shoving a drink menu at Bryan. "Those are the specials. If you think you can serve them and not slow me down, come on back. I appreciate the help."

Bryan skimmed the menu of staple cocktails with a Key West twist. He could make mojitos, margaritas, rum runners, and piña coladas in his sleep. Bryan stood, took a chug of his beer, and moved around the corner to slip under the flap.

The look on Tim's face was pure relief. "I'll handle the beer taps and bottles and either call out or jot down the orders for cocktails. Do not take orders or payment on your own. Send anyone who tries down to me."

"No problem."

Tim filled a cup with draft and nodded to the bulk supply of plastic cups lining the second shelf. "Everything's in plastic."

"Gotcha."

Tim shook his head, a tepid smile dusting his lips. "One of us is a fool, I'm just not sure which one."

Bryan lifted his hands and shrugged. Doing anything other than trying to investigate his brother felt like a gift. "Hit me with an order. We'll figure it out soon enough."

Eleven

The humid air smelled like a party. Base notes of spilled alcohol and cooking grease mixed with cologne and coconut sunscreen. Cigarette smoke and pot hovered like a cherry over the top. With the bass drum vibrating through her skull and colored lights pulsing overhead, Meg shouldered her way through the heat-sticky crowd, cursing Eva and her insistence that Meg "go out and have fun."

Despite a few minutes of joy in dancing to the music with friends, there was nothing fun about cruising between stinky armpits and soggy, sweat-soaked hair, desperate for a place to sit and catch her breath.

Barb had been working with Lily, filling orders, and teaching her the ropes, when Meg stopped by to retrieve her. Eva intercepted her at the door, insisting that Meg take a night to herself.

"What am I going to do by myself?"

"What do you like to do?"

Eva's question had stumped her. Meg couldn't remember the last time she'd done something fun just for herself. "I don't know." She'd wracked her brain, tried to think of something, and blurted the first idea that came to mind. "Read."

Eva had the nerve to roll her eyes. "No reading. Go out, meet people, talk to a stranger or two."

"Where?"

"Westies is having a band. You've got the poster in your window."

"That's for tourists."

"A band is for everyone. Besides, if fun was reserved for tourists, Key West wouldn't have any permanent residents."

Eva and her quick comebacks had boxed Meg into a corner. "Fine. I'll go see the band." She liked to support local businesses, and Tim was a friend. "But I'm not staying long."

"Why not?"

Meg had dipped her head sideways and gestured behind Eva where Lily worked with Barb at the counter. "Lily."

"We've got Lily. Go have fun. She can sleep at our place. You know she adores Ralph."

Lily did adore Eva and Barb's cat. Spending time with their pet might lessen Lily's requests they get one of their own. "I don't know." She'd looked down at her linen shorts and work top. "I'm not dressed to go out."

Eva dropped her chin and her voice. "Do you think there's a dress code?"

Of course there wasn't a dress code, but that wasn't the point. "I have work tomorrow."

"You work every day. One night off won't kill you."

As Meg lunged for a seat at the bar, desperate for water and a second to rest her legs, she begged to differ with Eva. One night off was killing her work shoes and her motivation to ever go out again. The band was good, and she'd had fun dancing with friends, but after fending off some handsy men, including one who'd grabbed her butt, she wondered if going out was worth the hassle.

Meg sighed as she sat, swiveling around to face the bar, and eyed the distance between her seat and the bartender with the impressive backside fixing drinks along the back wall. Meg knew all the regulars and this guy, with his shirt clinging to his athletic build, didn't look familiar. Tim must have hired a new bartender.

He turned, forcing Meg to lift her gaze. Bryan Westfall, with shaggy hair and a killer smile, brought two cocktails to Tim's daytime bartender, Kaya, before slinging his brown eyes in Meg's direction. She sat speechless, a tight fist squeezing her throat.

The smile leaked from his lips. He reached for something beneath the counter and came up with two plastic cups. "I can't take your order."

"What?" The band was starting up again and the lead singer joked with the crowd.

"I'm making drinks, not serving them." Bryan jerked his head down the bar where Tim and Kaya fielded requests from all sides. "You have to tell them what you want."

"I only want water."

He flashed a grin with enough wattage to send her body down a one-way street to awkward. Her physical reaction to him made her feel guilty, like she was no better than her sister—and look where that had got her.

"That I can do." He filled a glass with ice and used the soda gun to fill her drink, handing it over with a wary look in his eyes.

"Thank you." She sipped and watched him fill cups with ice. "What are you doing here?"

"Helping a friend."

"Tim?"

"He was shorthanded." Bryan lifted his hands before palming a bottle of rum. "I've got two."

She deliberately relaxed her face muscles when she felt them sagging into a frown. Since when was Tim *his* friend? And how could she hold a grudge against a guy who'd done something so selfless and nice? She leaned in to be heard over the music. "You're a bartender?"

"Used to be. Back in college."

Of course he went to college. Meg added another mark against him in her personal tally. "That's nice."

"It paid the bills." Bryan lifted his voice when the band started into another song.

"Two margs and a rum runner," Tim shouted from the draft pulls.

Bryan gave him a thumbs up and resumed his stance along the counter, freeing Meg to look her fill. *Okay, fine*, she admitted, as the guitar player began a complicated solo. Maybe Bryan wasn't as in-your-face good looking as his annoying brother had been, but he certainly held his own. But just because he was attractive didn't give him a pass. He never should have come into her store, gawking at them and leaving without a word. Meg felt sure if Lily knew who Bryan was, she'd feel as uncomfortable as Meg did now.

Meg shook her head, mentally scolding herself. It didn't matter what Bryan Westfall did or didn't do. His brother, the barnacle, had done enough. Meg downed the water, her parched throat grateful to the looker behind the bar. Now that she knew Bryan was at the bar and she'd rehydrated, it was time to go home—Eva and her instructions to stay out late be darned.

She stood from the stool, absently stepping onto someone's foot. She jerked her foot away but not before the guy who'd grabbed her on the dance floor leaned in and pressed his drenched shirt to her side. Meg apologized and tried to move away, but he'd boxed her between him and the bar.

"That's okay, pretty lady." His breath reeked of beer, his dilated pupils said he'd had one too many. "How about I buy you another drink?"

Grief shot like fireworks through her veins. Meg and Amanda would tag team guys at a bar the same way they used to tag team customers at the store. If Amanda were still alive, she'd be with her. If Amanda were still alive, she'd have Meg's back. "Sorry, but I'm on my way out."

"Come on, Red. What's the hurry?"

The overused nickname grated on Meg's nerves. No one who knew her would ever have called her Red. "My name's not Red or Ginger or Pretty Lady. And you need to step back and let me pass."

He did the opposite, squeezing his barrel chest against her, his sweaty shirt giving off the musty odor of a wet dog. She leaned back and crushed herself against the bar, imprinting her metal bra hooks into her back like a brand. Meg couldn't see Bryan, but she felt his presence behind her, heard his quick intake of breath.

"The lady said no." Bryan's voice, so affable and calm whenever they'd spoken, came out as a gruff and menacing growl.

The man's face reddened, and his nostrils quivered. "Stay out of it, barkeep."

"I'll stay out of it when you let the lady pass."

"And if I don't?"

Bryan was right behind her, his breath tickling her neck. "Do you really want to find out?" The deep timber of his voice sent a shiver down her spine.

The man's eyes shifted, and his posture slouched. "Give it a rest, Max." Tim's firm command from a few paces back left no room for doubt.

Max stayed put, squished against Meg. "I was just trying to buy the lady a drink."

"The lady's not interested," Tim said. "Move along or I get Stevo involved."

Whoever Stevo was, the mention of his name had Max backing up with his hands in the air. Meg took her first full breath that didn't reek of dirty bodies and booze. She looked at Tim, sparing a quick glance at Bryan. "Thank you."

Tim scowled at Max as he slithered back into the crowd. "Sorry for the hassle," he said to Meg and made his way down the bar.

Meg's gaze was snared by Bryan's intense blazing eyes. She turned and made a beeline for the door, unsure which man inside the bar she was running from more.

Twelve

Bryan tossed the bar towel into the sink and tapped Tim on the shoulder. "Be right back."

Tim nodded, his focus on the patrons demanding his attention.

Bryan dipped under the flap, zigzagged his way through the crowd, and exited just in time to see the swing of Meg's coppery hair disappear around the corner. He kicked his pace to a jog.

She stuttered to a stop and spun around with a hand clutching her chest, her eyes bulging, and her breath expelled on a forceful hiss. "You scared the life out of me."

He stopped in front of her as he released his own shaky breath. "Sorry."

"What are you doing?"

He hadn't thought, he'd just taken off after her. "Making sure you get to your car okay."

She stared at him with a wrinkle between her brows as if he'd suggested walking her to the moon. Despite the already sweltering temperature, Bryan's face heated with embarrassment. "That guy was pretty persistent. It doesn't take much for a drunk to lash out."

A gust of wind blew hair in her face. She brushed it away impatiently. "I can take care of myself."

"I'm sure you can, but for my own peace of mind, I wanted to see you to your car."

She placed a hand on her cocked hip. His eyes followed and lowered to her legs. The woman had a fabulous pair of legs. "Look, Bryan. I appreciate your help back there, but I grew up on this island. Dealing with drunks and fools is pretty much a requirement of residency."

He liked the sound of her voice, the way it lilted when she was angry, the way it pulsed like the beat of a song. He wanted to keep her talking. "This is my first time on the island. Where I'm from, when a man sees a woman getting hassled, he steps in to secure her safety. That's how I was raised."

Meg snorted, probably thinking of his brother. Corey was the ultimate hustler, swaggering around bars, leering at women. She straightened her back. "I was raised to mistrust strangers."

He gave her an are-you-kidding-me frown. "Owning a retail store? That sounds like career suicide."

She'd never done anything but scowl, so when her lips twitched and bloomed into a teeth-showing smile, he felt woozy and weak. Watching her face transform was like seeing the sun after weeks of pouring rain.

"Touché."

Bryan stared at her for a beat, afraid to say the wrong thing, tick her off, and make her storm away. "What do you say?"

Her smile disappeared and she blinked, her green eyes bewildered. "About what?"

"Can I walk you to your car like a gentleman? Maybe claw back some points for my gender?"

She tilted her head, her red hair billowing in the humid air. "If I say no, are you going to follow me anyway?"

"Yes." Bryan nodded. "I will."

"Fine." Her eye roll wasn't much of a speed bump when accompanied by a half-hearted smirk. "It's only, like, ten steps away."

His ego soared when she slowed her breakneck pace. "You never know what can happen in ten steps."

She stopped by an older sedan with dings and chipping paint, flashed him a flippant smirk. "Apparently nothing. This is me."

Bryan nodded, slipping his hands into his front pockets. He wasn't ready to let her go, not when she was being civil. "How far is home?"

"Key West is an island. Nothing's far."

He dropped his head and smiled. Man, she was pretty. The kind of pretty that stole his breath and gave him the bittersweet thrill of a savoring a moment that couldn't last. "Be careful on your drive."

She punched a button on her key fob and only one back light flashed. Bryan frowned before wiping his expression clear.

"I always am."

"Good to hear."

She eyed him suspiciously, jingling the keys in her palm. "You going to stand there and watch me drive away?"

He'd do anything to capture the moment like a still life in his head. "Can't be too careful."

"I'd better get going so you can get back to work." She got in, started the car.

He heard a whine that sounded like a loose belt and knew with a hundred percent certainty she'd never let him peek under the hood. He stepped to the side when she backed out, grimacing at the busted taillight as she pulled onto the main drag and disappeared into the night.

Bryan walked back to the bar, rubbing the aching hollowness in his chest, the salty air cooling his skin, his mind resolute. He wasn't going anywhere. Meg had burrowed under his skin like a tick, carving him out and leaving him restless. He knew he would only obsess and worry if he didn't stick around and see it through. With Meg's pretty smile on his mind, he entered the bar and rejoined the chaos.

The band had quit over an hour before and all that remained were the stragglers. Tim shooed Bryan to the other side of the bar and poured him a draft from the freshly tapped keg. The cold brew went down easy after a sweltering night on his feet. "Wow, that tastes good."

"You earned it, man." Tim used a spray bottle and clean towel to wipe the bar top. "I had my doubts, but you came through. I can't thank you enough. I'm not sure we would have survived without you."

"Happy to help."

Tim waited for Bryan to lift his cup before cleaning his end of the bar. "Any interest in a job? I could use another bartender."

Bryan took a sip, angled his head, watched Tim work his way down the bar. Now that he'd decided to stay, his offer was worth considering. "I'm not sure how long I'll be in Key West."

"Where's home?" Tim asked.

"Atlanta."

"What do you do?"

Not much, at least not in the next couple of months. "I'm a teacher. High school math."

"Huh." Tim rubbed his hand over his hair. "I would have said accountant or banker or something."

Bryan's low chuckle felt like a satisfying scratch. "Started out as a banker before I switched to teaching."

"Interesting career move."

"It was for me."

"So, you've got the summer off." Tim stopped in front of Bryan, rested his elbows on the bar, the rag dangling between them. "How about the job?"

Until tonight, Bryan had forgotten how much he liked to bartend. Meeting people, being a part of a crowd without having to be a part of the crowd. And he could certainly use the money. "Corey's lease is up next week. I don't have a place to live."

"If you had a place, how long could you stay?"

Bryan stopped thinking of the conversation as a hypothetical and considered his options. "If I had a place to live, I could stay through early August."

Tim tossed the rag, came to stand in front of Bryan. "There's a studio apartment upstairs. One bedroom, one bath. Small kitchen. Fully furnished."

"You in the landlord business?"

"It comes in handy. If you stay and work through the summer, I'll slash the rent by half."

"Seriously?"

Tim jerked a shoulder. "It's not occupied, and I need the help. Preferably help that requires minimal training."

"That sounds like an offer I can't refuse. Unless ..."

"Unless what?"

"Does your place have air conditioning?"

"Of course."

"Does it work?"

"Last time I checked. I'll make sure."

Bryan tapped his finger against the cup. "How soon could I move in?"

"You accepting the job?"

It was more than a job—it was an answered prayer. Bryan would've been a fool to turn it down and return home with so much unsettled in Key West. "Sold—on the job and the apartment."

Tim held out his hand for Bryan to shake. "Now that you're staying ..." Tim's grin dissolved, and he pulled his hand away. "What's the deal with you and Meg Holloway?"

Thirteen

Meg listened to Lily chatter about her night with Barb and Eva, how they'd eaten breakfast for dinner, watched a scary movie, and she'd slept with Ralph curled up at her feet. Lily's night off was more restful than Meg's had been.

All night long Meg tossed and turned with thoughts of Bryan Westfall—rugged, stubborn, complicated Bryan Westfall—filling her mind. His good looks weren't as obvious as the barnacle's had been but were made more attractive by his unaffected manner. His persistence had him walking her to her car even after she'd told him not to. And after pitching in to help Tim and then coming to her rescue, Bryan seemed nothing like his brother.

His brother had made a move on Amanda the minute they'd walked into a local restaurant where he'd been holding court at the bar. Wearing frayed jean shorts and a tattered t-shirt, he'd blown a cigarette ring in their direction and trailed Amanda and Meg with his eyes as they'd followed the hostess to a booth.

As soon as Meg saw Amanda's reaction, that saucy smile playing on her lips and her gaze flicking back and forth to the bar, Meg knew she was in for a battle. She waited until the waitress walked away with their drink order to say her piece. "Tell me you're not flirting with that waste of time over at the bar."

Amanda wiggled her shoulders and gave Meg a party-pooper glare. "He's cute."

"He's trouble. I can't believe you don't recognize the difference."

Amanda waved Meg's opinion away with the flick of her fingers. "Where you see trouble, I see fun. Besides, we've always had different taste in men."

"Obviously." Meg had pulled her eyes from the menu and peered over her shoulder toward the bar. The guy had the nerve to wink when he caught her looking. Meg was certain if she hadn't scowled at him, he'd have offered up a threesome. "Come on, Amanda. You can do better than that."

"Come on, Meg," her sister parroted. "You don't even know him. Stop being so judge-y."

"I know his type," she'd said, and then followed it up with a snarky response that sounded a lot like a challenge. "And so should you."

Meg had always wondered—would forever wonder—if she'd said nothing and let the moment play out, if Amanda would have concluded that the waste of space at the bar wasn't worth her time.

But instead of keeping her mouth shut, Meg had egged Amanda on, practically daring her to prove Meg wrong. Instead of allowing Amanda to figure out how cheesy and gross the human barnacle was, she'd rebuked her older sister and clouded her judgement, spurring Amanda into action. Instead of eating lunch and laughing over the abysmal pool of available men on the island, Meg had sat by and watched her sister make a colossally bad decision that would ultimately lead to her death.

And by voicing her opinion from the get-go, Meg had no standing to mount a defense a few months later against the trip Amanda proposed with the good-for-nothing who'd sunk every one of Meg's rock bottom expectations. The guy was a user and a loser and blowhard all in one, a garbage can burrito hidden beneath a layer of creamy goodness.

If only Amanda had looked beneath his good-looking surface and seen the dumpster fire underneath, she might still be alive. Might still be around to raise her daughter. Might still be here to help Meg sort through her knotty feelings about the barnacle's contrary brother.

Amanda's death meant Meg lost her sister, her best friend, and her confidant all in one. Swathed in loneliness, she couldn't hide the melancholy from her voice when Eva dropped by the next day, wanting details of Meg's night off.

"So," Eva said, wagging her brows and making Meg laugh. "How was the band?"

"They were good." Meg continued folding t-shirts and stacking them neatly by size, her gaze purposely diverted. "Kind of reggae and rock all in one."

Eva touched her shoulder, stilling Meg's progress and drawing her eyes from the task. "I'm not really asking about the music."

Annoyed at her motherly friend for quickly sidestepping Meg's see-through deflection, Meg decided to be honest. "At first it was weird—going out without Amanda."

"That's to be expected."

"I ran into some high school friends. We caught up and even danced for a while."

"That sounds fun."

"It was. But it was hot, and after a bit I got tired from being on my feet all day. And some of the guys got handsy trying to reel in a catch."

"That's not shocking. You're quite a prize."

Meg ignored the compliment and chewed her lip, debating whether to tell Eva the rest. She glanced over her shoulder to where Lily was color-coordinating the sale items on a shelf in the back of the store. Even though her niece was distracted by the task and the music piping through her earphones, Meg lowered her voice. "There's something I haven't told you."

"What do you mean?" Eva leaned in, her grin like a question and a prayer.

"Remember when I asked you about that guy who'd come into the store and freaked me out? A week or so back?"

Eva nodded, her forehead crimping in concern. "Was he there?"

Meg took a deep breath, checked once more to be sure Lily wasn't listening to their conversation, and waded into murky water. "His name is Bryan Westfall." She speared Eva with a pointed look, willing her to connect the dots.

"Bryan ..." Eva's eyes swelled, and her mouth swiveled open as recognition dawned. "Corey's family?"

"His brother. With Tim's help, I figured it out a few days ago."

"A few days ago? Why didn't you tell me?"

"I handled it." At least, Meg thought she had. After her emotional plea that may have kinda-sorta been a threat, she never expected to see him again. She gave Eva the blow by blow of what happened after Tim came clean and she discovered Bryan's identity. Eva listened with the intensity of a hawk on the hunt. "So imagine my shock to discover him serving drinks at Westies."

"Well, I'm not sure what to think. He sounds like a pretty decent guy."

That had been Meg's conclusion, too, but hearing Eva's take made her feel less relieved. If Bryan were the bad guy, he'd be easy to ignore. With his awe-shucks demeanor and boy-next-door good looks, he was like a crack in an otherwise perfect display case: flawed but still functional; annoying, but not dangerous. "I know."

"Why do you sound upset? That's good, right?"

"I'm not sure. I just ... I don't get his angle."

"You said yourself he was cleaning out the apartment and looking into Corey's last few months. What don't you understand?"

"Considering what happened between his brother and my sister, you'd think he'd avoid us and get in and out of town as fast as possible."

"It's hard to find answers without taking the time to look. And Amanda spent a lot of time with Corey in his last few months."

Too much time, but that was beside the point.

Eva studied her long enough to make Meg squirm. "Why does he bother you so much?"

"He just does. His brother was a cancer. Have you forgotten what he put us through?"

"Before or after he died?" Her question and tone were like a slap. "He's dead, Meg. I'd say he paid a price."

"And so did Amanda." More so, to Meg's mind. Amanda had lost a daughter, and her daughter had lost the most.

"Amanda was a grown woman who made her own choices. Just because you didn't agree with her choice, doesn't make Corey a bad guy."

"Come on, Eva. You met him. You know what he was like."

Eva touched Meg's arm, gave it a gentle squeeze. "Honey, he

wasn't who I'd have chosen for her, and I know you felt the same, but we didn't get to choose. She did. And it's not like he got her hooked on drugs or roped her into a prostitution ring. They were two consenting adults who took a trip to the beach and tragically died in an ocean that takes dozens of lives a year."

How could she say that? How could she *believe* that? "If it wasn't for him, Amanda wouldn't have even been on that beach. She'd have been here with Lily where she belongs."

"What happened was an accident. He's not to blame. And neither is his brother."

"I have to blame someone." Because if there was no one to blame, Meg didn't know what to do with the guilty ache threatening to drag her under. Without someone to blame, Meg would have nothing to do with the bitterness that had defined her life for the last few months.

Eva watched her with a mournful look of pity that soured Meg's stomach. "Sometimes accidents are just accidents, and no one's to blame."

Meg stood in her store, her stomach churning with anger and resentment, as tears crested in her eyes. If she couldn't blame the barnacle, the only one left to blame was herself. She'd provoked Amanda into talking to the barnacle the day they met. She'd covered for Amanda so they could be together on the island over and over again. And she'd fought with her sister about going away with him because she was sick and tired of taking care of Lily alone, and she'd known in her gut a relationship with him was a horrible idea.

As if Eva read her mind, she reached out and grasped Meg's hand. "You can't blame Corey or his brother any more than you can blame Amanda or yourself." She gave her hand a squeeze. "You can what-if the situation all you want, but you can't change the past." She gave her hand a final squeeze before letting go. "I think, if you could let go of all that bitterness you carry, you and Bryan would have a lot in common. You might be able to help each other."

Meg sputtered. She and Bryan had nothing in common. And she wouldn't—she couldn't—make friends with the enemy.

Fourteen

Bryan taped the last box of Corey's things and carried it to his truck, wiping the sweat from his brow. With the prospect of air-conditioned quarters looming in the very near future, he'd stopped his meticulous digging and started packing with the intent to get out as fast as possible.

It had taken him a couple of days to find organizations that would accept Corey's clothes and kitchen items and furnishings. He'd dropped off all the items he'd boxed for charity and arranged for another group to pick up the furniture. The remaining items he'd boxed to take with him to eventually go through on his own time at his own pace.

With the truck packed and the key back under the mat as the landlord instructed, Bryan was free to move into the apartment over Westies—only steps away from A Day's Wait and his inconvenient fascination with Meg Holloway.

He'd done his best to explain to Tim his interest in Meg. He and Corey had had a falling out, so Bryan didn't understand Corey's life or how he paid his bills, and Meg was a connection to Corey's life before he died. The not knowing was eating away at him and keeping him from the closure that would help Bryan and his family move forward back at home.

Tim had listened intently, a do-I-or-don't-I-trust-this-guy crevice between his brows. In the end, Tim must have believed Bryan, or he was so desperate for reliable help he'd agreed to the deal. Either that, or Tim had decided it was safer for Meg, for him to keep Bryan underfoot and under surveillance. If there was one thing Bryan gleaned from the information Tim shared about his background, Bryan knew Tim could easily keep Bryan in his sights.

No matter the reason, Bryan was grateful for the job and the chance to stay and get some answers.

After stopping in the bar to get the key, Bryan made his way up the stairs. As he unlocked the door, he couldn't help but wonder at where this trip had led him so far and where it would eventually lead.

The apartment was nicer than Tim had described, with its exposed brick walls and high ceilings. Most of the furniture was retro but functional (and free), so Bryan couldn't complain. He sat on the couch and leaned back, stacked his feet on the modern coffee table, and found it more comfortable than it looked.

The air conditioning not only worked, but worked well enough to cool the space and drown out the noise from the bar below. Whatever managed to seep through—especially at night—a simple white noise app should easily cover. All in all, it was a comfortable and convenient place to call home for the next two months.

After breaking the news to his dad whose only reaction had

been a grunt, Bryan figured it was past time to check in with Dustin.

"Hey, man," Bryan said when Dustin answered. "How's it going?"

"It's going. How are things in the Keys? You need a wingman yet?"

That remained to be seen—for them both. "The Keys are hot as three levels of hell and as humid as when you wore that sweat suit into the sauna when you were trying to drop weight for wrestling."

Dustin exhaled a rich and rusty chuckle. "I forgot about that. I almost passed out from dehydration."

"I'll never forget the way your eyes rolled back in your head. Scared the life out of me." In the pause that followed, Bryan's smile leaked from his face. Life sure was simple back then when their biggest worry was dropping weight for wrestling or passing an algebra test.

"So, what have you learned about Corey? Do I need to refer a lawyer?"

"From what I can tell, he didn't do much more than work a part-time job and party like a beach bum."

Dustin snorted. "Sounds like classic Corey. How'd he pay for rent in a tourist town with a part-time gig?"

"Good question. Finding the answer is part of the reason I'm staying."

"Part of the reason?"

Meg's smile flashed like a warning light in Bryan's head. "The other is a little more complicated."

"Lucky for you, complications are my specialty. What's going on?"

Until Dustin asked why he was staying, Bryan hadn't realized he'd called to talk through his conflicted feelings with a friend. "Amanda's sister, Meg. She's ..." Stunning and surly, like a sour candy in a glossy red coating. "She's something else."

"If she looks anything like Corey's usual, I assume 'something else' means she's hot. 'Complicated' means she's not interested."

"She wants nothing to do with me. She's ticked and her guard is up, big time."

"She's judging you by Corey."

"I know she is, and that's bad enough, but I found out Amanda has a daughter. From what I gathered around town, Meg is raising the girl on her own."

Dustin made a grumbling noise. "Hence the anger and resentment."

"The thing is, I want to help her—I need to help her—but she's snubbed me at every turn."

"Help her how?"

"I'm not sure, but I can tell she's struggling." He pictured her busted taillight and heard the belt about to snap. "She drives a junker and she works all the time."

"What do you want to do? Fix her car?"

"She wouldn't let me if I asked."

Bryan heard rustling paper and the sound of a door closing. "The police ruled their deaths an accident. Corey wasn't responsible for what happened to her sister."

"I know he wasn't responsible, but Meg didn't like him. I'd say, from her reaction to me, she pretty much despised him."

Dustin made a non-committal humming noise. "You and Corey weren't even speaking when they died."

"She knows, but she doesn't care. In fact, it's like a mark against my character." Bryan rubbed at the headache forming above his left eyebrow. "I know I sound crazy, but there's something about her that's got me by the throat."

"She must be *really* hot."

Bryan unclenched his teeth and the pressure in his head lessened. Lying to his best friend was a waste of time. "She's not ugly."

"So, when you say you want to help her, what you mean is you want to bang her."

Bryan closed his eyes, took a deep breath, and counted to five. "In what universe does the word help mean bang?"

"In my universe, where banging my wife would help my marriage."

From Dustin's snarky tone, Bryan knew things with Tegan hadn't improved. "No progress on the home front?"

"We just keep going in circles. She says I'm not happy, she says she can't make me happy, she says we can't be happy together unless I figure out how to be happy on my own. It's like an annoying song I can't get out of my head."

Bryan sat up and scratched his leg where his sunburn had started to peel. "Why don't you write her a song?"

"Write Tegan a song?"

"Back in high school, that time you and Tegan almost broke up, you wrote her a song and performed it at lunch in front of everybody. It worked back then."

"I haven't picked up a guitar in years." Dustin's voice sounded weary and worn.

"Maybe you should. You were good. And playing the guitar made you happy."

"You know what would make me happy?" Dustin's tone meant Bryan's prodding had worked. He'd rather his friend be annoyed than depressed. "Not talking about what makes me happy. I'd rather talk about you and the hot sister you want to bang. What's your plan?"

If being Dustin's punching bag meant helping his friend deflect his problems, Bryan would suck it up and take the poke. "I don't have a plan. And I never said I wanted to bang her."

"You never said you didn't." Bryan heard the discontent in Dustin's gruff sigh. "You're staying to keep digging about Corey and to assist the beautiful Meg?"

Bryan tried to shrug the uncertainty from his shoulders. Even talking it out didn't help unravel his jumbled emotions. "I'm going to keep looking through Corey's stuff, keep talking to people, keep trying to talk to Meg."

"You don't do well without a schedule."

"I got a bartending gig that kinda fell in my lap. It comes with an apartment with air conditioning that works, so that's a plus. And a little extra money never hurt."

"I suppose it's better than being a beach bum."

Bryan rubbed his peeling ankle with his other foot. "I'm too fair skinned to be a beach bum. Unlike my brother, I have a real job waiting at home."

"Just don't forget to come home. The hot girl may not be able to stand you, but I'm starting to miss your ugly face."

"Yeah? I miss your ugly face too. Give your wife a hug for me."

"How about I bang her instead."

Bryan scrunched his eyes closed, determined to bleach the image from his mind. "Whatever makes you happy."

Dustin's answering growl before he hung up was like music to Bryan's ears. Whatever was going on with Dustin and Tegan, Bryan hoped they'd work it out.

The pretty flower store sat just down the street from Westies like an oasis of color against the oppressive heat of the afternoon haze. Bryan had started to think of Key West as a self-contained sauna with steam rising from the blacktop and the oven-baked feel of the air.

Every morning he would look out his second-story window, hoping to catch of a glimpse of Meg Holloway. Every afternoon and a handful of times in between, he'd repeat the process. Not once had Bryan spotted her ground-eating stride or her hair blazing fire in the sun.

If he thought their proximity would be enough to ensure an encounter, he'd thought wrong. She was as busy and elusive as ever, her rusting beater of a ride parked in the back lot of her store from morning until night.

Without the convenience of a run-in, Bryan had to make his own luck. He could sit around and play defense, or man up and go on offense. With the clock ticking and his patience waning, especially after Dustin's comments had put ideas in his head— ideas that kept him up at night, tossing and turning even after a shift at the bar—it was time to make his move.

His plan was simple. Considering its location, Bryan wouldn't even have to pass in front of *A Day's Wait* to pop inside the flower shop and have a look around, to see if his instincts about Meg had led him in the right direction or directly off a cliff to his demise.

He stood outside just long enough to admire the tall urns filled with colorful blossoms and unusual greenery he couldn't name to save his life. His mother had a green thumb and a knack for growing things. If she were here, standing on the sidewalk in front of Blooming Glory, she'd have admired the flowers and admonished him for his lack of interest in her favorite hobby. With his mom on his mind, he pushed open the door.

If the outside made him think of home, the inside gave him hope he'd made the right decision. Floor to ceiling buckets held flowers of all shapes, shades, and sizes. Plants ranging in color from forest green to citrusy lime intermingled haphazardly, some with leaves spilling over the containers and drooping to the floor, others standing tall like soldiers guarding a palace.

And the smells. A dewy-fresh mishmash of every scent he couldn't name, a chilly blast of freshness that made his nose tingle on every inhale like a flurry of freezing air. Blooming Glory was an oasis of cool serenity among the desert of scorching heat.

He followed his nose throughout the store until a gray-headed woman in a smock dress poked her head around the corner from the back.

"Hello there," the woman said. "You caught me dozing. I didn't realize we had a customer."

"Great shop you've got here."

"Why, thank you. We certainly like it."

"I can see why." His gaze bounced from flower to flower. "If my mom were with me, she'd never want to leave."

"She'd have to take some flowers with her and bring the happy home."

Bryan chuckled. "You can bet she would."

"What brings you in today?" the woman asked. "Buying something for your mom?"

He would have to, he thought. It wasn't only his dad's job to keep her happy and afloat. "Not today. I'm looking for something special. For someone special."

"Making something special for someone special is our specialty." She extended her hand across the counter. "I'm Eva."

"Nice to meet you, Eva." He gave her hand a squeeze. "I'm Bryan."

Eva came around the counter and stood in front of him. She was short and round and reminded him of his grandmother with her sparkly eyes and cunning smile. "What have you got in mind, Bryan?"

"There's this woman."

"Ahhh," Eva said with a wink. "There usually is."

"We got off to a rocky start. I need to fix her impression of me."

"Flowers are a good first step. Tell me about her."

Bryan didn't think before he spoke and let the words fly from his mouth. "She's a beautiful mystery, and stubborn to boot."

Eva wandered among the buckets, nodding her head as if taking notes. "Well, when I think of a beautiful stubborn woman, these red calla lilies come to mind."

Bryan eyed the trumpet-shaped flower in rich red that reminded him of Meg's hair. "That's perfect."

"A nice pair to the calla lily is the peony, which represents honor." She plucked the stem of a round flower with folds of icy white.

"Pretty, and I like the meaning. You're batting a thousand so far."

"Music to my ears." She continued walking, studying the flowers with a crease between her brows. "These gold and bronze coreopsis are a stunning match with the calla lilies, and they bring out the fire of the reds."

"Sold."

"Let's see." She plucked a purple iris from a bucket and held it with the other stems. "This purple is a nice contrast and it's a symbol of wisdom."

"I know that one," Bryan said. "My mom had a patch of irises in our garden growing up."

"They're a showstopper in a home garden. See how the purple complements the grouping?" Without waiting for him to answer, she picked up another stem with bushy white flowers. "The lilac is a nice addition plus "—she pulled some green stems and held them all together for him to see—"the sage adds more wisdom and a pretty touch of silvery green."

"Eva, you're a genius. If this doesn't work to win her over, I don't know what will."

Eva's smile made him ache for his long-deceased grands. "I'll do my best to impress your girl. Can you give me an hour to put this together in a nice vase or a box?"

"A vase is perfect and take all the time you need." He followed her to the counter. "I'm working the lunch shift over at Westies."

"Oh, are you on the wait staff?"

"No, ma'am. I'm bartending for the summer."

"How nice. I know Tim needs some help." Eva pulled a sales order from beneath the counter and passed it to Bryan. "If you'll fill out the top part of this sales order, I'll work you up a price." She passed him a pen and got to work on an ancient calculator.

Bryan gripped the pen while a caution bell blared in his brain. Eva owned the store next to Meg. They had to know one another. She may even know about Bryan being in town. Even if she didn't, full disclosure felt like the right approach. He cleared his throat. "Before I fill this out, I should probably tell you the flowers are for Meg Holloway next door."

Eva's eyes blinked wide, her smile wobbling like a gelatin mold until it splattered into a scowl. "You're Corey's brother."

He flashed his palms. "Guilty as charged."

She took a breath and let it out, studying him over the readers perched on the end of her nose. "I don't know how to feel about this, Bryan."

"I'm not sure how you should feel about it either. Meg is mad at me, and I don't understand why."

"Meg is angry with your brother. She blames him for the accident."

"Yes, ma'am. I imagine she does."

She cocked her head but there was no judgment in her stare, only curiosity. "Do you think he's to blame?"

"For dying? I don't think so. Riptides kill without distinction."

"That's true enough." Eva studied him as if trying to read his heart. Bryan let her look her fill. "Are you playing games with Meg? Because if you are, I won't abide being used in the process."

"No, ma'am, I'm not. I told you straight out, I made a bad impression. I don't want to hurt her or cause her any harm."

"What are your intentions?"

The million-dollar question. "A truce. A friendship. Maybe some answers about Corey and Amanda."

"She won't talk to you about her sister. There's too much anger, too much regret."

Anger and regret were his constant companions, as much a part of him as his right and left arms. "There's nothing more painful than losing a loved one. Especially your only sibling."

"Was Corey your only brother?"

"Yes, ma'am."

"I'm sorry for your loss."

"I appreciate your condolence."

Eva glared at him, her eyes pinging back and forth between

his. "They were inseparable, Meg and Amanda. Meg sacrificed a lot for her sister. Amanda's death was more than a shock—it was a body blow. A weaker person wouldn't have survived."

"She's resilient and resourceful."

"She is, but Meg's not as tough as she looks. She puts on a good front, but there's a softness underneath—a softness I aim to protect. It's going to take more than pretty flowers for Meg to let her guard down."

Eva's warning solidified Bryan's resolve. "The flowers are just the opening act."

"There's no guarantee they'll work."

"I'm also resilient and resourceful."

"You'll need to be." She tapped a finger on the counter and stared into his eyes. "If you work your way in, you'd better treat her right or you'll have more than her Irish ire to deal with. You'll have mine."

Fifteen

Meg packaged the Key West ornament in bubble wrap and tucked it inside one of their logoed bags, before handing it to the customer. The woman and her husband were in town for the day, shopping along Duvall Street before they had to re-board the cruise ship.

"That should protect it until you get back to Virginia."

The woman looked inside the bag and smiled. "Perfect. I'd hate to get home and not be able to use it on the tree this year. We've collected so many we have a special travel tree for all the trips we've made over the years."

"What a lovely idea." Meg's smile masked her awe and her envy. What would it be like to explore parts unknown, so much so that she'd need an extra tree for all the ornaments?

Her husband sputtered, eyeing his wife the same way she'd eyed the ornament, with fondness and delight. "It only sounds lovely when you're not the one who has to put up two trees in the house."

The woman tapped her husband's belly and then squiggled her signature on the payment screen. "It's not that bad."

Meg printed the receipt. "Safe travels back home. Enjoy your holidays."

"Thanks. We'll think of you this Christmas when we decorate the tree."

Meg watched the couple exit. The holiday merchandise she'd had the funds to order would be delivered in a few weeks, but Meg kept a supply of ornaments on the shelves for those who bought vacation mementos to commemorate their trips.

The more she learned the books, the more she realized how hard it was going to be to keep the store in the black. Staying open longer during the holidays without the funds to hire extra help was like watching a hurricane form off the coast and not having any way to avert disaster. No boards for the windows, no sandbags to ward off a flood, no way to escape a direct hit. She would have to choose—work longer hours while juggling Lily's needs or keep regular business hours and lose the revenue. Losing the revenue could mean losing the store. It was an impossible choice.

And that was just the business side of life. Thinking about the holidays turned Meg's blood cold. Thanksgiving and Christmas without Amanda and her parents felt more like a funeral than a celebration. Meg would have to muster the energy and enthusiasm to put on a Thanksgiving spread, if only for Lily's sake. Would it be worth decorating their apartment when neither one spent any time there or felt any cheer in their hearts?

She shook her thoughts clear and eyed the clock. Lily would get dropped off from surfing camp in an hour, hot and cranky from a day spent outside. She'd traded four boxes of beach towels for a week of surfing camp to keep Lily busy and entertained while Meg worked the store. The loss of her dwindling stock was well worth it to keep Lily around friends and feeling like a normal kid.

The door bells chimed, announcing a customer. Meg slipped on her welcome-to-the-store smile and looked up to see a pair of long sunburnt legs and a face obscured behind a stunning flower arrangement in Blooming Glory's signature sea-green vase. Her stomach tingled with awareness and a chuckle escaped her throat. "What in the—"

The flowers dipped lower. A mass of windswept brown hair sent a shiver down her spine. Bryan Westfall stopped opposite the counter, a sheepish grin on his too-handsome face, an explosion of color and scent in his arms. "I come in peace."

"What is this?"

"An olive branch. Well, it's more like a bouquet branch, but I wasn't sure you'd get the meaning."

"You bought me flowers?"

"You don't like flowers?"

Before Amanda's funeral, Meg had adored flowers—the colors, the smells, the textures. All the endless combinations and feelings they provoked. Until the funeral home and the suffocating smell of flowers trying and failing to mask death and embalming fluid made her want to vomit on the spot.

"Flowers are okay."

"Only okay? Look at these colors. Your neighbor Eva is a magician."

"Eva made these for you?" The turncoat. She would be speaking with her neighbor as soon as Bryan left.

"Don't be mad at Eva. I told her who I was and who they were for. She warned me not to expect much."

"She did, huh?"

"Scouts honor. I'd flash the pledge sign but I'm holding this bouquet branch."

Bryan had the Westfall charm in spades, standing there flashing his dimpled grin and twinkling his innocent brown eyes with delight. Even her soaring endorphins slowed at his show-stopping appeal.

Meg would have been interested if she hadn't seen his brother in action, leaning on that same counter, enticing Amanda to ditch her responsibilities and go out with him and play. As if bar hopping and binge drinking trumped earning a living and raising a daughter. Amanda would giggle like a schoolgirl and beg Meg to close up shop, put Lily to bed, be the responsible sister and aunt. Meg would bite her tongue and agree, all the while cursing the slick-talking slime ball who'd wormed his way into Amanda's life and under Meg's skin.

She straightened her spine. "You wasted your money and Eva's time if you think flowers are going to change my mind."

He set the bouquet on the counter. The colors were fantastic—the rich hues drawing her eye and subtle scents tickling her nose. "I took a gamble. Most women like flowers."

"I'm not most women. If you hurry back, I'm sure Eva will give you a refund. She can probably sell the bouquet in the store."

"They're yours, Meg." His voice was like a deflated balloon. "I told her they were for a mysterious and stubborn beauty, and this is what she created even before she knew they were for you."

"Why would you waste your money? Do I look like I can be bought?"

"That wasn't my intent." He rubbed his temple and shoved his hands into his pockets. "I'm not here to hurt you. Usually, people get to know me before they hate me."

Meg rolled her eyes. He flustered her more than she was willing to admit. "I don't hate you. Like you said, I don't know you. But I knew your brother. And he was trouble."

"And if I'd known your sister, should I have judged you by her? Were you and she one and the same?"

The accusation stung, if only because it was logical. She was losing her argument and her temper, infuriating her more. "No."

"Then maybe you can give me the same courtesy. Corey was my brother, but we were very different. I assume the same can be said of you and Amanda."

"She and I were different. She was fooled by your brother's charm. I'm not so easily fooled."

"Corey always did have a way with the ladies." Bryan's expression turned serious, and he stared over her shoulder into the past. "Even without much to back it up."

Meg startled at the melancholy sound of his voice. "You sound jealous of your brother."

He shrugged his impressive shoulders. "I used to be. He was older, good looking, smart. He never had to study, had lots of friends, lots of girlfriends."

"You didn't?"

"I did okay, but not like Corey. He was one of those kids who seemed to have it all. Everything came easy for him. Too easy."

He could have been talking about Amanda—high school Amanda with her legions of boyfriends and gaggle of friends. Being Amanda Holloway's sister had given Meg the kind of credibility she'd never have earned on her own. Until her last boyfriend tarnished Amanda's reputation and left her pregnant and alone. "Amanda was like that—popular and admired."

"They cast a big shadow. It's hard to figure out who you are when you're trying to be just like your sibling."

Meg's temper melted like chocolate in the sun. She studied his face, got snagged by his eyes. Yes, he looked like his brother—the generous mouth, the dark eyes, the easy manner—but there was a depth to him that didn't exist in his brother, a quiet understanding that made her knees weak. Before she could muster a response, he flicked a finger over a red blossom and gave her an unassuming smile.

"Enjoy the flowers, Meg. I'll see you around."

As soon as Lily got dropped off at the store, Meg sat her behind the counter and told her she'd be right back and to call if a customer came inside. Lily was too tired to complain. She plopped onto the chair Meg had dragged behind the counter and began doodling on a piece of paper. Meg went through the back door, and after a quick knock, entered the back of the flower shop.

Barb jerked around, a smile on her weathered face. "Hey, Meg. What's shaking?"

"Is Eva around?"

"She's up front with a customer. Can I help you with something?"

Meg pursed her lips, listened to Eva prattle on to an indecisive shopper, and knew she only had a few minutes to say her piece. "Did you know about the flower arrangement Eva made for me?"

"The calla lilies and peonies? Yes, I did it myself."

"Why?"

"Well …" Barb set the pink bushy stems aside and wiped her hands on her apron. "When a customer comes in and wants a bouquet made, we tend to follow their instructions."

"Do you know who they were from?"

"A Mr. Westfall, according to the receipt."

Meg folded her arms across her chest instead of flailing them in the air like she wanted. "I know Eva told you who he was."

"She did. She also told me he came clean about who he was and who the flowers were for."

"That doesn't make it okay."

"That a handsome man bought you flowers? I'm not sure I follow your logic."

"His brother was a handsome guy too. Look where that got Amanda. Look where it got Lily."

Barb leaned against the counter, her hands on either side as if bracing for Meg's temper. "Honey, I don't think he's a bad guy. If he were trying to trick you—and I can't see a motivation for that—he wouldn't have told us who he was. Eva thinks he's harmless."

"That's not up to Eva."

The woman in question appeared in the doorway. "I'm not allowed to have an opinion?"

Meg glared at her substitute mother. "I'm aware of your opinion. I don't understand how everyone can so easily give him the benefit of the doubt."

"And I don't understand why you can't."

Meg knew she was being irrational, even without the pitying looks on Barb and Eva's faces. "His brother stole everything from me and from Lily." She tried but failed to keep her volume in check. "Why isn't that enough?"

As if to scold her, Eva's voice remained calm. "Would you have preferred I refuse him business? How long would we stay in business if we decided who was worthy to buy flowers?"

Meg uncrossed her arms and fisted her hands at her sides. "You know how I feel about him. You knew the flowers would upset me, and you did it anyway."

"I told him you'd be upset. I also warned him not to play with your emotions. He doesn't strike me as someone trying to pull the wool over your eyes, Meg. I think you're being unfair."

"I'm being unfair?" She spun around and gripped the edge of the counter, felt the sharp metal edge dig into her palms. "He's a living reminder of that scum who took my sister."

It was Barb who spoke in her quiet, measured tone. "And you're a living reminder of the pain his brother left behind. He's searching for closure. Put yourself in his shoes. What if you and Amanda hadn't lived in the same town? What if you hadn't talked every day or even every week? Wouldn't you want to speak to the people who knew her and could tell you about her last few days?"

She dropped her head, exhausted and drained. "Of course I would."

"I think that's all he wants," Eva said. "And maybe a little consolation from someone in a unique position to understand what he's been through."

Angry, shame-fill tears swelled in her eyes. Meg swiped them away before turning to face them. "You think he's going to be comforted by what I have to say about his brother?"

Eva's look was full of pity and understanding. "I think he's prepared to hear whatever you have to say. He chose to seek you out, Meg. He can't blame you for telling your side of the story."

Meg didn't think she could talk about his brother and offer comfort. But he was here, and he wasn't giving up. And neither was Eva or Barb. "Fine. I suppose I could give him a chance."

Barb gave an approving smile. "I think it would do you both good to talk."

"I don't know how to reach him."

"He's working for Tim." Eva inclined her head in the direction of the bar. "You might want to start there."

Meg dropped Lily and Cammie at the beach hut for surfing camp the next morning and drove directly to the store. It wasn't unusual for her to start her day before opening hours, but this morning would be spent on personal business.

The whole night she'd wondered and worried about talking to Bryan Westfall. If all he wanted were details to find closure, she could give them—the unvarnished truth—and maybe he'd leave and never bother her again. Never remind her of the person who stole her sister. Never stir uncomfortable feelings of longing and regret.

She parked behind her building and walked directly to Westies, eyeing the lights shining in the upstairs apartment. Good, she thought. She'd get information from Tim about why he'd hired Bryan and how long he intended to stay. She smelled coffee and heard voices from the kitchen when she stepped over the gate to the outdoor dining area of the bar.

Her stomach tingled with awareness and her nervous fingers tapped on the bar. After listening to the muffled chatter from the kitchen, she called out, "Hello?"

One of the line cooks poked his head out of the kitchen. "Hey." He nodded a greeting. "We don't open til eleven."

"I'm looking for Tim. Is he around?"

"He's not in yet."

Meg chewed her lip and considered her options. Once the store opened, she wouldn't have a chance to speak to anyone, and she really needed to put Bryan and his questions in the rearview. "I'm Meg Holloway from A Day's Wait down the street. Is Tim upstairs? I saw a light on walking over."

The man waved the large chopping knife in his hand. "That's Bryan, the new bartender."

What the … *he's living above the bar*? "Bryan Westfall?"

The guy's shoulders grazed the bandana shielding his hair. "I guess so."

"Okay, thanks." Meg stared at the hallway she knew led to the upstairs apartment. She could put it off and let it fester, or confront him and get it over with. Fueled by curiosity and an irrational sense of irritation, she took the stairs two at a time, pounding on the door before she changed her mind.

Bryan opened the door wearing nothing but a towel cinched low at his waist. Beads of water dripped from his hair and his chest.

Meg blinked, swallowed the jolt of shock, and stumbled back. Lust shot like a lightning bolt to her libido. She shook her head to stop her mind from leaking out her ears.

He cinched the towel tighter, a shocked expression on his rugged face. "Oh, hi. Uh"—he stepped back and held the door open—"come on in."

She forced her feet to cross the threshold, close enough to smell the soap on his skin, feel the heat from his body. She stopped by the couch and turned to face him.

"Have a seat. I'll just … uh, put some clothes on. Be right back."

Meg watched him disappear into the bedroom, swinging the door closed behind him. The door banged against the jam and ricocheted open an inch. Meg saw the towel hit the ground and caught a glimpse of taught white flesh before she turned around and exhaled a ragged breath.

Don't think about him naked in the next room. Don't obsess about his broad chest and tapered waist, his sculped back and long lean legs. Don't wonder what he would do if you pushed the door open, strode inside the bedroom, and ran your tongue from his navel to his neck.

Bryan reappeared in record time, stopping a foot away from her, finger combing his hair away from his face, forcing Meg out of her head and back to reality where she wasn't ruled by urges. "What can I do for you?"

Meg blinked the hunger from her eyes and tried to focus. What was she doing here again? "I'm sorry. I'm sorry to show up unannounced."

His hair sprung free and frizzed around his temple. "It's no problem. I'm glad you stopped by."

"Eva told me you were working at the bar. I didn't realize you'd moved in."

He shrugged and flashed his choir-boy smile. "Tim needed a bartender. I needed a place to stay."

"How long?" she asked.

"Excuse me?"

His presence was a problem. Her reaction to his presence was an even bigger problem—for both of them. She folded her arms across her chest. "How long do you intend to stay?" She held her breath, waiting, worried for his answer. Anything longer than a few days would mean nothing but trouble.

Sixteen

Bryan was in danger of getting whiplash from Meg's seesaw reactions. He'd hustled from the bathroom, fresh from the shower, to find her standing on his doorstep like a fuming fantasy in white shorts and a football-field green top. He'd been too surprised to do anything but gawk as she gave him an appraising up and down, the blush on her cheeks a few shades lighter than her silky red hair.

When he'd come out of the bedroom after getting dressed, she'd seemed flustered, and if he didn't know better, by the way her skin flushed and her eyes went hazy, she seemed *attracted* to him. Until she'd pulled herself together with one impressive breath. The woman lassoed her emotions faster than a seasoned cowboy captured a runaway steer.

He needed to answer her question before she lassoed him too. "I have the summer off. I told Tim I'd stay through early August."

Disappointment flared across her features, sinking her lips into a frown, weighing her shoulders into a slump. "All summer?"

"Technically, more like half."

"You don't have to get home?"

"Not really." He'd been disliked before, but not quite so obviously. So painfully. His ego could only take so much. "Look, I'm not going to harass you all summer. I'm just tying up some loose ends and getting Corey's affairs in order."

She straightened, shoving her nose in the air like the aristocrats she favored. "Is that what we are—Lily and I—loose ends?"

Bryan needed caffeine so his mouth would stop digging him into a deeper, more cavernous hole. "Ah ..." He jerked a thumb over his shoulder where his coffee maker sat like a beacon. "Would you like some coffee?" When she shook her head and took a breath, Bryan kept on talking. "Because I need caffeine in the morning to function."

Her lips slammed into an adorable pout before he turned his back and walked into the makeshift kitchen.

He needed coffee because pouts weren't adorable. Angry women showing up on his doorstep at the crack of eight shouldn't cause his fuses to burn or his fingers to tingle with awareness. Shouldn't turn apprehension into anticipation with the crook of her cynical brow.

He made a full pot in case she changed her mind and set his favorite flavored creamer on the counter as an enticement. See, it shouted, I'm not a cave man. He knew how to use a coffee machine. He bought creamer—*hazelnut* creamer. She could trust him. Despite his brother. Despite his inconvenient and obviously one-sided attraction.

She followed him into the space, stared at him like a bug under a microscope. "Why do you have the summer off? Do you work construction or something?"

Bryan couldn't help it. He glanced down at his body. "Do I look like I work construction?"

Her arms flopped at her sides. "I have no idea what you do."

"I'm a teacher."

"A teacher?" She jerked her head back and lifted her brows as if he'd said stripper or rocket scientist. "What grade?"

"High school. Math."

"Huh." The crease between her brows wasn't going away, and neither were the bees dive-bombing his stomach. "I always hated math." She gave him another up-down he didn't know how to interpret. "But I never had a teacher who looked like you."

Her response sounded like a compliment and had him contemplating a smile. Fortunately, the coffee maker beeped, saving him the humiliation in case it wasn't. He filled a cup with the steaming brew and held it out to her like a white flag.

She huffed and reached for the mug, setting her purse down on the counter to add creamer and stir. "Thanks."

He fixed another cup, poured creamer until his morning crack resembled the color of toast, and turned to face her. "Shall we sit?"

She didn't answer, but swiveled and walked to the couch, easing onto the end as she cradled the cup in her hands. Bryan took a seat on the adjacent armchair, sipped his coffee, and considered an entry that wouldn't send her running for the door or throwing hot coffee in his face.

She beat him to the punch. "Before you go and make me mad again, I want to thank you for the flowers. They're beautiful. I'm sorry my reaction was less than grateful."

The apology had cost her. He'd never heard someone say thank you in a way that sounded the opposite. "You're welcome. And just so we're clear, you and your niece are not loose ends." He took a gulp and winced as the hot liquid burned his throat. "My mom and dad ..." He set the mug on the coffee table and steepled his hands. "They're struggling. Corey's life down here was a mystery. His living arrangements, his job, his friends. They need to know something. We all need to know."

She sat, seemingly unmoved by his words, staring intently at him with no expression on her face.

"Corey hasn't been present in our lives for a while and now he's just gone. I know, as close as you and your sister were, you can't understand what that's like, but his death doesn't seem real. Understanding what his life was like before he died seems like the only way to move forward."

"What did he do?" she asked.

He was surprised she didn't know. "He rented jet skis and taught wind surfing."

She shook her head. "No. Why didn't you speak? Why didn't you know anything about your brother's life?"

He would have to tell her the ugly truth if he wanted any information in return. He knew it would hurt—digging up the old bones and bringing them into the light—but he hadn't realized how much it mattered what she thought of him. "Corey dropped out of college more times than I can count—each time promising it would never happen again. The longest he ever stayed was a semester and a half."

And every time Corey would come to his parents for another chance, he would swear he'd changed, would swear he'd take school seriously, would swear he'd learned his lesson. Every time was a lie. Bryan had had to take out loans to go to school because Corey had proven to be such a bad investment.

"He eventually stopped trying and moved on to risky investments. He'd burned the financial bridge with my parents, so he started coming to me. I was paying off my student loans, trying to get my feet under me and figure out my life. I gave him money at first. He was my brother and I loved him. I didn't want him to go hungry or be homeless." Bryan had thought Corey pathetic for not doing the work, for not putting in the time, for taking and taking and taking from their parents with nothing to show in return. "He kept coming back for more. Eventually, I said no. He accused me of being the favorite, called me selfish for not parting with a sliver of my big fat salary, said I didn't understand."

"I thought you said you were a teacher."

"I am now, but out of college I worked in financial services. I did ... fairly well."

"And he stopped calling?"

"Pretty much. I tried to keep in touch, but he'd be short with me if he answered at all. When he did take my call, he'd ask for money. Corey always had some scheme to make millions. All he needed was a little seed money and he'd pay me back in spades."

"He was a drifter and a user." Meg's harsh tone said more than her words.

Bryan didn't know whether to agree. He knew what he knew. He wanted to know what she knew.

Meg set her coffee down and reached for Corey's picture where Bryan had leaned it against a book on the end table. "Your brother was too good looking. His looks are what got my sister killed. Amanda was a sucker for a good-looking guy."

Bryan watched Meg as she studied the photo, mumbled under his breath. "He got all the looks."

Meg shot him a squinty-eyed stare that felt weighty and full of meaning. "He didn't get them all." She set the picture face down. "Amanda would have spent her life trying to save him, dragging Lily into his sordid mess." She sighed and softened her tone. "I don't know what I can tell you that will help. I hardly knew your brother. I didn't like him."

She was a different person when she let her guard down. The small glimpse of the tenderness Eva described had the power to slay him a thousand times worse than her anger. "Anything you tell me will help. It doesn't have to be flattering. It only has to be true."

She stared at him, blinking once, twice before she inclined her head toward the door. "I have a delivery coming soon. I have to get to work." She picked up her cup and took it to the sink, grabbing her purse from the counter before turning to face him where he stood by the door.

Bryan didn't want Meg to leave. He didn't know where they stood or if she'd ever talk to him again. Didn't know if the panic he felt deep in his gut was from not finding out more about Corey or not being able to puzzle his way through her contrary layers.

"I don't want to like you," she said, looking directly into his eyes. "It would be easier to hate you, to write you off as a jerk the way I did your brother."

"I kinda thought you had written me off as a jerk."

She shrugged, her expression soft and impossibly beautiful. "When you've won over everyone I care about and they all think I'm being mean, I suppose I need to consider that you may be a decent guy."

It felt like the nicest compliment. "I try to be a decent guy."

"I guess we'll see." She stepped toward him, and he opened the door. She stopped before walking through and lowered her voice. "I won't talk about your brother in front of Lily. She's been through enough."

"Understood."

"Come by the store. Lily's in camp this week from eight to four. If she's not around and I'm not too busy, I can probably answer your questions."

His shoulders sagged with relief. "Thank you. I appreciate your help more than I can say."

She inclined her head and gave him a closed-mouth smile. "Don't thank me yet." She breezed past him, her scent like a slap to his face.

Bryan closed his eyes and inhaled her fresh laundry smell. He knew with crystal clear certainty he would replay their encounter in his mind a million times over and she'd be the star of his dreams that night.

Seventeen

Meg was glad for the busy day of customers wandering in and out of the store. Some were in the mood to buy, some were in the mood to look, some sought refuge from the blistering heat. The steady stream of people kept her out of her head, unable to replay the morning with Bryan that had left her shaky and confused.

The man was an enigma. Good looking and smart, thoughtful and serious, with a sly and self-depreciating sense of humor. He wasn't anything like his leech of a brother. He had a job—he was a teacher, for goodness' sake—and he seemed sincere and patient. She'd been less than friendly, and he'd gone out of his way to be nice. Under normal circumstances she'd have felt guilty for her behavior.

These weren't normal circumstances.

They'd both lost their siblings. They were both trying to understand and come to grips with their new normal. He needed closure. She needed a way forward.

Meg could help him fill in some gaps, but there was no one to help her. She was stuck. As stuck as she'd been when she graduated high school and had no money for college. As stuck as she'd been with her mother's diagnosis when she'd had to run the store and raise Lily with Amanda, her dreams and hopes eclipsed by worry for her mom, her sister, and Lily. By the end of the summer, Bryan would have some answers. Meg, on the other hand, was permanently stuck and permanently stressed.

Hours later, Lily entered the store, her skin the color of walnuts, her hair lightening to platinum the way her mother's had every summer when Amanda was a girl. Meg looked up from restocking their signature yellow bags. "You're back already?"

"It's after four."

"Really?" Meg pulled her phone from her pocket. Between the steady flow of customers and too much time in her head, the day had whizzed by. "How was camp?"

"It was all right."

"Just all right? I thought you loved it?"

Lily slumped her slender shoulders. "Cammie's mad at me."

Meg stuffed the last of the bags under the counter and stood. "Why?"

"They moved me to the advanced group and she's still with the beginners."

"That's not your fault." She pointed to the back of the store. "Go put your stuff away. There's a snack in the fridge. Let me check on these customers and I'll be right there."

Meg assisted a middle-age woman buying a present for her grandson. She bagged the youth size t-shirt and watched the customer leave before checking on Lily in the office. Meg leaned against the doorway so she wouldn't miss an incoming shopper.

"What happened?"

Lily flicked a baby carrot between her fingers. "Cammie thinks I'm showing off."

Lily wasn't an attention seeker. If anything, since Amanda's death, she'd tried to blend in. "It's not showing off to do your best."

Lily pursed her lips, her expression so like her mom's it made Meg's pulse jump. "She can't find her balance on the board, and when she gets frustrated, she gives up."

"It's hard for Cammie to watch you do better at something, but that's her problem."

"I know, but she's acting like I'm doing better to make her look bad in front of the boys."

And so it begins. "I see."

"I don't even like the boys in the advanced group. They think Cammie's acting like a baby."

Friends and boys were a toxic mix during adolescence and beyond. "Sounds like they might be right. But Cammie's your friend. I hope you weren't agreeing with the boys or making Cammie feel worse because she was struggling."

"I tried to show her how I figured out how to stay on the board, but she wouldn't listen. She barely talked to me in the car."

Meg knelt, gripping the edge of the desk, so she and Lily were eye to eye. "She's upset with her herself and taking it out on you. That's not fair and it's not nice. But you're friends. One surfing camp won't change that."

Lily's blue eyes flashed. "What am I supposed to do? Mess up to make her feel better?"

"No. Do your best. It's up to Cammie to improve. You're there to learn. It's only natural you learn at a different pace."

Lily dug her fingernail into the carrot, her lips in a frustrated pout.

If Meg knew her niece—and she did—Lily had more on her mind than just Cammie's behavior at surfing camp.

Lily set the carrot on the desk and glared at Meg with Amanda's steely resolve. "I know you want me and Cammie to be friends because you like her parents, but she's been mean before."

Meg stood and crossed her arms, unease tickling the base of her skull. "What are you talking about?"

Lily's cheeks flushed and she averted her eyes. "Never mind."

"Tell me what she did. I'm not going to get mad at you."

Lily shoved her hands under her legs and stared at the desk. "Gina told me Cammie said some stuff about Mom after she died."

Meg's stomach shriveled and her voice came out on a hiss. "What kind of stuff?"

"It doesn't matter."

"It's okay." Meg touched Lily's leg. "You can tell me."

Lily dropped her gaze to her lap, her cheeks a smear of pink under all that brown. "She said … she said Mom was a …"

Meg lowered her head, hovering over Lily to hear the mumbled insult. "A what?"

"A slut."

Meg gasped, jolted back to high school when her sister's pregnancy came to light. Like a fresh cut over an old wound, the label sliced Meg in two. "Look at me." She waited for Lily to lift her eyes. She firmed her voice. "That's not true. I'm her sister. I would know."

Lily nodded but stayed wilted in the chair.

"You don't believe her, do you?"

Lily answered with a halfhearted head shake.

"Your mom hardly dated." Insult lent her voice a defensive edge. "And when she did, it was one man at a time. I can count on one hand the number of guys she went out with since you were born."

Lily picked up the carrot, folded and unfolded it in her hands, her gaze darting to Meg's. "What happened to my dad?"

Her whispered query shot through Meg like shrapnel to the gut. Never, as far as Meg knew—and she would have known—had Lily ever asked Amanda about her father. Which left Meg in the default position of answering the loaded question. She swallowed past the lump of dread in her throat and said, "What do you want to know?"

"Who is he? *Where* is he? How come I don't know his name?"

Meg squeezed her eyes shut, cursing her sister's untimely death. Lily wasn't a baby. Of course she'd be curious to know about the man who gave her life. Meg and Amanda had been too busy getting through the day to day to discuss how to answer the question Lily would inevitably ask—a question Meg never intended to answer.

"Remember when you took health class and we talked about how babies are made—the man has the sperm, and the woman has the egg?"

Lily shook her head, her cheeks the same rosy pink as when she'd come home with the permission slip. "That's not what I mean."

"I know, but hear me out. A dad is someone who stays, someone who participates in raising a child. Yours didn't, so I've never considered him your father. In fact, I'd say the only man who was ever a father to you is in Orlando."

"Grandad?"

"Yes. He was here, he helped raise you, he loves you even though he had to go away with Gram."

"Okay. But who is he?"

Lily could find out on her own, but she needed to hear the

truth from Meg. "He was your mom's boyfriend in high school. He was older." Too old, Meg thought, to be sniffing around a girl Amanda's age. With Amanda's limited experience. With Amanda's giving heart.

"Is he dead too?"

"I don't know. I don't know anything about him now."

"Why not?"

Meg wished she could tell Lily her dad was a man she could look up to and admire. A soldier serving the country, a police officer killed in the line of duty, a fireman who lost his life saving others from certain death. But she'd never lied to Lily, and she wasn't going to start now. "He left your mom before you were born, and he's never come back. It's not your fault. He didn't leave you—he didn't even know you. He left your mom pregnant and alone."

Lily took a deep breath, staring at the carrot in her hands. "Do you think if he knew about me, if he got to know me, he'd come back?"

How many times, how many ways could one girl's heart break? And how many times was it left to Meg to break it? She softened her voice. "No, honey, I don't. He was a grown man who ran away from his responsibilities. What little I knew of him, and the fact that he's never come back, tells me you're better off without him."

The words sounded hollow, and by the devastated look on her face, landed like a salt in Lily's wounds. It was past time for Meg to dig deep and address the bigger issue with humor and humility. "Listen. Your mom is gone, your grandad is taking care of Gram in Orlando, and you're stuck with me. I get it. It totally stinks."

Lily's eyes filled with tears, but she didn't disagree. Meg inwardly winced, but she didn't react. This wasn't about her. Lily's need to know about her parents didn't have anything to do with Meg. "Don't believe any gossip about your mom. She was a wonderful person and a great mother. Don't let other people tarnish her memory."

Lily nodded, jutting her jaw back and forth like she didn't know what to do with Meg's advice.

Meg had never felt so useless as a proxy-parent. Even though the door bells rattled announcing a customer, she didn't budge. "People shouldn't judge you by your parents—good or bad. No matter what anyone says about your mom, it has nothing to do with you."

"It doesn't feel that way."

Meg squeezed Lily's shoulder and looked her dead in the eyes. "I know it doesn't, and that stinks too. Your mom wasn't a slut. Knowing that—and believing it—is the only thing that matters."

Meg heard the customer approach and straightened to greet them. "Hi." She pasted on a freeze-dried smile. "Can I help you find something today?"

Eighteen

Bryan's hands didn't shake as he approached the entrance to A Day's Wait, but that didn't mean he wasn't nervous to see Meg again. Nervous to discover if she'd be warmer around him or if she'd look at him like the nuisance he'd become. He'd intentionally given her a day to think about what he'd asked of her and to figure out if she liked him or not.

Bryan liked her enough for them both. He'd thought of nothing and no one else since she'd surprised him at his new apartment. Guilt niggled at his subconscious. He was in Florida to find out about Corey's life, not get involved with a beautiful and exciting woman with a direct connection to his brother.

His life was full of irony, putting people in his path at inconvenient and inappropriate times. Bryan had stopped trying to figure out life's twists and turns around the time he'd quit his well-paying job to become a teacher. He intended to stick to that plan, as far as Meg was concerned.

If he pushed Meg for too much information, if he tried to explore his growing attraction, she would push him right out the door and out of her life. Having already committed to hang around for the summer, Bryan didn't want that to happen. He didn't mind hanging out on an island filled with flamboyant people doing curious things at all hours of the day and night, but that wasn't why he'd come to Key West.

The door bells tinkled as he entered, a playful touch he was too freaked out to notice his first couple of times in the store. He stopped just inside the entrance, this time to admire the space and not the woman who'd snagged his attention on his previous visits.

If he'd had to describe A Day's Wait in one word, it would've been quirky with its varied giftware and welcoming style. From the cool gray walls hung t-shirts and hats for all sizes and sexes. There were beach bags and bathing suits, lotions and potions, candles and coasters and so much more.

He'd just wandered over to inspect a fun display of sun care items when Meg appeared from the back, her hair in a long braid hung over her shoulder like the silky tail of a fox. Her expression morphed from friendly to aware when she spotted him and headed his way.

"Hi." She gripped a box to her chest and stared at him with her big green eyes.

"Hi." Bryan needed to remember why he was there—for information about Corey—and not to get lost in her gaze, feel buzzy and heady in her presence, or get distracted by her elusive and sultry scent. "Is now a good time?"

She pulled the phone from her back pocket, glanced at the display, and tucked it back in her shorts. *Lucky phone.* "Yeah, now's good. Today's not a cruise day, so it should be pretty quiet."

"A cruise day?"

"A day without cruise ships docking in the harbor means less foot traffic for the store."

"Ah." There was a lot more to running a gift store than he'd ever imagined. He looked around. "I like your shop, by the way. It's fun and inviting."

"Thank you." She set the box on the counter and faced him. Bryan had never seen her so unsure of herself, folding her fingers together and then pulling them apart to tap against her legs. She eventually shoved them into her pockets. "What can I do for you?"

"You said to come by when Lily wasn't here so we could talk about Corey."

She ran her tongue around her teeth as if dislodging something unpleasant. "I'm not sure how much I can help."

She was backtracking fast, but he wouldn't let her off the hook. "Like I said, anything is better than nothing." He looked around. "Is there somewhere we can sit and talk?"

After a long-suffering sigh, she motioned to the back of the store. "We can use the office."

He followed her to the back, admiring the sway of her hips and the way she filled out her shorts while giving himself a mental scolding. He couldn't afford to get distracted when she'd finally agreed to talk and they had a few moments alone.

While the store was quirky, the office was bedlam. Two desks sat against the wall—one cluttered with papers and files and knickknacks and boxes, the other with a computer and keypad. Boxes stacked three deep and ceiling high lined the opposite wall.

"Wow," he said, blinking at the boxes. "This is the belly of the beast."

"It's organized chaos." She picked some files off one of the desk chairs and placed them on the cluttered surface. "Maybe not so organized."

"How do you keep track of all this stuff?"

She offered him a seat at the desk with the computer. "We have a program that keeps track of the inventory. It's …" She scrubbed her hands over her face. "I have a love-hate relationship with our POS system."

Bryan eyed the boxes. "You have to manually enter all the merchandise?"

"Yes, and I'm a little behind. More than a little behind. Our holiday stock keeps arriving and I can't seem to make much headway."

And time spent talking about Corey was time better spent on work. "If you're too busy I can come back later."

"Tomorrow or the day after won't be any better. I'm in a constant state of catch up."

He rubbed his hands against his legs as guilt and worry twined their way up his gut, choking the breath from his lungs. "You're shorthanded because of Amanda." It wasn't a question, and she didn't have to answer. The way she chewed her lip and inclined her head told him everything he needed to know. "How can I help?"

"What do you mean?"

"I'm here, taking up your time when you obviously have a mountain of work to do. So, put me to work. We can talk while we inventory."

She blinked her eyes, shaking her head as if she'd heard him wrong. "I … I can't ask you to do that."

"You didn't ask. I'm offering." When she simply stared at him, he went with instinct. "Look, Meg, I'm a fill-in bartender with a lot of time on my hands. You need help and I'm twiddling my thumbs at home." Avoiding going through the last of Corey's things. Every time he peered into a box, his gut twisted with dread. What would he find and what he would do if he found nothing? "I'm going crazy in that apartment."

"Bryan …" The bells on the door announced a visitor, drawing her attention to the front of the store.

"Go, see to your customer. I'll wait here."

She eyed him warily, pointing a finger at his face. "Don't touch anything."

He gave a low chuckle. "I wouldn't know where to begin."

Bryan watched her disappear behind a display and glanced around the office. He leaned over the desk to study a picture of Meg and Amanda taped to the wall. Side by side, the resemblance was striking. Despite the difference in their coloring, they had the same heart-shaped faces, the same full, pouty lips. The camera captured the mischievous gleam in Amanda's eyes and the love and affection between the sisters.

Poor Meg, swamped with work while mourning her sister and business partner, raising her niece on her own. Her hostility toward him made so much sense when he took a big step back. From the very beginning, his gut had told him Meg needed help. Looking around the crowded office, he finally figured out what that meant.

Bryan straightened when Meg reappeared, smiling and leaning against the desk like he hadn't just been ogling her picture.

"Sorry," she said. "Just a browser. I think half the people who come in just want a break from the heat."

Bryan sympathized. He still wasn't used to the humidity. "Can't blame them there."

"So … where were we?"

He gave her his most encouraging smile. "We were about to work our way through your inventory."

Nineteen

Meg knew Bryan's offer was the lifeline she needed in the jungle of wall-to-wall boxes—and the distraction she craved. She'd spent the morning worrying about Lily and how the rumors about her mother had made her feel. But offers came with strings. She'd been outmaneuvered by a Westfall before. She wouldn't make that mistake again.

"Look, Bryan, I'm going to answer your questions. You don't have to dig through merchandise to get them."

"You'd be doing me a favor." He splayed his fingers across his chest, drawing her eyes to his build. His presence made the office feel even more cramped. "I want to help. I need to keep busy."

He seemed sincere, and she's always gotten a sense about him like he couldn't sit still. Who—other than someone with boundless energy—would have volunteered to bartend for Tim during a sold-out concert? "I can't pay you. If I could afford help, I would have already hired someone."

"I not looking for money."

She folded her arms across her chest and tried her hand at a menacing glare. "What are you looking for? Besides information about your brother."

He shook his head like it was a trick question. "Nothing. You need help and I have a lot of free time."

"It's exhausting."

Bryan did that thing men do when they're insulted, jutting his head back and scoffing audibly. "I have a strong back."

"It's tedious work."

"I'm a teacher. I'm used to monotony."

He had an answer for everything. And she couldn't remember why she was working so hard to send him away. "Fine. You can help."

"Great." He glanced around, rubbing his palms together like he couldn't wait to dig in. "Where should we start?"

Meg pointed at the wall. "Pick a box. They all need to be sorted."

He chose a box at random, plucking it up and setting it down as if it weighed nothing, his muscles bunching with the effort. Meg did her best not to swoon. He really did have the perfect body—athletic and rangy, buff but not beefy like a guy who spent all his time in the gym.

She handed him the box cutter and he made quick work of the tape. "Hand me that invoice before we get started."

Bryan did as instructed.

Meg opened the software to the inventory page. "Pull an item from the box and tell me what it is."

He unwrapped something brick-sized and laughed. "It's Christmas flip flops."

"Don't make fun." She eyed the pair he held featuring surfing Santa on the souls and candy cane striped straps. "Those sell out every year."

"I can see why."

"The invoice says thirty pairs in two different designs."

"Let's see." He reached in and started unwrapping, stacking them neatly into a pile on the floor. "Yep, fifteen of each."

She updated the inventory page and started printing tags.

"Oh, cool." Bryan stepped over and gawked at the device. "You print the labels right from there?"

"Technology is a wonderful thing."

"Can I put the tags on?" He had the eagerness of a toddler asking to play with a new toy.

Meg pulled the sheet of barcodes and showed him where to affix the label. "Just like that."

He followed Meg's lead, carefully lining up the barcode with the end of the tag. "How's that?"

"Perfect. If you weren't working for free, I'd hire you."

"I told you I don't need your money."

"Good thing," she mumbled to herself. "I don't have any to spare."

When Bryan grimaced, staring at her with pity on his face, she wished she'd kept her thoughts to herself. She tried to ignore the uncomfortable silence and focused on the invoice. "What's next?"

Bryan dug through the box, unwrapping items like a kid on Christmas morning. He'd comment on each one, as if the boxes had just shown up on their doorstep and hadn't been carefully considered and ordered with their customer base in mind.

He unrolled an item and shook his head as he read the front. "Who would wear a 'Time to Get Basted' apron on Thanksgiving?"

Meg pinned him with an are-you-kidding-me smirk. "You've been in Key West long enough that I shouldn't have to answer that question."

He nodded his head, conceding her point, and continued counting the aprons. "This is fun."

As one box turned into a half-dozen, Meg realized she was having fun too—and it had more to do with enjoying Bryan's company than taking inventory. Every time a customer came into the store, she felt a ding of disappointment she had to step away. And every time she returned, he flashed a too-charming smile that made her stomach flop to her knees.

It had been a long time since someone outside the family had helped with inventory—someone other than Lily who wanted nothing to do with helping at the store. When guilt tried to take hold, it couldn't when she remembered how Bryan had insisted. Even when Amanda had been alive, Meg had been too busy trying to mentally stage the items in the store to appreciate and admire the items they'd ordered. Meg felt Bryan's eyes on her as she stretched her neck from side to side.

"Do you want me to take over?" Bryan asked. "Give me a quick tutorial and we can switch places. I feel like I'm having all the fun."

"No." Meg kneaded her neck. "I barely know what I'm doing."

Bryan stepped over and shoed her hand away, squeezing her shoulder muscles and using his thumbs on her neck. "You're all knotted up."

"Oh, God." His hands were like magic, easing the tension in her neck, feeding the ache in her soul. The sound she let out was as close to a sex noise as she'd ever made in public.

His hands stilled before starting up again at a slower, almost suggestive pace. Up her neck, across her collar bone, rounding her shoulders with his long, strong fingers. His low hum was deep and intimate. "I take it that feels good."

Her eyes drifted closed. "If you keep that up, I'll be a puddle on the floor." The breathy sound of her voice was like a neon billboard. She was aroused and losing her foothold on reality. How long had it been since she'd been touched by a man? A year? Closer to two?

The bells clinked but she didn't get up. The customer could wait. It felt so good to have a man's hands on her body. Even a man she barely knew. Even a man she barely trusted.

"Aunt Meg?"

Meg's eyes flew open, and she shot from her chair, flinging it backward into Bryan's crotch.

"Oof," he mumbled and stepped back.

"Lily?"

"Hey." Lily's eyes flipped between Meg and Bryan as she strangled the towel hanging over her shoulder.

Meg's face heated. She'd lost track of time and lost her mind, letting Bryan massage her shoulders. "I didn't realize it was four."

"Who's that?" Lily inclined her head at Bryan.

"Ah …" *Crap. Crap. Crap.* "This is Bryan. Bryan, this is my niece, Lily."

He stepped forward, his hand extended for a shake.

The formal move caught Lily off guard. She shuffled toward him, her skinny arm outstretched. "Hi."

"Bryan is helping with inventory."

"Cool." Lily stood, shifting from foot to foot. Bryan's presence messed with her routine. After camp, she'd put her stuff in the office, eat her snack at the desk, and wander next door to visit with Eva and Barb. With merchandise everywhere and Bryan in her space, she didn't seem to know where to go.

Bryan broke the silence by clearing his throat. "I probably need to get going."

Grateful she didn't have to kick him out, Meg nodded but didn't meet his eyes. "Thanks for the help."

"No problem. Let me know when you need a hand."

"Will do." Meg scooted past him and opened the back door, ushering him outside like a teenager caught with her boyfriend. She shut the door in his face and turned to smile at Lily, certain her cheeks were flaming red. "How was camp?"

Lily set her towel on the desk and looked at her like a disapproving parent. "Who's your new boyfriend?"

Busted, Meg searched the mini fridge for the apple slices she'd cut for Lily that morning, anything to avoid the suspiciously amused look on her niece's face. "He's not my boyfriend."

"He was touching you," Lily said. "You were making noises."

She squeezed her eyes tight and then faced her niece. "I was not."

"Yes, you were." Lily wrinkled her nose. "He looks familiar."

Any mention of Bryan's connection to Amanda would only confuse Lily and cause her pain. "He came to the store once."

Lily stared at Meg with narrowed eyes.

Determined to change the subject, Meg handed Lily the apples and asked, "How did everything go? Any issues with Cammie?"

"She did better today, but she's still with the beginners. We just kinda ignored each other."

That was one way to solve the problem. "Do you want me to call her mom?"

Lily dropped the apple slice on the way to her mouth. "Please don't."

"If you think this will blow over, I won't call her."

"Getting her mom involved would make everything worse."

"Okay." Meg held her hands up and started stacking merchandise back into boxes. She and Bryan hadn't made as much progress and she and Amanda typically did, but with Bryan's help they'd at least made a dent. "I won't call her."

"So, what's the deal with you and Bryan?" Lily gave his name a sing-songy lilt.

"There is no deal. We're friends. He helped me with inventory."

"That's not what it looked like."

Meg couldn't look at Lily, not with her face on fire and her palms sweating with nerves. "That's what it was." She shrugged, as if she'd be able to slough it off if she found Lily in the same position with a boy.

Meg remembered stumbling into the stock room over a decade ago to find Amanda and Deke pressed against the wall, his hand down her pants. They hadn't even heard Meg come in. Meg asked her sister that night if she'd gone all the way with her older, more experienced boyfriend. Amanda had looked at her and laughed, denied the truth written all over her face. The sisters shared more than their features and enviable metabolism. Neither one could tell a lie without blushing.

"Since when do you invite guys to help with inventory?" Lily asked, pulling Meg out of her memories.

Meg ignored the insinuation and motioned to the endless pile of boxes. "Do you want to help inventory all this stuff?"

"No." Lily's response was quick and decisive.

"Then I have to look elsewhere so I can get it on the floor in the fall."

"You don't have to be so mean about it. I was just asking."

And Meg was being defensive because she felt guilty. If Lily hadn't walked in, she didn't know what would have happened. Would Bryan's hands have continued wandering? Had she wanted them to? Would he have dragged her to her feet and kissed her? Would she have kissed him back?

She folded the boxes and knew the answer was yes. Meg would have kissed him. She might even have made the first move. Something was seriously wrong with her if a nice gesture from a good-looking guy turned her to putty. How easy could she be?

But Bryan wasn't just a good-looking guy. He'd been persistent and helpful and, despite his coming around for information about his brother, he hadn't asked a single question about him in the hours they'd spent going through merchandise. Meg had relaxed in his presence and learned a bit about the man who made her squirm.

Bryan was patient, and funny, and genuinely nice. He had a way of looking at Meg that made her feel like he had nowhere he'd rather be or nothing he'd rather be doing than sorting through giftware in a dusty old stockroom for hours on end.

But that was foolish schoolgirl thinking.

Bryan wasn't in Key West to get to know Meg. He was here for his brother—looking for information he suspected could implicate the barnacle in something seedy or illegal. Bryan's instincts about his brother matched Meg's. How many times had she warned Amanda to be careful around a man whose sole goal in life was to discover a pot of gold?

Lily stood, scooping the uneaten apple slices into her palm, and dropping them into the trash. "I'm going next door to see if Barb and Eva need help."

"You don't think I need help?"

"You had help today, and it's not my problem you kicked him out."

"I didn't kick him out. He had to go."

"Whatever." Lily smirked, turned on her heel, and left.

Meg stood in the stock room, her emotions swirling. Irritated at herself. Anxious about what Lily perceived. Suspicious of and fascinated by a man who kept surprising her around every turn.

She was acting as reckless as her sister—her dead sister. Bryan had a job and a family back home. He wouldn't stay. She couldn't leave. Whatever sparked between them would fizzle out eventually. She wouldn't—she couldn't—get burned in the process.

Meg looked up from the computer to find Eva at the door, a mischievous grin on her face. "I hear you had a visitor."

She should have known Lily would tell. Meg struggled not to roll her eyes. "I did."

"According to your niece, you two looked pretty chummy."

Meg recorded a figure before facing the firing squad. "He helped me with inventory."

"That was nice of him."

"He's a nice guy."

"Nice looking, too."

Meg leaned back in the chair and linked her fingers over her belly. "Why, Eva. Are you interested in the man?"

Eva gave Meg an I-see-right-through-you scoff. "No. But you are."

"And you know this how?"

"Oh, come on. I saw him go into your store hours ago and then Lily said she caught you together. She said you acted embarrassed."

Awareness jolted Meg upright. "You didn't tell her who he was, did you?"

"No, but she called him Bryan. I assumed she knew."

"She doesn't know, and I don't want her to find out."

Eva crossed her arms against her ample chest. "She's not stupid, Meg. She'll figure it out eventually."

Lily wasn't stupid, but neither was Meg. Involving Lily in Bryan's deep dive into his brother's life was out of the question. Nothing he discovered would bring Amanda back. "Knowing who he is and why he's here would only confuse her."

Eva studied Meg, the worry line between her brows deep and pensive. "You don't seem all that confused anymore. What did you find out?"

"He's a teacher from Atlanta. He's also generous with his time and has a self-depreciating sense of humor."

Eva nodded like a dog with a bone. "What else?"

"His parents are struggling."

"As are yours."

"As are mine." Meg stood and placed a hand on Eva's shoulder. "I see what you're doing. I don't need you playing matchmaker."

"I don't think I have to. You're already smitten."

Meg cursed her Irish skin. "What I am is grateful. He was a big help today."

"You think he'll be back?"

She hoped so—despite all the reasons he shouldn't. "Probably. We never got around to talking about his brother. Plus, he likes to feel useful."

"There's plenty to keep him busy here." Eva wagged her brows. "And I'm not talking about the store."

Twenty

Bryan added ice, rum, mint leaves, and simple sugar to the beverage shaker and rattled it like a maraca in a mariachi band. He poured the mojito cocktail into a highball glass and set it atop the waitress's tray. Bryan had quickly graduated from making drinks to using the register after a tutorial and an afternoon shadowing the head bartender.

Bartending was easy and enjoyable work. Bryan liked mixing cocktails and making friends with the island's guests and colorful inhabitants. In the nineteen eighties, the Key's residents' one-day resistance to roadblocks along Highway One created the now fabled Conch Republic—a badge the islanders wore proudly. Bryan wondered if Meg considered herself or Lily a Conch.

He'd thought a lot about the woman who intrigued him and the child who intimidated him in the days since he'd seen them last. The woman was as hard to crack as a Rubik's Cube—cold one minute, laughing the next, melting beneath his fingers like ice cream on a hot summer day. Talking about the store relaxed her, had her dropping her guard, showing him more of the woman who lie beneath the beautiful surface. She was short-tempered and quick witted, slyly shy, and fiercely protective of her niece.

He grabbed an orange, cut it into perfect slices, deliberated how he'd find a way to see Meg again soon. A man walked up, his shadow arriving first, derailing Bryan's train of thought. He glanced up, but couldn't see much beyond a tall form in the glare of the setting sun filtering through the palm fronds.

"What can I get you?" Bryan asked, loading the slices into a condiment tray.

"A cold beer and a place to stay in exactly that order."

Bryan jerked his head up at the familiar voice and squinted into the face of his oldest friend. "Dustin? What are you doing here?"

"I just told you. I need a cold beer and a place to crash. Tegan threw me out."

Disappointment settled like a weighted blanket on Bryan's heart. No. Just no. Not them. Anyone but them. "Why?"

"Beer first." Dustin collapsed onto a stool, flinging his arms over the bar, and rubbing his travel-weary eyes. "Please. It's been a long day."

Bryan retrieved a cold mug, poured Dustin a local IPA he knew his friend would enjoy. As the golden liquid filled the glass, Bryan reminded himself to tread lightly. Dustin was his best friend, but Tegan was a friend too. She hadn't exactly come running to Bryan with their marital problems, but he couldn't trash-talk her for casting Dustin aside without knowing her side of the story.

He placed the beer in front of Dustin, nudged his shoulder when he kept his eyes closed.

"Thanks, man."

"What happened?" Bryan asked. "And how did you find me?"

"It's an island." Dustin turned the glass in his hand. "And you told me the name of the bar."

"Tegan really threw you out?"

"She asked for a trial separation, as if coming home to me every day is such a trial."

"I'm sorry, man. That stinks." And it didn't sound like the Tegan Bryan had grown up with and adored.

"Like roadkill on hot asphalt." Dustin saluted Bryan before taking a sip. He set the cup down and scrubbed his hands over his face. "My marriage is over."

"A separation doesn't mean divorce."

Dustin seared him with a steely stare. "What else would it mean?"

Bryan searched the gold-streaked sky for a silver lining. "A break? A time out from all the fighting to remember why you love each other?"

"It's a semi-permanent break that leads to divorce. If she's miserable being married to me, do you think she's going to be even more miserable without me? No," he answered before Bryan could comment. "She's going to cut her losses and move on. This whole separation is just her way of easing her conscience when she finally asks for a divorce."

Dustin didn't need a thousand questions or a lecture on fighting for his marriage. He needed an ear, a beer, and a soft place to land. "You don't know that for sure."

"Trust me. I don't know much these days where Tegan is concerned, but this I know. We weren't fighting so much as freezing each other out. And she's done."

A couple approached the bar, pulling Bryan away from his heartbroken friend. He fixed their drinks and started a tab while keeping an eye on Dustin.

The guy was wrecked, with bags under his red-rimmed eyes and his normally proud posture slouched under the weight of his troubles. Bryan hardly recognized the sad, broken man in front of him when all their childhood memories were of a playful kid with a quick smile and a penchant for getting them into trouble.

"What happened to the counselor?" Bryan asked.

"I told Tegan I wasn't spending three hundred bucks an hour to have a stranger question my love and commitment to the only woman I've ever loved and committed myself to. We could have flown to Fiji for what we paid that overpriced windbag who answered every question with a question."

"Why didn't you?"

"Fly to Fiji?"

"Go somewhere—anywhere—and reconnect."

"Tegan said if I wasn't willing to go to counseling, she wasn't going on vacation."

They were both too stubborn for their own good. "So that's it?"

"Apparently my refusal to continue with counseling was her breaking point." Dustin finished his beer. "I know this is the last thing you need right now, but can I stay?"

"Of course you can stay. I need to check with my boss—he's my landlord—but stay as long as you need. It's a one bedroom, so you're stuck on the couch."

"Wouldn't be the first time." He squeezed the bridge of his nose and looked up at Bryan with worried eyes. "What am I going to do?"

With his string of go-nowhere relationships, Bryan was the last one Dustin should've asked. "Take some time. Figure things out."

Dustin stared at his empty beer glass. "I love her, man. I don't know who I am without her."

"You're Dustin Carver, and you're the same as you've always been. Just ... sadder."

"I can hardly remember my life before her."

Bryan could. He and Dustin were always together, shooting hoops, talking smack, navigating adolescence while riding high on testosterone. "Before Tegan came along you were a good athlete, an above-average student, and obsessed with music."

"I don't remember that guy."

"I do." Bryan smiled, remembering. "He was the life of the party."

Dustin fiddled with the paper napkin on the bar. "There's no life left in this party."

"Sure there is." Bryan grabbed a ticket from the waitress and began fixing drinks, his eyes fixed on Dustin. If he and Tegan had both dug their heels in—as Bryan had seen them do on many occasions—a little break didn't mean a permanent break. That a little absence makes the heart grow fonder theory wasn't the worst idea in the world. Or was it?

Twenty-One

Meg couldn't get Bryan Westfall off her mind. It had been days—four to be exact—since he'd stumbled into her store and taken up residence in her mind. Lily's merciless teasing hadn't helped her forget the man. Or his muscles. Or his manners.

She kept telling herself he'd be back. He needed information and she had some to give. His relentless pursuit wouldn't end because they'd called a truce.

Or would it?

Maybe she needed to apologize for kicking him out as gracelessly as she had. Of all times for Lily to come back and catch her unaware, catch her falling under Bryan's spell and under the feel of his hands on her body.

Stop. She had to stop thinking about how good it felt to be around him, to be touched and seen. When she needed help, there he was offering it up without her having to ask. Making her laugh and remember all the reasons she fought so hard to keep the store open and in the black.

He'd opened more than the boxes. He'd opened her mind and heart to the possibility of more. More help. More touches. More feeling like a worthy and desirable woman. Little did he know, the combination was the kryptonite that could topple her well-constructed walls.

Try as she might, Meg couldn't talk herself out of wanting to see him again. Courtesy alone meant she owed him a thank you. What better way than to stop by the bar and present him with the trinket he'd enjoyed the most in their time together—a funny, harmless gift of thanks where she could gauge her feelings in real time instead of on a continual loop in her head.

When Lily was busy helping Eva and Barb, Meg fetched the item and wrapped it in the store's yellow paper with pink and orange twine. He'd laugh at the silliness of it once again and maybe invite her in or volunteer to help her again. Either way, no matter what happened, she owed him a proper thanks.

After locking up the store, she walked to Westies with the breeze ruffling her hair. The bar was moderately busy for a Monday, and on a night like tonight when there wasn't a band, music piped from well-disguised speakers. Tonight's selection was jazzy and slow.

The mellow music fit Meg's mood. Any more time spent inside her head debating whether to instigate contact with Bryan was worse than just getting it over with, regardless of the outcome. That she'd applied a coat of gloss to her lips and brushed her hair before coming didn't mean anything. After a day spent in the store moving stock and dealing with customers, she would have done the same no matter where she was going.

She found Tim behind the bar wearing a smile and one of his endless band t-shirts. "Hey, Tim."

"How's it going, Meg?"

"It's going." She scoped the bar, waved at a friend eating nachos with her husband. "I was looking for Bryan."

"He worked the lunch shift." Tim cocked his head in the direction of the stairwell that led to Bryan's apartment. "Not sure if he's home."

His smirk did not go unnoticed. "Thanks."

"Are you two …?" He let the implication linger but his eyes stayed steady on her face.

"We're friends, Tim." Meg kept her voice flat. "Helping each other out."

Tim nodded, not offended but not entirely convinced. "Okay. He's a good guy—not that you asked my opinion."

"I value your opinion. Always have."

"Then I'll tell you he seems legit. Shows up on time, works hard, helps out whenever he can."

"Yes, that's my impression too." And Tim's opinion mattered. As a former military guy, he could sniff out a fraud better than most. His backing of Bryan gave Meg an added measure of comfort and boosted her attraction. "Not much like his brother."

"Can't really speak to that more than the handful of times I saw the guy, but Bryan's different. He's not a drifter like Corey. He's grounded and mature. I wish he were staying longer than the summer."

Meg's seesaw emotions kicked into high gear. *He's a great guy. He's leaving. He's attracted. He's the barnacle's brother.* And the last guy she let her guard down enough to trust had left her high and dry. She shook her worries clear and focused on the now. "Me too. I'll see you around."

Like the last time she approached his apartment, she ascended the stairs quickly before she could change her mind. If Bryan was home and they talked about his brother, his reason for seeing her would become crystal clear. She took a deep breath and knocked on his door.

Her stomach took a header when a man answered. A man who wasn't Bryan.

"Hello." He blinked his blue eyes at Meg as if she'd been placed there for his enjoyment.

"Ah ... hi." Meg tucked her hair behind her ear and tried to peer behind him, but he was too tall and broad. "Is Bryan here?"

"Meg?" Barefoot and dressed in a t-shirt and basketball shorts, Bryan shoved the guy aside. "Hi."

"Hi." Meg glanced between the men. "Is this ... a bad time?"

"Not at all." Bryan waved her inside, and they watched her move into the apartment like a circus animal on display. Bryan motioned to the tall guy. "This is my friend Dustin. He's visiting from Atlanta."

"Nice to meet you, Dustin." Meg held her hand out for a shake.

Dustin had a firm grip and a lopsided smile. "Nice to meet you, Meg. I've heard a lot about you."

"Really?" Her curious gaze winged to Bryan.

"Dustin was just leaving."

"I was?"

Bryan fixed Dustin with a pointed stare. "You were going for a walk to clear your head, remember?"

"Oh, right." Dustin nodded slowly. "On a ninety-degree evening. In a hundred percent humidity. Yep." He pointed over his shoulder. "I'll just get my shoes and go."

Bryan led her into the kitchen. "Can I get you a drink? Some wine or a beer?"

"No, thank you." Alcohol wouldn't do anything to help Meg figure out her reaction to seeing Bryan again when he'd kicked out a friend so they could be alone. Better to stay clear-eyed and focused on her reason for dropping by. "I came by to give you this." She pulled the package from her purse.

The smile that claimed his face only illuminated his gorgeousness. "For me?"

"Don't get too excited. It's a silly thank you for your help the other day."

"This doesn't look silly." He pulled the colored twine and ripped the paper, and the wattage on his smile surged to blinding. "The bikini couple snow globe!" He shook the plastic bauble and watched the beachgoers through a burst of plastic snow the same way he had when he'd first pulled one from a box in the stockroom—as if it were the most magical thing he'd ever seen. "I was going to come by this week and buy one."

Pleasure rolled through her like waves at the ocean. The pull she'd felt toward him in the stockroom swelled in his small kitchen unearthing an inconvenient and intoxicating attraction. "I saved you a trip and a hefty markup."

Meg startled when Dustin reappeared. She'd been so enchanted by Bryan's reaction she'd forgotten Dustin was still in the apartment.

"Whatcha got there?" Dustin asked.

Bryan lifted the snow globe. "Meg owns a gift store. I helped her unpack some boxes and she brought me this as a thank you."

"Cool." He spared the snow globe a fleeting glance before zipping his eyes back to Meg. "Got any more?"

Meg snorted, an unfeminine sound Amanda would have fussed at Meg for making. "You want one too?"

Dustin shook his shaggy brown hair. "I meant the boxes. Bryan's been a great host, but I'm losing my mind in this apartment."

Questions clogged Meg's tongue like cars during rush hour. Why was Dustin stuck in Bryan's apartment? It wasn't like Bryan worked all the time. "A lot, actually. I'm sure you have better things to do while you're visiting."

"Not really. I could use a distraction."

"We both could." Bryan stepped beside his friend, pulling Meg's attention back to him. "But only when it's convenient. We don't want to intrude."

Meg shaky smile tried and failed to take hold. "I swear I didn't come by to recruit you."

"We offered." Bryan stepped into the living room, scooped his phone from the end table, and passed it to Meg. "Give me your number so I can call when we've got time. Make sure you're not swamped."

Meg plugged her number in his phone, handed it back. "Are you sure about this?"

"You know I'm happy to help." He elbowed Dustin's gut. "And Dustin's smarter than he looks."

"Hey." Dustin shoved Bryan in the shoulder.

Meg's heart ached at their playfulness. Whatever Bryan and Dustin's relationship, they were as close as brothers. As close as Meg and Amanda. "I'm grateful for the help." Swamped by feelings of melancholy and confusion over what she'd just offered, Meg stepped to the door. She needed out of the apartment and into the hot air where she could analyze the baffling chain of events where a thank you gift resulted in double the help for her store.

Bryan met her there and reached for the knob. "You're welcome to stay. I was just about to order dinner."

"Thanks, but I've got to get Lily."

"Raincheck?"

Meg was tempted by Bryan's suggestion—too tempted. She inclined her head and couldn't stop the teasing pout of her lips. "Maybe."

Bryan's grin was quick and lethal. "Maybe's not a no."

Meg wasn't too out of the game that she didn't recognize flirting—or couldn't do some of her own. "It's also not a yes."

Bryan's hand settled low on his abdomen. "I guess I've got some work to do."

The coy noise she made was like waving a green flag at a race—this game—whatever game they were playing—was definitely on. "I guess you do."

Twenty-Two

Bryan faced the door and took a moment to savor the small victory. If he'd been alone, he would have pumped his fist in the air or performed a happy dance around the apartment, but with Dustin behind him, he prepared to temper his response.

Dustin crossed his arms, a you're-busted smile on his annoyingly smug face. "Well, well, well. Living proof why you're still here when all you've got is a couple of boxes left to sift through. That girl is smokin'."

Bryan ignored him and sank onto the couch, placing the snow globe on the coffee table and pulling up the menu of his favorite pizza place on his phone. "I told you she was attractive."

"Come on, man." Dustin followed, folding his big body into the chair. "She's hot." He sat forward. "Have you banged her yet?"

Bryan inhaled and did his best to remember Dustin's heart was bruised and battered. Battered or not, the banging talk had to stop. "What are you? Twelve?"

Dustin let out a spine-scraping chortle and sat back, folding his hands over his belly. "That means no."

"That means none of your business."

"Dude, it's okay. She's totally into you."

Bryan couldn't help it. He dropped the phone and leaned toward Dustin, eager to hear his friend's assessment. "You think so?"

"Yeah. She brought you that snow globe. She gave you her number." He wiggled his fingers in front of his face like he was casting a spell. "You two played that little flirting game by the door."

Instead of feeling better, Bryan brooded. Calling their interaction a game made it feel like a game. Bryan didn't know much about Meg, but he knew she didn't play games.

Dustin studied him, a wrinkle between his brows. "What's with you? I haven't seen you so anxious around a woman since Tina Bowers in the seventh grade."

Tina and her tight shirts and cutoff shorts had put him through months of agony. He'd finally worked up the nerve to ask her out when Brett freaking Hodges with his stupid skateboard and stupid Livestrong bracelet swooped in and stole her away. *How you feeling about that bracelet now, Brett? Lance Armstrong was a cheater!* "That's a memory that doesn't need resurrecting."

"So, what gives?"

"I don't know." He rubbed his breastbone where the ache she created wouldn't go away. "I think she's into me, but she's hard to read. Sometimes, when she forgets our connection is Corey, she warms up and lets her guard down. But as soon as she remembers, it's lights out. She's got me in knots."

"So, you like her-like her, and not just because she's hot?"

"If she were just hot, I'd pack up and head home. I mean,

her sister and my brother—that's weird. But she's vulnerable and feisty and shouldering a huge amount of responsibility. Without Amanda, she's raising her niece and running the store on her own. It's impressive."

"So is this crush you've got." Dustin sat forward and put his elbows on his knees. "Since I'm here and in no condition to help my own messed up love life, I'm going to help you with yours."

Uh-oh. The last time Dustin offered to help, Bryan ended up making a fool of himself at a basketball game asking a girl to prom. The whole evening had been a disaster. "I think I'd rather you didn't."

"Think about it. This unboxing gig is the perfect opportunity to spend time with her without any pressure."

"Yes, I know. Which is why I offered. And now you'll be there."

"Not for long. I'll help because she needs it, but at some point, when the timing is right, I'll slip away and leave you two alone to explore your feelings."

Dustin knew and understood him too well. "I'm not asking you to bow out, but I'd appreciate if you did."

"No worries, man. Trust me, I don't want to be a third wheel." Dustin dropped his head and scowled at his linked hands.

Bryan didn't want to poke his nose into Dustin's business, but turnabout seemed like fair play. "Have you heard from Tegan?"

"Nope." He exaggerated the p with a popping sound. "I knew I wouldn't."

"Seriously?"

"Come on, Bryan. It's Tegan. You know how by-the-book she is. If she asks for time, she wants time."

"How does that feel—not talking when you've been together since you were kids?"

"It sucks balls. But I know her—at least I used to." His sarcasm was as thick as the stubble on his chin. "She's serious about a separation." Dustin sounded resigned, as if he'd accepted his fate.

"You seem to be taking it better than before."

"Not really, but I've decided to play the long game. I need her to miss me—to miss us. If I text her or call her, she won't miss me. She can't miss me unless I'm gone."

"You couldn't have gone any further south."

Dustin nodded, staring at the floor. "What if she doesn't miss me?"

His whispered question exposed his greatest fear and made Bryan sick with worry. "She does."

"How can you be sure?"

He wasn't sure, but Dustin needed a pep talk, not a reality check. "Because I know you, and I know her, and I know you both together. You're a unit. If you take one piece away, the whole thing falls apart."

Dustin's gaze was like a tase to Bryan's chest. "Is that supposed to make me feel better?"

"She's probably falling apart without you."

"What if she's not?" He sprung from the chair and prowled the room, his long stride eating up space. "What if she's planning the rest of her life without me?"

"Do you really want to play the what-if game?"

"Why not? I play it all day long. Why shouldn't you join the fun?"

Bryan regretted broaching the topic instead of waiting until Dustin was ready to talk. He could have listened instead of opening his big mouth and making things worse. "Because it's a waste of time. Because I think you're doing the right thing—giving her space. I think that's all you can do." Bryan stood up, walked to Dustin, placed a hand on his shoulder. "Every relationship has highs and lows. You'll work this out. You love each other. When the rest of the stuff falls away, you'll always have love."

"That's just it," Dustin said, his voice breaking. "I'm not sure she loves me anymore."

Bryan felt the earth shift beneath his feet. He had a couple of certainties his life. Teaching was his calling, he would forever live in Corey's shadow, and Dustin and Tegan would always be in love. "Did she say that to you?"

"Not in so many words. But what is this break if not a torturous, slow-motion goodbye?"

How would Bryan know? Between his string of fizzled relationships and being stuck inside his head since his brother died, he'd been too oblivious to notice Dustin's life was falling apart. "Think of it like a pressure valve. When you two were together and things weren't going well, all that pressure built up and needed a release before one of you said or did something you couldn't take back." He poked Dustin in the chest. "I know you. You say mean things when you feel cornered."

Dustin knocked Bryan's hand away. "Really? I say mean things?"

"All the time."

"Yeah? Well, Meg's out of your league."

Bryan felt his chest expand at Dustin's playful tone. "She *is* out of my league. But I'm more patient than I used to be. More calculating."

"Mr. Romantic. I'm sure Meg would love to hear you're using your nerdy math brain to plot a vacation fling."

The smile leaked from Bryan's lips. Serious Meg would never

agree to a fling of any kind. He ran his hands through his hair and considered who, exactly, needed a reality check. What was he doing, trying so hard to connect with a woman who lived hundreds of miles away?

Dustin noticed the change. "Stop overthinking."

"I'm not."

"Yes, you are."

"I'm not this time."

Dustin pointed at his face. "Yes, you are."

Bryan ambled back to the couch. If they'd been in middle school, Bryan would have made Dustin go home. But they weren't in middle school, and Dustin had nowhere to go. "You hungry?"

Dustin sat in the chair, looked at Bryan. "That's a silly question. You know I'm always hungry."

Twenty-Three

Meg checked her phone after helping a customer, cursed the blank screen and herself for feeling disappointed Bryan hadn't reached out. She was being stupid, acting like one of Lily's boy-crazy classmates. She was a grown woman with a business to run and a niece to raise. She didn't have the time nor the energy to pursue an ill-fated relationship with a complicated man who'd be gone in a matter of weeks.

If only he weren't so attractive. If only he didn't stir up longings and feelings better left ignored. If only he didn't have such a notorious connection to the man who'd stolen her sister and left her and Lily alone.

It was better if he didn't call. She didn't need any more challenges in her life, not with her car barely starting, a mountain of unpaid bills, and a sad pre-teen with nothing to look forward to but a long, boring summer at the store.

Truthfully, Meg had had more than a few moments to work on inventory in the last few days, but she'd waited for Bryan and Dustin's help. Why nag her moody niece or dig into a box alone when the three of them could tackle so much more all at once?

Meg's nerves twitched when her phone dinged an incoming text. She left the phone tucked in her pocket as she refolded some shirts and straightened a display. Her itchy fingers pulled the phone from her pocket, and she read the text from the unfamiliar area code.

It's Bryan. I checked the cruise calendar and there aren't many ships in port today. You busy or can we come by to help?

The track team in her stomach took off at a sprint. Bryan was complicated, but he was present and consistent and offering help. She'd be a fool to turn him down. Wouldn't she?

I'm here if you want to come by.

She almost made it to the bathroom to check her appearance when the bells on the door jangled and she turned to see Bryan enter with Dustin on his heels. "We were in the neighborhood."

And they'd probably seen her gawking at her phone like a love-sick puppy. Fantastic. She flashed a smile she hoped blinded her blush. "Hi."

Dustin's gaze was everywhere, nodding his head with an appraising look on his face. "Nice place, Meg."

"Thanks. Have a look around."

He sidestepped Bryan and made his way down the perimeter of the store. "Don't mind if I do."

Bryan, wearing shorts and a yellow t-shirt that brought out the gold in his eyes, smiled at Meg. "Thanks for letting us come by."

"It's been slow, and Lily's gone for the day. But I'm not sure why you're thanking me."

Bryan angled his head to where Dustin browsed her merchandise. "He's in a weird place. I'll explain later, but getting out of the apartment and doing something productive is just what he needs."

"I'm glad my messy stock room can help."

"Where's Lily?" Bryan asked. "Another camp?"

"She's on a road trip with Barb."

"Really?"

"They went to a floral wholesaler in Miami. Lily's developed an interest in the floral business, so Barb's teaching her the trade. Honestly, it's been a nice distraction for her. She—" She stopped when she heard music playing from the back of the store. "What in the world?"

Bryan's smile bloomed and he shook his head. "That's a blast from the past."

Meg didn't flinch when Bryan's hand whispered across her lower back as they followed the music, but the heat that spread through her midsection caused other reactions to fire. The subtle spice of his cologne tickled her nose. The deep timber of his low chuckle sent vibrations low in her belly. And the warm sensation of having men in the store brought back bittersweet memories of when her dad was at the helm of A Day's Wait.

It was Dustin strumming a cheap ukulele he'd plucked from their meager collection of kids' toys and singing about trees of green and red roses too. Meg recognized the song and Dustin's raw talent. His voice drifted off with the last bars, his face a mask of heartbreak. When Bryan and Meg applauded, he opened his eyes.

"That was beautiful," Meg said. "Your voice is amazing."

Dustin shrugged and looked at the toy in his hands. "It could use a tune." He dropped the ukulele into the bin. "Honestly, so could I."

Bryan slapped Dustin on the back. "It's good to hear you singing again. Man, that brings back memories."

Dustin flashed a sheepish smile. "A kid's toy is about my speed these days. I'm rusty."

"I'd pay to hear you rusty." And Meg would love to be able to stir people's emotions without even trying. "That was amazing."

"I used to play." He flopped his hands before shoving them into his pockets. "A lifetime ago."

"You should tell Tim," Meg suggested. "He lives for music and he's always willing to host new bands."

"I'm not exactly a band."

"He has singer/songwriters play all the time."

Dustin was shaking his head before she even finished talking. "I haven't played for a crowd since high school. Heck, I haven't even picked up a guitar in years."

"It's like riding a bike—obviously—or you wouldn't have moved me with your voice and some flimsy plastic strings."

Dustin narrowed his eyes at Meg, a comma between his brows. "I came here to unpack boxes, not rekindle old fantasies."

Meg recognized the thread of hope in his voice. Performers were like artists, caught in the tug of war between passion for their art and fear of rejection. But she'd lit a spark. If she pushed too hard, he'd dig in his heels, but if she let the idea fester, it might catch fire on its own. "Fine. If you'd rather waste your time on useless busywork, I've got plenty of that." She opened the storeroom and stepped to the side.

"Wow." Dustin scanned the room. "You weren't kidding."

There was no use feeling embarrassed by the bank of boxes staring them in the face. "Procrastination is my middle name."

"We're kindred souls, you and I." Dustin rubbed his hands together. "Where should we start?"

Meg parked herself behind the computer and motioned to the wall of cardboard. "Pick a box."

Bryan grabbed the boxcutters, cutting and unfolding a box, and handing the invoice to Meg. She didn't have to explain the process, not since Bryan took control and directed Dustin to unpack the merchandise and count the supplies.

They made quick work of the first box and were halfway through the second when the bells on the door chimed, alerting Meg to a customer. "Oh, shoot." They were getting so much done she'd forgotten the store was still open. She marked the invoice for where they'd left off. "I'll be right back."

Bryan watched Meg leave and faced Dustin where he stood scowling at an open box. "You okay?" he asked.

"Yeah. Sure." Dustin blinked as if coming out of a daze. "Why?"

"You seem a little distracted." He'd deny it, but Bryan knew him too well. Playing an instrument—even a toy ukulele—and singing had jarred loose memories of when he'd spent countless hours strumming and singing the soundtrack of their youth. Hearing Dustin play brought back so many good memories of them camping in the backyard with nothing but junk food, comic books, and Dustin's faithful guitar.

"I'm fine." He looked around the storeroom. "She's got a pretty good mess on her hands."

Bryan let Dustin's deflection slide. It was enough to know his wheels were spinning from Meg's suggestion he play for an audience. "She does." Bryan took his own survey and noticed how little progress Meg had made since his last visit to the stockroom. "It worries me."

"Why?"

Bryan gestured to the boxes. "It's too much for one person. And she doesn't have any help."

"What are we—chicken liver?"

"I mean permanent help."

"Why doesn't she hire someone?"

"I don't think she can afford to, and with her sister gone …" Things were worse. He didn't have to know Meg before Amanda's death to understand the burden she carried.

"I get it, man. I'm on it."

"What are you talking about?"

"I'm freeloading off you and driving us both crazy sitting around all day wondering what Tegan's doing, what she's thinking, if she's missing me or drawing up divorce papers. I may as well help out a friend."

"What are you saying?"

"If I can manage multimillion dollar projects, I think I can handle a gift store. It's not rocket science."

Bryan bit his lip to keep from smiling at the image of Dustin manning the register at Meg's quirky little shop. "You want to work here?"

Dustin dropped his head and picked at the ketchup stain on his shirt. "I think I need something to do other than sit around and mope." He dropped his shirt and glanced around the stockroom. "She needs help—a lot of it from the looks of things. Two birds, one stone."

"I'm not asking you to do this."

"I'd be doing it for Meg." His lips quirked with a playful grin. "And if I'm here, gathering intel, that wouldn't be such a bad thing, right?"

Bryan's spine itched. *He* wanted to spend time with Meg, get to know her, figure her out. But if his best friend worked at the store and learned about her life, sharing that with Bryan at home would be normal, right? "I don't know. It seems a little underhanded."

"I'd be helping her out of a jam."

"I was supposed to help Meg." It was ninth grade all over, only this time, Meg was the prize—not Tegan. "You're stealing my thunder. *Again.*"

Dustin ran his tongue along his teeth the way he did when trying not to lose his patience. "Technically, Tegan was a free agent, and you knew I'd liked her since before you two hooked up in middle school. Besides, middle school doesn't count."

Tell that to his twelve-year-old ego. "You still broke bro-code."

"This time, I'm married—at least for the moment. And if things work out with Meg, maybe you'll finally forgive me for dating your middle school ex. Never mind that she's stomping my heart as we speak."

"The last time you tried to help, I ended up asking the wrong girl to prom." Bryan would never forget the announcer at their high school basketball game calling Ashley Pinson to center court instead of Ashley Parker. Bryan was too embarrassed to humiliate the girl—and himself—in front of the whole school, so he took her and missed his chance with the perky cheerleader he was supposed to ask.

"Hey"—Dustin pointed at Bryan—"that wasn't my fault."

"Are you kidding me right now?"

"That was twelve years ago. Isn't it time to let it go?"

"Easy for you to say. You got lucky on prom night."

"Not feeling so lucky right now." Dustin peeked out the door before continuing. "Do you want to rehash old mishaps or talk about all the ways my working with Meg will be good for you?"

"That was hardly a mishap." But Dustin was right. Bryan did need to let go of the past and focus on the present. "Good for me how?"

"If I'm here helping, she might have more time to go out and have fun with you."

"If I can get her to go out with me."

"I can give you some pointers." Dustin pulled something from the box, frowning at the bubble-wrapped gift. "On second thought, you're on your own. I haven't had moves since high school."

Bryan ignored him and sat at the desk. "Tell me what that is and how many are in the box."

Dustin unwrapped the gift and scratched the stubble on his chin. "I have no idea what this is." As he unwrapped, a smile fanned across his face. "They're Santa and Mrs. Clause salt and pepper shakers." The pair attached magnetically—and quite creatively—at their laps. "Nice. Our little Meg has a naughty side."

"It's Key West. She knows her clientele." Bryan pointed at the box. "How many?"

"Six. Maybe five if I buy a set for Tegan. Remind her how it's done."

"Very funny."

"Or very instructional." Dustin rewrapped the shakers and glanced at the door. "Sounds like Meg is done." He walked to the back door, looked up and around. "Is this thing going to set off an alarm if I open the door?"

"Where are you going?"

"Giving you a head start. Go on and make your move."

"We just got started. What am I supposed to tell her?"

"Tell her I ate something bad for lunch."

"We ate at the bar. I'm not doing that to Tim."

"Then tell her I got a call. Geez. Be creative." Dustin pointed at the box they were working on. "Use the shakers if all else fails. I'll see you at home." He disappeared out the back.

Bryan pinched the bridge of his nose and tried to come up with a believable lie. His mind, like his refrigerator at home since Dustin moved in, was completely empty.

Twenty-Four

Meg straightened the stack of tissue paper and made herself walk slowly back to the storeroom. The whole time she helped the customer, she felt sure Bryan and Dustin were talking about her and the sad shape of the store.

She ticked off a list of things that needed tending. The display window needed updating, the shelves needed a good dusting, and the endless bookkeeping duties that had piled up faster than Lily's laundry at home needed to be addressed. She was doing the best she could and when she looked around on her way back to the stockroom, it was obvious her best wasn't good enough.

Meg halted inside the storeroom. Bryan stared absently at the computer, and Dustin was nowhere in sight. "Where's Dustin?"

Bryan straightened as if she'd caught him looking at porn. "Ah … he had to go."

"I thought he had nothing to do."

"His lawyer called."

"His lawyer?" A tight fist grabbed Meg by the stomach and pushed her heart up into her throat. Despite his affable manner, Dustin could be a hardened criminal or sex predator for all she knew. "Is he in some kind of trouble?"

"Marriage trouble. He and his wife are ..." Bryan scratched the back of his neck. "They're taking a break."

Meg's stomach unfurled and her heart settled back into place. No wonder Dustin had that faraway look in his eye. "I'm sorry to hear that. Have they been married long?"

"Six years, but they've been together since high school."

"Oh." Meg linked her fingers and brought them to her chest. She knew firsthand the sweetness of young love blooming into adulthood. "My grandparents were high school sweethearts. I hope they work it out."

"Me too. He's ... he's a mess."

Meg's heart broke for Dustin. Every time she talked to her dad, he sounded more and more depressed. She couldn't blame him. Every day he watched his wife slip farther and farther away while he dealt with the shocking death of his daughter without the loving support of his partner. "That's why he's visiting?"

Bryan wrinkled his nose. "It's not so much a visit as an escape." He stood and skirted the desk. "Are your parents local?"

"They're in Orlando." She cleared the emotion from her throat. Saying it out loud, no matter how long it'd been, felt like a knife to the gut. "My mom has early Alzheimer's. She's in a special facility."

"Meg." His hand came to rest on his heart. "I'm so sorry. That must be incredibly hard."

"It is." She could talk about it—about her mom—without breaking down. "She was full of life, witty and creative. I miss her. I miss them both. She doesn't even know about Amanda."

The guilt on Bryan's face was unmistakable. "You're kidding."

"We told her, obviously, but it didn't compute. My poor dad is grieving Amanda while his wife slips away day by day." And from the look on his face, her saying that out loud was like a knife to Bryan's gut.

"I'm ... I didn't know."

She shrugged and looked away, intent to change the subject. "How could you?"

The gritty sound of Bryan's voice shocked her, had her looking up into his hardened stare. "I could have shown up sooner instead of putting it off when it was more convenient or when I thought it'd be easier to swallow."

Meg wanted to soothe him and lighten the heavy mood. There was no use lamenting what he couldn't change. "Hey, you're talking to a world-class procrastinator. You don't have to feel bad for putting it off. Most people avoid facing hard stuff head on."

"You didn't."

"Yeah, well, I didn't have a choice." Her sassy smile slipped. It was time to take her own advice and face a hard truth, stop dancing around the reason they were together. "You haven't asked about your brother."

He looked down at his hand where it rested on the desk. "I'm avoiding that too."

"Why?"

His finger traced a long-ago scratch Lily had made with a toy car. "We're getting along, you and me, and talking about my brother upsets you. I'm guilty by association."

Busted, her face flushed. "You told me once not to judge you by your brother. I'm trying because I don't want you to judge me by Amanda. I loved my sister, but we were very different people."

"Tell me about her. Tell me how you're different."

Thinking about Amanda sent Meg spiraling into a dark hole she'd rather avoid. And their differences were too many to count. Better to keep things light. "For one thing, I never would have given your brother the time of day."

His eyebrows lifted and he blinked his brown-gold eyes. "That's because you're smart."

"My balance sheet says otherwise." The pointed way he watched her, ticking his fingers on the edge of the desk, his broad shoulders rising and falling with each inhalation of breath made the air crackle with tension. The last time they were alone in the stockroom, he'd touched her. She'd wanted him to. Meg deliberately broke the spell, motioned to the computer. "Was there a problem?"

"Ah, no." Bryan stepped away from the desk. "Before Dustin left, he was unloading, and I started updating online."

Alarm bells clamored. If he'd screwed something up just as she was getting the hang of things … Meg stepped to the computer and wiggled the mouse, leaning over the desk. Everything looked as it should, but the guilty look on his face when she walked in made her more than a little suspicious. "What did you input?"

"The rest of the box." He stepped behind her, bent over her shoulder, and pointed with his finger at the screen. "Here and here. We were about to start on another box when his lawyer called."

His breath feathered her ear, his sandalwood scent infusing her nostrils. Meg tried to clear the desire from her throat and checked the numbers against the invoice. "Everything looks good." Why was her voice so thick and throaty? "Shall we keep going?" She turned her head, but Bryan hadn't moved. His body bracketed behind hers, his lips inches away. Meg's pulse punched the base of her neck, and she couldn't stop blinking. When she worked up the courage to lift her eyes to his, they were dark and hooded and dipped to her mouth. She licked her lips, breathless, waiting.

"I think we should."

Meg felt his voice, scratchy and low, at the base of her pelvis. He grasped her lightly at the shoulders and turned her to face him, aligning their bodies. Standing close, too close, dangerously close, he burrowed his fingers into her hair.

He was giving her time to say no, to push him away while he explored her face, his eyes searching from brow to jawline and everywhere in between.

"So beautiful," he murmured and lowered his lips to hers.

The first pass was soft and intimate, just a brush, a mingling of breath. Meg could have stopped—the look in his eyes dared her to stop. She gripped the edge of the desk and waited, panting, and primed for more.

With a look of triumph, Bryan pounced. He took and took and took, wild and wet and wicked, he plunged.

Meg groped, her fingers scraping wherever they could reach— his back, his waist, his hair. Everything but Bryan faded to black. The annoying buzz of the half-fridge disappeared. The musty smell of cardboard vanished. Meg was trapped between the feel of his satin tongue in her mouth and the throbbing ache between her legs. Embarrassing, primal sounds escaped her throat as the kiss went on and on and on.

Somewhere in the recesses of her mind she heard the door bells jingle and the faint chatter of shoppers in the store. Her hands moved to his chest and with pressure and a good deal of regret, she pushed him away. "Bryan, wait." Meg sucked her swollen lips into her mouth and tried to catch her breath.

His hair was wild from her fingers, his eyes glazed with passion. He looked like she felt—ravenous, and nowhere close to full. He sucked air as if he'd just run a race instead of scooping out her brains with his tongue.

"Don't say you're sorry," he said, his voice as scratchy as the marks she'd left on his chest. "Because I'm not. Not one little bit."

Oh, this man, his words. He was a Westfall all right. Slick as they came. "I have a customer."

"I'll be here when you're done." He ran a hand through his hair, mussing it more. "There's something I need to explain."

The best she could do was nod. He stepped back and let her escape.

Meg wanted to run, to burn off the restless energy and focus her spinning nerves. But she couldn't. She blinked her eyes clear and tamped her aching need. She sidestepped the customers, welcoming them to the store with a strangled voice, and sought refuge behind the counter.

What could he possibly have to explain after kissing her stupid? Was he married? He didn't wear a ring or have the telltale tan line that gave it away. Maybe he was engaged. He was probably engaged. Disappointment and longing settled deep in her bones. It didn't matter. He wasn't staying. Indulging in mind-melding kisses—while addictive—wasn't good for either of them.

Twenty-Five

Bryan stepped back and watched Meg scurry out of the stockroom, his heart hammering, his body hungry with need. He sighed, long and deep, and rubbed the ache in his chest with a hand that wasn't quite steady. He hadn't meant to launch at her the way he had, drawing her up, backing her against the desk, fusing his mouth to hers like a frantic baby suckling his mother. The urgent need shocked him, had him questioning his control.

She'd destroyed him with her greedy mouth and roaming hands, meeting fire with fire. There was no staying away from her now, not now when he'd tasted her flavor, felt the force of her need. He was in so far over his head. Meg had the power to crush him if she decided he wasn't worth the risk.

And what a risk he was. His brother and her sister dead. His stint in her hometown temporary. Her niece and store here. His job and life in Atlanta. Their grieving families.

With one touch of her lips, his mission in Florida turned a one-eighty. Corey was gone. Knowing what he'd done to make ends meet took second place to Meg. All he could see was Meg. Her courage in the face of tragedy. Her determination to shield her niece. And buried beneath a mountain of responsibility, a woman with flesh and blood needs he yearned to fulfill.

All he had to do was convince her to give him a chance. A big ask under normal circumstances. With everything stacked against him and the tactical error of showing his hand too soon with that kiss, he was in for the fight of his life.

His adrenaline pulsing, Bryan pushed away from the desk and roamed the cramped room with his hands clasped behind his neck. He prowled the small space from door to door, his focus on the woman whose voice he could hear in the other room like a whisper against his skin.

A slash of bold red and aquamarine caught his eye, drawing him to the corner of the room. He dropped his hands to brace himself and stare at the handful of canvas paintings leaned against the back wall partially hidden by boxes. Without much room to get a good look, Bryan chose one and carried it to a spot where the lighting was better and he could look his fill.

It was the ocean and the sky at sunset in soft focus. He recognized the point at the end of the island, the stand of mangroves, the crystal water, the blazing sky at dusk. It was exactly the image of Key West he'd take with him, that ethereal quality of the elements that seem too bright, too stunning to be real. He could taste the salty water, feel the heat of the sun on his skin.

"What are you doing with that?"

Bryan startled, jostling the painting in his hand. He hadn't heard Meg enter. "Sorry, I saw it behind the boxes and wanted a better look. This is …" He struggled to find a word to express how it made him feel, serene and awed. "Fantastic."

Meg seemed flustered, her mouth in a tight line. "It's not for sale."

"Why not?"

She lunged for the painting. "I was just messing around."

Bryan held it away from her reach. "Wait. *You* painted this?"

"Yeah." She tucked her hair behind her ear and jerked her shoulders. "So?"

"Meg, I'm blown away." The daring strokes, the vivid colors, the soft lines that drew him in. Of course it was her. Everything about her was intense and enticing. "You're unbelievably talented."

"I'm actually not."

"What?" He sputter-laughed. "Are you kidding me?"

"It's not a big deal. I used to paint."

"Used to?"

She was so uncomfortable, even the tips of her ears were red. "It's not like I have the time." She wiggled her fingers at him. "Can I have that, please?"

He placed the painting in her outstretched hands in a calculated move to keep her busy. "Sure. I want to get a look at the others."

"The others? Bryan, wait."

With the painting in her arms, she couldn't stop him from scooting behind the boxes and extracting another. This one was a streetscape of the cottages that dotted the island. The detail was exquisite. The palm fronds and elephant ears, the picket fence, the cat on a porch rail, the streetlamp standing sentry.

"Did you paint this one too?"

She looked guilty, as if she'd done something illicit instead of creating something beautiful. "Yes."

"I'm no art critic, but I love these. You've captured the island— its beauty and uniqueness—so perfectly. These would sell, Meg. You have to know they would sell."

"Maybe. But this is a gift store, not an art gallery."

How could she deny her obvious gift? Meg was an onion he'd only begun to peel. And like everything else with Meg, he had to take it slow and ease her into the idea. "Would you sell one to me?"

She chewed her lip, suspicion seeping from every pore. "Why?"

He wanted to kiss her again if for no other reason than to wipe the frown from her face. "Why does anyone buy a piece of art? It speaks to me. Your work moves me, Meg."

Her lips quirked before she averted her eyes and leaned the painting against the desk. "You don't have to say that."

"You don't want to hear the truth?" He couldn't keep the bite from his voice.

She straightened her posture, crossing her arms over her chest, and gave him a look that would leave a mark. "I do want the truth. Are you engaged?"

"*What*?"

"You kissed me and then said you had something to tell me."

He'd always thought himself clever, but keeping up with Meg was like attempting a spelling bee drunk. "No. How could you … I'm not engaged."

She just stood there, a lofty look on her face like she didn't quite believe.

Bryan flipped the question. "Are you seeing someone?"

Affronted and visibly annoyed, she flashed her palms. "In what free time?"

"Good." Bryan let go of the breath he held, lightheaded with relief. Her question, while unexpected, opened a shortcut to his goal. "I want to see you."

She licked her lips as if tasting him and remembering. "You're seeing me now."

"I want to get to know you, Meg." He motioned to the painting by her feet. "There's a lot I don't know."

"I don't think that's a good idea."

He'd miscalculated and pushed her too far, too fast. But he was too far gone to turn back. "You said you wanted the truth. Well, here's the truth. I want you. This kind of connection is not something you walk away from because it's a little messy."

"A *little* messy?"

He ran a frustrated hand through his hair. "I know it wasn't just me." And he didn't want to badger her into admitting to what was still sizzling between them in the small and dusty room.

Her shoulders sagged on an audible sigh. "It wasn't just you. But that doesn't make it right."

"Right or wrong, we can't pretend it didn't happen. At least I can't."

"Bryan ..." She had no defense. They both knew it. "You're only here for a couple of weeks. I'm not interested in a short-term fling."

"Neither am I. Which admittedly makes this complicated."

"Complicated?" Her snort was haughty and harsh. "Your brother and my sister make this complicated. You, living hundreds of miles away, make this impossible."

He could push her, and she would fight him. Or he could table it until later giving them both time to think. "Nothing is impossible." He glanced around the room. "Except maybe this inventory."

"You don't have to stay." She turned her back to shuffle papers on the desk. "I can finish up on my own."

He kept his voice deceptively light. "In what century? Besides, I have good news. It's what I wanted to tell you when you asked if I was engaged."

She cast him a wary glance over her shoulder. "What is it?"

"It's Dustin. He wants to work here."

"Work here?" The knocks kept on coming, one after the other after the other. Meg could hardly keep up after seeing Bryan holding one of her paintings on the heels of their toe-curling kiss. "I'm not hiring."

"He doesn't need money."

"Everyone needs money."

"He's staying with me for free." Bryan used his fingers to tick away his answers. "He's on paid leave. And he's bored out of his mind."

"So, take him around the island. There's lots to do and see on Key West."

"He's done some sightseeing on his own when I've had to work. He's seen it all."

She doubted that. The only way to see everything on the island was by land, sea, and air. "He could rent a boat. Tour the island or go fishing."

"Dustin gets seasick."

"What about a seaplane ride out to Dry Tortugas? Or a helicopter ride?"

"He doesn't like to fly."

Once again, Bryan had an answer for everything. With her back to the corner, Meg's instinct was to fight. "Why does he want to work here?"

Bryan lifted his hands in a helpless sign of appeal. "Meg, you're swamped. He can help. He wants to help. And so do I."

"You've been here all afternoon and the only thing we've

accomplished is one box." And a mind-bending kiss that led them lip-deep into muddy water. *And* his panic-inducing discovery of her work. She should have done a better job concealing the paintings. It hurt to see them and remember a time when she could paint and had hopes of making art her career. Stacked in the back of the stockroom collecting dust, they were a bittersweet reminder of the dream she'd never realize.

"I'll admit I got distracted, but I'm still here and I've got all day. Let's get to work."

She thought he'd bolt after confessing some deep dark secret. Standing in the same small room where he'd reduced her to an aching pile of need, she wasn't sure which scenario she preferred. She pointed at him, gave him her best stern face. "No more kisses."

His answering smirk sparked a flame low in her belly. "Can't make any promises."

She ignored both him and the urge to stoke that flame back to life and sat behind the computer.

They worked companionably for the next hour, making their way through three additional boxes. Every time she went onto the floor to help a customer, when she came back, he'd pulled another painting from the back and set it by the others lining the wall. She deliberately ignored them and went back to work behind the desk.

By the time they finished a fourth box, it was late enough to close the store for the night. She locked the front door and turned off the lights in the main room. When she returned to the stockroom, all her paintings were dispersed around the room, and she could no longer ignore them or Bryan who stood staring at them against the walls. "What are you doing?"

"I'm deciding which one I want to buy."

"I told you they're not for sale."

"Then how about a barter? My time for one of your paintings."

The look he gave her, all smug and satisfied, grated on her nerves if only because he knew she couldn't refuse.

She narrowed her eyes at him, tried to figure out his angle. "They're not worth that much."

"Art is worth whatever someone is willing to pay." He moved around the room, eyeing each painting, lifting them up and looking them over. "My boss at the bank had this huge abstract painting in her office. It looked like a finger painting some kindergartener had done." He set one painting down, moved on to the next. "She loved telling everyone she paid thousands for the work by some up and coming artist. I thought she was crazy."

"Art is subjective." While abstract art wasn't her thing, Meg could appreciate the freedom and vision it took to create.

"I get that, but I like your work. I can look at it and know what I'm supposed to see." He nodded at the one in his hands. "This fishing dock with the lighthouse in the background. I can imagine myself there, looking out across the water. I can feel the breeze pushing against the humidity in the air."

His words thrilled her, sprouting hope like a tiny seedling buried deep in her soul. He'd described exactly how she wanted someone seeing her work to feel—grounded on that rickety dock. Her throat tightened when he set the painting on the floor and stepped down to stare at one of the last ones she'd completed.

"This one, though …" He picked it up, studied the lone figure leaning against a scarred table. "This one breaks my heart."

"It's my dad. The way he'd look at my mom after her diagnosis. He loves her so much, so completely."

"He's tormented."

"Yes, he is."

He turned his head and pinned her with a sober stare. "Has he seen it?"

She fiddled with the hem of her shirt, willed the building tears not to fall. "He tried to be so strong for her, for all of us. 'It's going to be okay,' he'd say. 'We're going to fight this.'" She swiped at the pathetic tear that tried to escape. Tears were as useless as hope— she'd wasted enough time on both, only to be let down again and again. "He's fighting a losing battle."

"You should show him."

"I can't. I captured a private moment. I think he'd feel … embarrassed."

"A man who loves his wife the way your father loves your mother would never be embarrassed by this. It's raw and real and unbearably beautiful."

She turned away and slammed her eyes closed, tried to stop her chin from trembling. The only chance she had of composing herself was to change the subject. "Is that the one you want?"

"No."

Surprised, Meg turned to face him.

"It's not meant for me. But this one …" Bryan picked up a seascape. "This fishing boat. It's morning, right? Going out to sea?"

Meg's voice squeaked from the emotion still tightening her throat. "It's a hard life and so much a part of the island."

"I love how you can't make out the name on the back in the glare of the morning sun, but you can see the flag flying proudly. It's the optimism of everyday life in America. Every day is a new chance to make something of yourself. Can I have it?"

How did he do that? How did he look at her painting and know exactly what she felt while painting it, know exactly what she wanted someone to feel when they looked at her work? Other than her family—her mother, especially—Bryan was the first person who ever looked at what she did as something other than a silly hobby or a way to pass the time. "What will you do with it?"

"Look at it every day. Remember how many people get up and go to work—to do hard, grueling jobs—without any glory or any guarantees their efforts are worth the price to their bodies, their families, their bottom line. They just do what needs to be done."

"Like teachers."

He tilted his head in a maybe, maybe-not kind of way. "I guess so. There's not much glory in teaching except knowing you tried to make a difference in someone's life."

Every word from his mouth made her like him more. Meg needed to lighten the mood before she did something stupid and kissed him again. "If you can get someone to like math, I'd say you're making a difference."

His lifted his chin, his lips curving. "I can't make them like it. I can only try and make them understand how important it is." His gaze darted from the painting in his hands to her face, his brows lifted in question. "What do you say?"

"It's yours." How could she say no when he'd made it his with his vision? "I hope you don't regret your offer."

"Are you kidding? I just made the deal of a lifetime."

Twenty-Six

Dustin arrived the next morning, his hair wet from the shower, smelling of soap and the smooth nutty flavor of freshly brewed coffee. "Morning, Boss."

Meg stood behind the counter staring at him, wondering just what she'd gotten herself into the day before. She still felt unsteady after spending the day with Bryan. She'd never met a man who got her as much as he did. And that made him dangerous—to her heart and her psyche.

Once upon a time, she'd given both freely to someone who'd proved unworthy. It took heartache and time to see the situation for what it was: a fun distraction wrapped in a meaningless affair. If she'd left the island with Zander and followed him to Chicago, they'd have imploded. She'd have been back within months with her tail between her legs. Two creatives were destined to come to blows.

"I'm not your boss."

"Sure you are." He set one of the two paper cups he held on the counter in front of her. "Bryan said you like it sweet."

Bryan. Just the mention of his name sent her pulse jumping. "Thank you."

"You're welcome." He glanced around with the enthusiasm of someone who was going to drive her nuts. "Where should we start?"

"Well, if—" Lily emerged from the back of the store and stopped when she saw Dustin. She waited, as she'd been taught, for Meg to finish with a customer. Meg berated herself for not anticipating Dustin's arrival and coming up with an explanation that didn't relate back to the barnacle. "Lily, this is Dustin. He's going to help out at the store."

"Hi." Lily eyed Dustin curiously. She probably couldn't figure out where Meg found all the strange men to help.

Dustin's smile was warm and friendly. "Hi, Lily. Nice to meet you."

Lily flashed a closed mouth grin and dragged her eyes back to Meg. "Can I have my phone?"

"You know the rules. You don't get to play on social media just because you're bored."

"I don't want to get on social media. I want to show Barb the design boards I made for the stuff we got yesterday."

She'd been giddy the moment they returned, talking a mile a minute about ribbons and foams, water tubes and wires. For someone so bored by everyday life, Lily had a real passion for the flower business. These days, whatever put a smile on Lily's face got the green light from Meg. "Fine. Thirty minutes, tops." She handed the phone over to Lily before she disappeared to the flower shop next door.

"Cute kid," Dustin said. "How's she doing with … everything?"

"Everything?"

"You know …" He stuck his hand in his pocket and shucked his shoulder. "Her mom and all."

His question startled Meg. Most people avoided talking about Amanda, as if asking Meg about her sister would make her crumble into a sloppy mess. "She's struggling. We both are. I had her in counseling right after, but she didn't want to go and I couldn't force her. "

"Yeah, I bet. It's hard losing someone so unexpectedly. I mean, it's different when someone old or sick dies. Then it can be kind of a relief. But the young and healthy …" He sighed, looked over her head, searching what Meg suspected was a vocabulary richer than hers. "It's tragic and hard to comprehend. Especially for a kid."

"It is." And she wouldn't—she couldn't—say anything more. "Did Bryan tell you I can't pay you for your help?"

"I wouldn't take your money." He sipped his coffee, leveled her with a blue-eyed stare. "I like your painting, by the way."

Her work was getting seen whether she wanted it to or not. "You want one too?"

Dustin choked on his sip and coughed. "Bryan would kick me out if I came home with one of your paintings. He feels like he won the lottery."

Her cheeks flared—and not from embarrassment. The memory of Bryan's kiss had her up half the night. "If you change your mind and don't want to help, all you have to do is say the word."

"Understood. Now, what can I do? More boxes?"

Meg glanced at the back of the store. "I can't guarantee I'll be able to input the merchandise. With a port full of cruise ships and Lily underfoot, we probably won't get much accomplished."

"Show me how to use your system and I can do it myself."

Her suspicious nature reared its ugly head. If he knew the system, he could rob them blind. "I don't think so."

"Meg, please." He clutched his chest as if offended. "I worked at a record store though high school and college. It's probably all the same."

"I doubt that."

He walked behind the counter and crowded her space with his tall, long-limbed presence. "Show me."

She was too shocked by his boldness to react, and he didn't give her time to object before he pointed at the screen. "Yeah. It's similar." He picked up the barcode scanner. "You use this to scan the barcode and the rest is easy-peasy."

"That's for checkout. The inventory is different."

"I get the gist. Show me where you input the data."

She exited the screen, brought up the inventory. "You count the merchandise and make sure the numbers of items received matches the number ordered, print the barcodes, and place them on each item."

"Gotcha."

A customer entered, demanding Meg's attention. "Stack the inventory slips on my desk."

"No problem," he said. "You go on, see to your customer. I'll get started in the back."

She watched him go, a dump truck of jitters cratering her gut. "If you have any questions, ask Lily."

He lifted a hand and kept walking. Dustin and Bryan were a shocking shift in her luck. So why couldn't Meg relax?

Hours later, during a break in foot traffic, Meg poked her head in the back. "Sorry I've left you alone for so much of the day."

Dustin taped a box closed, labeled it, and set it aside. "That's okay. You've been busy."

"So have you." A dozen boxes had moved from one side of the room to the other. "You've made serious progress."

"Not just me. Lily's been a big help."

"Lily?"

"Your niece is a pistol. She keeps checking on me to make sure I'm not screwing up." He wagged his brows and pointed his chin in her direction. "She reminds me of someone else around here."

"Where is she?"

"Next door at the flower shop. When she realized I knew what I was doing, she bugged out of here quick. She does not want to help with inventory."

"Tell me about it." Meg wandered to the computer, checked his work, fingered through the invoices. Everything appeared to be in order. "You work fast."

"I like to feel useful." He opened another box and unfolded merchandise. "Being busy stops my mind from wandering." He took the pencil from behind his ear and marked off on the inventory sheet. "You didn't tell Lily about Bryan."

Meg's stomach slumped and she struggled to close her mouth. "What do you mean?"

"She didn't know he was Corey's brother."

Of course Lily would ask. Meg should have been prepared. "You told her."

"She wanted to know how I ended up here." He picked up an item and set it aside. "I told her I knew Bryan. She seemed confused so I made the connection."

Guilt stained her cheeks and spread like fire through her veins.

Meg should have been the one to tell Lily. Her niece would hold it against her—with good reason. "Was she upset?"

Dustin jerked a shoulder, continued unwrapping and counting. "I don't know her well enough to measure her response, but she seemed surprised."

Meg rubbed the ache in her temple, willed the headache away. She'd mishandled the situation badly. "I'm sorry to put you in that position. I don't … we don't talk about him."

"Corey?"

Meg nodded, gritting her teeth at the sound of his name. Saying his name made him human. Thinking of him as a flesh and blood man meant Meg would have to sympathize. "That may sound cruel, but I'm trying really hard to keep her mom's memory alive in a positive way. Talking about him only reminds Lily of her death."

"I get that."

Dustin didn't seem to pass judgment. An idea sprouted and searched for daylight the way a worm digs through soil. Why couldn't Meg ask Dustin about the barnacle? After all, he'd brought him up. "How well did you know the b—Bryan's brother?"

Dustin stood and wiped his hands on his shorts. "We grew up together—me and Bryan and Corey."

"Was he—" She bit her lip, determined not to steer him. "What was your opinion?"

His hands landed on his hips, his gaze distracted. "Corey was one of those guys who had it all—looks, smarts, talent—the whole package. He could make you laugh and rob you blind without blinking an eye." He shook his head, his focus back on Meg. "We were too young and too awed to see his flaws."

Meg tried to imagine a youthful barnacle—his weathered

face softened, his eyes less cynical. It was difficult to picture him without a cigarette dangling from his lips or his jaw set in a cocky line. "What kind of flaws?"

"Oh, you know. He was an odd combination of lazy and restless. He was good at everything, but nothing ever got him excited unless he was working an angle. Everything with Corey was a wager. He was constantly chasing that high."

She made a noise of agreement in her throat she instantly regretted when Dustin cocked his head at her.

"You agree?"

"I barely knew him."

"Meg …"

If she told him what she thought of the barnacle, he would tell Bryan. Maybe, in the end, it would soften the blow. "He treated my sister like a conquest. She was too blinded by his looks to see he was using her."

Dustin narrowed his eyes. "Using her for what?"

"Amanda was beautiful, and he liked having her on his arm. He liked that she was known and loved on the island. She gave him an easy in with the locals he couldn't earn on his own."

"That sounds like Corey."

She knew she wasn't wrong. Meg only wished Amanda had seen what was so obvious to her. "He and Bryan were close?"

"When they were little, sure. Bryan idolized Corey. We both did."

"Bryan said they had a falling out."

"It was bound to happen. Corey left home and never looked back unless he needed money. Bryan gave him all he could, and it was never enough." Dustin looked down and shuffled his feet before lifting his eyes to hers. "It eats at him. He can't forgive himself for letting their relationship dwindle to occasional phone calls. He feels responsible."

"That's crazy."

"Not to Bryan. He's an optimist. He really thought a little tough love would get Corey to grow up and take responsibility for his life." Dustin shook his head and sighed with the certainty of someone who knew them both well. "Being on the outside let me see things Bryan couldn't. The truth is, Corey was okay with disappointing people because he didn't care about anyone but himself."

Twenty-Seven

Done with his shift, Bryan sat sipping water, resting his aching feet, and waiting for Dustin to come back from spending the day with Meg. The bar had been hopping from the time the day-travelers arrived until the time they had to be back at the dock to re-board their ships. Bryan was tired, but not too tired to interrogate Dustin.

That tight feeling in his ribcage was envy. Bryan was mature enough to admit to his immature feelings. While Bryan had kept drinks and food flowing for well-meaning tourists, Dustin got to spend the day with the woman who'd hooked Bryan without even trying. He simply couldn't get her out of his mind.

Tim appeared from the kitchen, a box of liquor in his grip.

Bryan moved to stand. "Need a hand?"

"I got this." Tim waved him off. "You just got done with your shift."

Grateful, Bryan eased against the seat. "Busy day today."

"Lots of ships in port." Tim pulled the bottles, began stacking them under the bar.

Bryan gave an agreeable nod while craning his neck to check the entrance for Dustin.

"You okay?" Tim asked. "You seem a little distracted."

Bryan leaned his forearms against the bar. "Sorry. Just thinking about something."

"Something or some*one*?" His smirking grin made Tim's question rhetorical.

Bryan couldn't fathom how Tim kept tabs on everything that went on around the island. And a man who knew everything was an untapped source. "Did you know Meg used to paint?"

"Sure." He tossed the empty box to the side and began wiping glasses from the dishwasher. "She used to drag her easel all over town. She was good, from what I remember."

She was better than good. He'd done a fair amount of sitting and staring at her picture propped against his mantle. "Her work's amazing. When did she stop?"

Tim angled his head, made a let-me-think face. "I don't know. Couple years ago, maybe. Right around the time her mom and dad left the island."

She'd called painting fooling around, so it made sense that when her parents left Meg and Amanda in charge of the store, she'd given it up. "You knew her parents?"

"Everybody knew her parents. They're good people. Shame about her mom. Last I checked, she wasn't doing very well. Steve's gotta be a mess."

"Steve's her dad?"

"Yep. Meg's mom, Celia, she was something else. Kind of a

modern-day hippy, she was loud and friendly, and talented like Meg. Used to ask me for bottles all the time and then she'd bust them up and make things out of them like frames and coasters. Cool stuff that caught the light." He looked over at Bryan, a curious look on his face. "You and Meg a thing now?"

Bryan wanted them to be. He wanted nothing more than to know if Meg walked in, he could go up to her and kiss her and let everyone know she was his. "I'm working on it. She's … a little gun-shy."

"I can see that." Tim pulled glasses, used a rag to dry the rims. "I mean, you're not planning to stay, right?"

"Not planning on it." But that didn't mean he hadn't run some crazy, what-if scenarios through his head. He was a teacher. He'd signed a contract for the year back home, but he could break it. He could teach from anywhere. But when he reined himself back to reality, he realized even thinking like that was insane. They'd kissed—once—and he was daydreaming about a future the way he used to fantasize about him and Tina Bowers walking hand in hand around the middle school campus. A hand on his arm jerked him out of fantasyland.

"Hey." Dustin squeezed his shoulder and took a seat next to Bryan.

"Hey. How'd it go?" Bryan asked.

"Good." Dustin leaned on the bar, motioned hello to Tim. "Got a lot accomplished."

"Dustin's helping Meg at the store," Bryan explained to Tim.

"I'm surprised she let you. That girl never asks for help."

"We didn't give her much of a choice." Dustin pointed at a tap. "Can I get a beer?"

"Coming right up."

Dustin turned to Bryan and lowered his voice. "I met the niece. She's spunky and very protective of Meg. I like her."

The cruel fist of envy squeezed Bryan's ribcage tight. "What do you think?"

"She's like a little adult. I guess that's natural, considering everything she's been through."

Tim set Dustin's beer in front of him. "Meg is an adult."

Bryan heard a note of distrust in Tim's voice, wondered if Dustin did too. "He's talking about Lily."

"Ah." Tim pursed his lips. "I guess you're right. She's had to grow up fast. Although, honestly, most kids around here are wise beyond their years because of where they live and what they see every day."

"Did you grow up here?" Dustin asked.

"Noooo." Tim gave an amplified head shake. "I never would've made it into the military if I'd had this as my playground. I probably would've ended up underground."

Envy turned to worry in a heartbeat. What would Meg do if Lily went wayward in the land of parties and plenty with no one here to help?

A guy approached the bar with yellow-tinted sunglasses, a trucker ball cap, and a guitar case slung over his shoulder. He reached across the surface and knocked knuckles with Tim. "Hey, man."

"Rourke." Tim's smile widened. "Good to see you."

The guy smelled faintly of weed and incense. "Thanks for letting me play tonight."

"Anytime." Tim dipped his head to his shoulder. "The stage is always open."

"Appreciate it, man." Rourke eased back, smiled at Bryan and Dustin, and made his way to the stage.

"I know, I know." Tim flashed his palm. "He looks like an addict, but his voice sounds like butter. Stick around and you'll see."

"Hey," Bryan straightened, flicking a thumb at Dustin. "Are you open to new talent?"

"Why?" Tim asked. "You in a band?"

"Dusty here is an amazing singer and guitar player."

"Bryan ..." Dustin's growl was a low warning.

Tim looked at Dustin like a dog with two tails. "You got a demo or something?"

"I haven't played in years."

"It's like riding a bike." Bryan clapped Dustin on the shoulder, gave him a don't-blow-this squeeze. "You were great the other day. Meg thought so too. She's the one who suggested we talk to Tim."

Dustin lasered Bryan with a side-eyed stare. "That was a kid's toy."

"Exactly. Imagine what you can do with a real guitar."

"I don't have a guitar."

Tim leaned his palms on the bar and lifted his stubbled chin. "I've got one in my office."

"You play?" Bryan never pictured stealthy Tim as a performer.

"Just a fan. A couple years ago, a band jacked up a huge bar tab for their friends and family, and then lit out before settling up. They left behind an acoustic guitar." He looked at Dustin. "I have no idea how good it is, but it's yours if you want to give it a go."

Bryan watched Dustin's face, saw his eyes light with interest, watched him run his fingers over the growth on his neck the way he'd touch the neck of a guitar. "I guess I could take a look."

Tim tossed the dishrag aside, a challenge on his face. "Follow me."

Twenty-Eight

Meg dragged Lily away from the flower shop and ushered her to the car with the promise of ordering a pizza for dinner. She had a coupon and she wanted to earn some goodwill when tackling a difficult subject.

It was past time she explained Bryan to her niece.

Lily buckled her seatbelt, fiddled with the bracelet she'd made from floral wire, and looked out the window as if she didn't have a care in the world. But if what Dustin said was true, that he'd told her Bryan was the barnacle's brother, Lily was putting on a good show.

Meg turned the radio down and cleared her throat. "Thanks for helping out with inventory."

"I didn't do much."

"Dustin said you were a big help."

Lily mumbled, shrugged, and ended the conversation by returning her attention out the window.

Lily was upset, and it was going to take more than pizza to make things right. Meg signaled and turned into their complex, her limbs heavy with defeat, and scowled at the ugly building. Coming home to this place was a daily reminder of how much their life had changed.

The place Meg had shared with Amanda, in a second story walk-up in a former bed and breakfast, had charm and character and friendly neighbors who treated them like family. Meg and Lily's current apartment was like Meg's car—in need of a paint job and major repair.

Meg parked and gathered her things from the backseat while Lily dragged her feet through the parking lot and up the outside stairs. Lily leaned against the door frame, picking at a hang nail, and waited for Meg. She scooted inside and disappeared into her bedroom the moment Meg unlocked the door.

Determined to clear the air, Meg dumped her bag by the door and flipped through the junk drawer for the pizza coupon, calling in their usual order of pepperoni and mushrooms. She would give Lily time to cool off and be alone while they waited for the pizza to arrive. Meg would use the time to change her clothes and figure out the best way to explain Bryan's presence in their lives.

Amanda's absence was like a wound that would never heal. No matter how much time had passed or how much experience Meg had with raising her niece, dealing with the emotions of a pre-teen were better handled by two. Amanda and Meg's twin-tracked negotiation technique was how they'd gotten through Lily's first twelve years. But with Amanda gone and Lily's hardest years looming like a flashing cautionary light in the distance, Meg worried about her ability to raise Lily alone.

Parenting was and should be a two-person job. But like it or not, Meg was solely responsible for raising Lily into adulthood. The easiest way—the only way—to move forward was to be honest—something she should have done the moment Lily met Bryan.

The doorbell rang, and Lily emerged from her room and took her seat at the table.

Meg paid and carried the box into the kitchen. "Did you wash your hands?"

"Yep."

Meg kneaded her twitchy hands in her lap, waited for Lily to coat her slices with parmesan before tackling the sticky subject. "I know why you're upset with me."

Lily set her pizza down and wiped her mouth very deliberately before lifting her gaze to Meg's. "I'm not upset."

"You should be." Meg reached for a slice just to have something to do with her hands.

Lily dropped her eyes to her dinner, poking the crust with her finger. "Is this about Bryan?"

"I'm sorry I didn't tell you."

Lily's scowl screamed betrayal. "Why didn't you?"

The greasy smell of the pizza and Lily's snappishness made Meg's jittery stomach queasy. "At first, I was trying to protect you. I didn't know him, Lil. I didn't trust him."

"And now you do?"

"I know him better." A *lot* better since he'd kissed her brainless and taken up residence in her mind. "He's a nice guy. And he hasn't given me any reason to think I can't trust him."

Lily watched Meg the way a detective watches a suspect—like she was looking for a crack in Meg's story.

Stalling and trying to act natural, Meg took a bite and chewed, swallowing past the anxious lump in her throat. "I never would have let him or Dustin near you if I didn't think they were okay."

Lily pulled a pepperoni from her slice and set it aside. "I like Dustin. He doesn't treat me like a kid."

Point for Lily. "He called you a pistol."

Lily's lip quirked and quickly disappeared. "Why are they here? What do they want?"

The cheese curdled in Meg's stomach. "Bryan and his brother weren't close like your mom and I were. He hadn't talked to his brother in a while, and he's struggling to understand his brother's life before he died."

"What does that have to do with us?"

Lily was asking the same questions she'd asked Bryan. He still hadn't given any answers. "Your mom and his brother were together when they died and before. I think he wants to know about their relationship."

"What difference does it make?"

"Grandpa had the same questions after your mom died. 'Who was this guy? Why were they together? How long had they been dating?' They're normal questions from people who weren't around."

Lily sank in her seat, shredding her napkin to pieces, her voice like a whispered confession. "I didn't like him."

Meg reached across the table and gripped Lily's hand, regret punching Meg in the face. She should have talked to Lily sooner. She should have done a lot of things differently. "I know, honey. I didn't like him either."

Lily's lip quivered, her tone wobbly. "I was mad at her. I miss her so much, but I'm still mad at her for going away with him and never coming back."

Meg's heart shattered like a fragile glass keepsake. She stood and pulled Lily into her arms, holding her limp-legged niece as she crumbled into a sobbing mess. When her tears transitioned into hiccups and gasps, Meg pushed the hair behind Lily's ears and wiped the wetness from her cheeks and cupped her face in her hands.

"It's okay to feel mad—no one can tell you how to feel—but you know she never would have left with him if she thought she wouldn't come back. She loved you more than anything in this world."

"I know." Lily nodded, wheezy and weak. She reached for a napkin and blew her nose with a honk.

"You need to try and let go of the anger." The words boomeranged, slapping Meg in the face. *She's not the only one.*

The truth, buried deeper than Amanda's shiny wooden casket, threatened to buckle Meg's knees. It was time—past time—for Meg to grow up and show Lily the way forward. She swallowed, licking her lips before pressing them together. "The truth is, just because we didn't like him, doesn't mean they were doing something wrong."

Lily's mouth parted and she blinked at Meg. "Why didn't you like him?"

Meg sat down and took her time placing her napkin on her lap and lining up her glass of water, waited for Lily to take a seat. There were so many reasons but only one that mattered. "He wasn't good enough for her. For either of you."

Lily's mouth twisted into a grimace. "Yeah. He wasn't."

Being honest meant setting it all free—including things she'd rather not say out loud. "I've been sad and mad and in a bad mood since your mom died, and that's because I miss her so much, and I'm struggling to run the store and take care of you by myself. It's a lot and I'm scared I'm screwing everything up."

"You're not screwing up."

"I am and I will—probably a lot. But Lily …" She reached across the table again, waited for Lily to offer her hand. "You got the short end of this stick, but I'd be so alone if it weren't for you." Her voice thickened with emotion. "I may get cranky and short-tempered, but without you, I couldn't get out of bed in the morning."

Lily's smile lightened the mood. "We don't *have* to get out of bed in the morning."

The laugh in Meg's throat felt rusty and raw. "I do if we want to eat and have this crappy roof over our heads." She motioned to the table. "See, I've ruined dinner. Now our pizza is cold."

Lily looked at her plate. "I like cold pizza."

Just like your mom. "If you don't want to be around Bryan or Dustin, I'll make sure they don't come around. I will always put you first, no matter what."

"I like Dustin." Lily shrugged, idly turning the parmesan bottle in her hand. "If you trust Bryan, I don't care if he comes around."

"If you change your mind, all you have to do is say so. This apartment and the store are your safe places. I won't have anyone make you uncomfortable in your safe places."

Lily picked up her pizza. "Okay."

"I promise I won't keep important things from you again. I never intended to get to know Bryan. I didn't want his help." Meg exhaled, blowing the frizzy ends of her hair out of her face. "I wasn't very nice to him. But he made friends with Eva and Barb, and he works for Tim. They vouched for him. He's nothing like his brother."

"You like him—the way my mom liked his brother."

Admitting her feelings out loud—even to a twelve-year-old—was like wishing on stars. Meg dropped her head to hide her blush. "Maybe a little."

Lily took a bite and chewed, a serious look on her too-smart face. "I've decided I'm never going to date. Boys aren't worth the trouble."

Meg sputtered. *If only that were true.* Suddenly starved, she picked up her slice. "I'll remind you of that in a couple of years."

Twenty-Nine

B ryan heard the telltale ticking of Meg's car as it approached the bar on her way to the store. Like his grandmother's old sewing machine chugging away on a quilt, it got louder and louder the closer Meg came to the base of his window on her way to her parking area.

He'd given Meg space and time to think about him and to get used to having Dustin around. After his first day at the store, Dustin said Meg had let her guard down and let Lily hang around the back with Dustin where she laughed at his corny jokes and kept him company. Bryan wished it had been him getting to know Lily and hanging out with Meg, but knowing they were with Dustin, and he was helping her work through her backlog, was good enough for now.

Bryan wondered if Meg thought about him and the kiss they'd shared. He'd thought of little else. In a frightening replay of middle and high school, Bryan allowed Dustin to feed him intel and give him pointers on the best way to proceed. Dustin seemed to think Meg's questions about Bryan and their childhood was proof of her interest. Bryan wasn't so sure.

With his best friend's go-ahead that the time was right, Bryan walked to her store. The first thing he noticed was the display. When Dustin told him Meg had changed the window display, Bryan thought she'd spent a couple minutes swapping out swimsuits and beach towels. Now that he'd seen her paintings and knew how talented she was, he shouldn't have been surprised by the showmanship.

Gone were the kites and pinwheels and in their place was a giant crepe paper wave swooping along the back and side walls. Surf boards of varying sizes sat upright next to mannequins in sport suits. A sea of mismatched beach balls covered the ground and the stuffed cats peeking out of the balls made the whole scene reminiscent of the Hemingway grounds a few blocks away. Meg had created an artful display that drew the eye and the shopper.

Bryan knocked on the locked door and then cupped his hands around his eyes to peer inside.

Meg glanced up from the counter and greeted him with a shy smile. She walked to the door and let him in with the flick of her wrist. "Hi."

Flesh and blood Meg, fresh and dewy and smelling like a spring meadow, had his heart accelerating as quickly as the temperature outdoors. "Good morning. Sorry for stopping by before you're open."

Meg stood back so he could enter. "You don't have to apologize."

Bryan motioned to the window. "Meg, the display looks amazing."

"Thanks." Unlike the wary, guarded way she'd treated her art, Meg seemed proud of her work on the window by the way her smile lingered. "It's kind of what we're known for."

"Your window displays?"

"When I have time to work on them, yes. Thanks to Dustin— and you—I've had the time. It's made a difference in our foot traffic, and as a result, our sales."

"It's time well spent. Your creativity is off the charts."

"My mom was the best at design." Meg gestured to where Lily folded towels. "This one was Lily's idea. She's becoming quite the surfer."

This was different. Instead of shielding Lily from him, Meg deliberately pulled her into the conversation and boosted Bryan's confidence. "Hi, Lily."

The girl looked over, smiled and waved. "Hey."

On the heels of Dustin's encouragement, Bryan felt a sea change in the air.

"So, what brings you by?" Meg asked. "If you're looking for boxes to inventory, Dustin's got you beat. He finished up last night."

"He told me. I'm glad it's working out for both of you."

"I'm not sure we're helping him, but he's been a big help to us."

"Trust me, he's better. Between working here and practicing the guitar, he's a lot better. He's still sad, but the distraction helps."

"He's playing again?"

"Yes, that's actually why I'm here. Since you were the first to suggest Dustin play at Tim's place, I thought you should be the first to know he's booked this Tuesday from seven to ten."

Meg's face lit with delight. "That's awesome. Did you hear that, Lily? Dustin's playing at Westies tomorrow night."

"Really?" Lily clasped her hands and gave her aunt a wide-eyed appeal that looked just like she'd given the pleading-face emoji. "Can we go? Please?"

Meg hesitated, but only for a second. "Yes, but not for the whole set."

"Yay!" The girl clapped, dropping her towel into the bin. "Can I tell Eva and Barb?"

"Sure." Meg watched Lily take off and didn't look back at Bryan until the door slammed shut. "Dustin was here most of the day yesterday and he didn't say a word."

Bryan scratched the back of his neck. "I think he's a little nervous."

"Dustin?" Meg walked to the counter, slipped behind, and resumed whatever she'd been doing when he interrupted. "He doesn't seem the type."

"It's been years since he's played." Bryan followed her to the counter. With only the worktop between them it would be so easy—too easy—to lean across and touch his lips with hers. "Even longer since he's performed in front of an audience."

"He'll do great. He's so natural with people." She chuckled, shaking her head. "You should see him with the older ladies. He has them eating out of his hand."

"He's like that on stage." Bryan leaned an elbow against the counter and watched Meg use her tapered artist's fingers to stack bags and fold colorful paper inserts. Everything she did, every move she made, was graceful. "He's been practicing at home, trying to pretend it's no big deal, but I can tell he's excited."

"Good for him." Meg tossed the empty box to floor. "He goes quiet sometimes. I can tell he's thinking about his wife."

"Going on two weeks with no contact. He's trying not to freak out."

Meg folded her hands atop the counter and gave him a curious stare. "What's she like?"

"Tegan?"

"I don't mean to pry." Meg reached for a pen and started twirling it through her fingers. "I think the people they are with says a lot about a person."

Bryan had to think hard to bring Tegan to mind—her glossy, dark hair; her quiet demeanor—when standing so close to Meg. "On paper, they make no sense. He's messy and loud and has never met a stranger. She's always put together, smart as a whip, and a little reserved."

Meg pursed her lips, drawing his attention to her mouth. "Opposites attract—or so they say."

"He's always been obsessed with her. I hope she doesn't do something stupid and end it for good."

She leaned closer. "Do you think there's someone else?" Her softly stated question was like a feather tickling his face.

"I don't think so, although I haven't talked to her in a while. Their problems started around the time we found out about Corey so ..." There was no use explaining. Meg knew how the world stopped spinning once they got the news. Nothing had existed ever since except for the stinging rush of grief and guilt and the numb going-through-the-motions feeling. Thanks to time and Meg, Bryan was just starting to recover. "I work the lunch shift tomorrow. How about I walk over around six and we make this a date?"

Her shoulders squared and her posture went ramrod straight. "A date?"

"Sure. You, me, and Lily. I'll buy you dinner."

Her green eyes lit, but when she started chewing her lip and looked down, Bryan figured she was trying to come up with a reason to say no. He wouldn't give her the chance.

"It's just dinner, Meg. A meal between friends watching Dustin perform."

"I suppose," she said after a long beat of silence, "since we'll all be there and it'll be dinnertime, it only makes sense."

"Great." Bryan did a mental high-five and tortured himself by placing his hand over hers on the counter. "I'll see you tomorrow."

Lily peeked her head into the bathroom and watched Meg apply lipstick. "You look pretty."

"Thanks." Meg capped the tube and tucked the hairbrush into her purse. Her nerves were on full display, making her hands shake and her stomach churn like the ocean during a storm. A storm was brewing all right, a storm named Bryan. "You ready?"

Silly question. The girl had been bugging Meg for over an hour. "Guess what?" she said. "Eva and Barb are coming too."

"That'll be nice for Dustin to see familiar faces in the crowd."

Bryan had called it a date and included Lily. No matter how much she tried to tell herself he was only being nice by inviting them to dinner, Meg's head and heart said otherwise. The man had every intention of getting her alone and recreating that kiss that had had her tossing and turning in bed.

She wasn't so out of the game that she hadn't recognized his subtle and not-so-subtle flirtations the day before. The casual compliments about the display and her talent. The way he kept looking at her mouth. His tactical move of leaning his body toward hers so she could smell his spicy aftershave and remember what it felt like to be in his arms.

"Ooh," Lily squealed. "There's Bryan." She jogged to the door and unlocked it.

The man made an entrance. With a retro rock t-shirt that could have come straight from Tim's closet and khaki fishing shorts, Bryan looked good enough to make Meg drool. From the back of the store, she watched him greet Lily with his heart-stopping smile and his signature easy charm.

He looked cool and comfortable and totally at ease while she'd spent the day trembling with anxiety, wondering how the night would end. Meg forced herself to move out of the shadows and into the front of the store. When Bryan saw her, his hand went straight to his stomach, rubbing the band's Celtic-inspired logo and scanning her from head to toe. Lily watched their greeting with eager, observant eyes.

Meg tried not to squirm under his appreciative stare. "Hi, Bryan."

"Meg. You look …" He inclined his head and inhaled as if smelling a savory meal. "Fantastic."

If Meg's hot cheeks didn't give away her nerves, her clumsy fingers at the neckline of her slit-sleeved mini dress did the trick. "Thank you."

"I'm the luckiest guy in the Keys to get to take the two prettiest girls out to dinner."

"Is Dustin at Westies?" Lily asked. "Is he getting ready?"

Bryan slipped his hands into his pockets. "He was still at my place when I left." He looked at Meg, his shoulders rising. "Shall we go?"

Bryan held the door for them, and Meg locked it behind her. "How's he doing?"

"He's nervous." A few steps beyond Blooming Glory, Bryan

settled his hand at the small of Meg's back. "He thinks he's going to bomb."

Dustin wasn't the only one plagued by nerves and dodging explosives. Bryan's fingers at the base of Meg's spine set off some spectacular blasts of their own. Meg struggled to keep up with the conversation with heat pooling low in her belly.

"He's going to do great." Lily skipped ahead. "He's so good."

"That's what I keep telling him." When Bryan grinned at Lily, Meg's heart took a painful thump. Not since her grandfather had a man looked at Lily like a person and not a nuisance. "He doesn't believe me."

"He'll believe the crowd," Meg said. "Westies' patrons love live music. They'll make him feel welcome."

Bryan stopped at the entrance to the outside area and ushered them in with the wave of his arm. "Ladies, after you."

He led them to a table in front of the stage with a reserved place card. Bryan winked and whispered in Meg's ear, "It pays to have connections."

And manners. He sat Lily and Meg before taking the chair beside hers. Her stomach rumbled as he passed her a menu.

"Grouper is the fish of the day—in case you're interested."

She was interested, all right, and not in the fish.

The waitress seemed surprised to see Bryan. "Hey. You don't spend enough time here?"

"Hey, Kelly." Bryan draped his arm along the back of Meg's chair, his fingers brushing her shoulder. "Do you know Meg and Lily Holloway?"

Kelly pointed her pen at Meg. "The gift store, right?"

"A Day's Wait."

"That's right. I love that store. Got my mom some funny slippers for Christmas last year."

"Those are—" Meg stuttered when Bryan feathered his fingers along her arm, "—big sellers."

"She loves them. I'll be back again this year."

"I start putting our Christmas merchandise out in September, so come by anytime."

Kelly scoffed and shook her head. "Gets earlier and earlier every year. What can I get you all to drink?"

Meg ordered a mojito and Lily asked for a Shirley Temple. Bryan ordered a beer.

Lily waved her arms when she saw Eva and Barb. "Over here," she shouted, earning a censuring glare from Meg.

Bryan stood, whispering something to Kelly, and greeted Eva and Barb. "Ladies, would you like to join us?"

"Oh." Eva fluttered her fingers. "We don't want to intrude."

"I already asked Kelly to bring more chairs."

"Please?" Lily clapped, bouncing on the tips of her toes.

Barb lifted her brows, leveled Meg with a skeptical stare. "You sure you don't mind?"

"Please, join us," Meg said. With her daytime neighbors at the table, her night out with Bryan would feel less like a date and more like a gathering of friends. "We just ordered drinks."

Meg's nerves went from screeching rock to soothing jazz in the time it took the hostess to bring two more chairs and place settings. Even with the lessened tension, Meg couldn't deny the twinge of disappointment at having to share Bryan's attention. *It's for the best. We have no future.* She shook her thoughts away and asked Eva and Barb about the surge in foot traffic, trying her best to pay attention while eavesdropping on Bryan and Lily's conversation about her newfound love of surfing.

Bryan leaned into Lily, giving her his full attention. "Your aunt says you're really good."

Lily's face pinked and she tucked a lock of white-blonde hair behind her ear. "I don't know about that. But it's fun."

"I've never surfed in the ocean. We spent our summers water skiing, tubing, and wake boarding on the lake."

"That sounds fun."

"It was a blast." His voice turned wistful, and Meg wondered if he was thinking of his brother. "Those were good times."

"Cool." Lily stared at the table, turning her fork repeatedly. "I can teach you to surf if you want."

She'd caught Bryan off guard by the dazed look on his face. "Really? You'd show me how to surf?"

"Sure. It's not hard. The waves are small so it's not like it's dangerous."

Meg twisted the napkin in her lap, worries stacking like chips on a poker table. *The barnacle's brother and Amanda's daughter in the water together? Terrible idea. And what if Lily gets attached? He's leaving at the end of the summer.*

Dustin ambled onto the stage, fiddling with his guitar and the microphone stand, scattering Meg's thoughts. What was she doing, spending time with Bryan? Adding Lily to the mix? This could only lead to disaster. She sensed him staring and turned her head in his direction.

Bryan's mouth had a tripwire attached to Meg's heart. Every time he flashed that panty-melting smile, she felt it implode in her chest like an explosive. Her body's reaction was the wakeup call she needed. Lily's attachment was the least of Meg's worries.

Thirty

Bryan sensed a wave of optimism on the warm breeze that fluttered the table's napkins and ruffled Meg's hair. He and Lily were bonding, Meg was starting to relax, and thanks to the running commentary of Barb and Eva, Bryan was getting a firsthand look at the friendship that made up Meg and Lily's makeshift family.

It was a wonder he could concentrate on anything other than Meg. She had no idea how beautiful she was, sitting there playing with the straw of her drink, her eyes shining in the muted light, laughter on her lips and desire thrumming in every glance they shared.

Their food arrived as Dustin introduced himself to the crowd as someone who hadn't picked up a guitar in years. He asked the audience to go easy on him and then dove into a unique rendition of the Eagles' "Peaceful Easy Feeling" that left everyone—Bryan included—stunned. Dustin's raw talent flowed through the popular cover and left the crowd juiced for more.

One song bled into the next until he was taking requests and looking like the Dustin of old. After nearly an hour and a half of non-stop songs, Dustin took a much-deserved break and headed for their table.

Bryan stood, knocking Dustin on the shoulder so hard he had to take step back. "You killed it, man. I knew you would."

Dustin exhaled, wiping the sweat from his brow with a small towel. "That was fun."

Meg grazed his arm with her fingers. "Dustin, that was fantastic. You're amazing."

He ducked his head, embarrassed by the attention. "I don't know about that."

"Young man," Eva said from across the table. "That was impressive. We came here to support a friend and we'll be leaving as fans. You're gifted."

Lily shoved a paper placemat in his face. "Can I have your autograph?"

The Dustin of old would have eaten up the compliments and scrawled his name on anything in sight. This Dustin, wounded from Tegan's rejection, took the praise like a side of humble pie. "Come on, kid. I wasn't that good."

When Lily's smile faltered, Dustin placed a hand on her shoulder and reached for the placemat with the other. "But if you insist." He looked from face to face. "Does anyone have a pen?"

Bryan reached for the pen inside the receipt holder and handed it to Dustin, watched him scrawl his name and hand the paper back to Lily.

"That and a couple bucks will get you a cup of coffee."

Lily folded the paper and blinked her big blue eyes at Dustin. "I don't drink coffee." She carefully slid the paper inside her pocket like it was something to cherish.

Dustin shook his head at her and pointed at the bar. "I'm going to use the bathroom and hydrate. Anyone need anything?"

Barb and Eva stood. "We're heading out," Barb said. "It's past our bedtime. Bryan, thank you for dinner, and Dustin, the entertainment was first class."

"We are too," Meg said. At Lily's whimper of protest, Meg gave her an apologetic stare. "I told you we couldn't stay for the whole set."

"Thanks for coming, ladies. I appreciate the support." Dustin scooted past and disappeared into the crowd.

Bryan tucked his chair beneath the table and looked at Meg. "I'll walk you back."

Eva raised her hand and her voice, stopping everyone from moving. She eyed Barb with a mischievous grin and tucked Lily into her side. "Why don't you let the old gals take the young gal home and you two stay for Dustin's second set? I feel bad, with us leaving all at once." She looked down at Lily. "How about a sleepover? You can help us unpack the delivery from the supply store in the morning."

Bryan wanted to hurdle the table and kiss Eva on the mouth—until he looked at Meg. Her expression was like an acrophobic who'd been pressured into a roller coaster ride.

"That's okay," Meg said. "You two are exhausted."

"Please, Aunt Meg? Please?"

Meg eyed at the faces around the table. She was outnumbered and she knew it. "Fine. As long as she goes to sleep and doesn't stay up until midnight like last time."

"I promise," Lily said. "I'll go right to sleep."

Meg stepped over, gave her niece a hug. "Be good. I love you."

"I will," Lily said. "I love you too."

The moment she turned back to Bryan, Meg's nerves were on full display. The frantic way she gripped the back of her chair. The way her leg bobbed as if she had to use the restroom. The way she wouldn't meet Bryan's eyes for more than a second after an evening of long, lingering glances.

"Can I get you another drink?" Bryan asked.

Meg licked her lips, glanced around. "I probably shouldn't."

He'd fought too hard to get Meg alone to discourage her from lingering. He leaned in, the silky strands of her hair tickling his face, and issued a challenge in her ear. "That's how good stories start."

She twisted her lips, a flash of agreement in her sea-green eyes. "I suppose one more won't hurt."

Supremely satisfied, Bryan led her to the quietest end of the bar. He placed their order and nudged Meg onto an empty stool, her skirt hitching mouthwateringly high on her thighs. He dragged his eyes back to hers. "I knew you and Lily were close with Eva and Barb, but I didn't realize how close until tonight."

"They're family. Especially since my parents left the island. I don't know what I'd do without them."

"I don't think you're going to have to find out. They love you and Lily like their own."

Meg tilted her head and Bryan resisted the urge to sniff her silky red strands. "What's that saying?" she asked. "Friends are the family you choose. In this case, it's true."

"Do you celebrate the holidays together?" He settled for wrapping his arm around her chair and fingering the ends of her hair.

Meg shook her head around the straw in her mouth. "Barb's daughter and grandkids live in Tampa so they usually go together to Tampa for Thanksgiving and Christmas."

"Are you able to take time off? See your parents?"

"Not over Thanksgiving, but I'll send Lily up for a few days over Christmas. They'll need each other, especially this year."

She didn't need to explain. Bryan dreaded the holidays more than usual this year. He didn't think it could get worse than the will-he-or-won't-he of every Thanksgiving and Christmas as they waited word of Corey's maybe arrival. Until it did. "What about you?"

"I've got the store. The holidays are busy times in the retail market."

Her lack of enthusiasm told him everything he needed to know. Her work and the first holidays without her sister left little room for cheer. He sipped his beer, watching her mood slip over the lip of his mug, and decided to switch gears. "You said the people they are with says a lot about a person." He set his glass down and tried out a teasing smile. "Tell me about your ex-boyfriends."

She choke-laughed and deflected. "There's not much to tell." There wasn't much she *wanted* to tell.

"Okay, I'll go first because I'm sure you're dying to know about the women in my past."

As expected, Meg rolled her eyes. But the way they zoomed back to his, her body stilled and leaning forward, she couldn't hide her interest.

"I kinda-sorta had a thing with a fellow teacher back at school. It was progressing nicely until I got the call about Corey. It was too new to withstand my abrupt absence and the heaviness of losing a sibling. I heard she's dating the football coach."

"Ouch."

He wrinkled his nose. "Not so much." He could barely remember their time together. "My longest relationship was right out of college. Melinda Jackson. Pretty blonde teller at the bank where I worked. We were getting serious and then I decided to change jobs."

"Wait." Meg straightened and put a hand on his arm, shooting firework flares up his shoulder. "Are you saying she dumped you because you left your job?"

"Afraid so."

"That's so ... shallow."

"Maybe, but in her defense, I was making a decent salary with a runway for more, living in a nice condo, driving a nice car, when we started dating." And if she didn't want to be with him as a teacher, she wasn't with him for the right reasons.

"And you had to give that up?"

"I traded the foreign car for a domestic truck, sold most of my suits, moved to a smaller apartment. My runway got considerably shorter." And he would do it all over again if given the choice.

An adorable wrinkle appeared between Meg's brows. "You're more than what you do or how much money you make."

"That's true, but I left banking because it was just a paycheck. All that mattered was the almighty dollar. I didn't like who I was, chasing my tail, chasing money. If I didn't like myself, she didn't like the real me anyway."

"Why teaching?"

"I started volunteering with a Big Brothers program through work. It changed my life. I realized how many kids needed help, how few men there were willing to make a difference."

Her mouth softened, and he'd have sworn her eyelashes fluttered. "Your girlfriend should have appreciated your decision, not dumped you."

He shrugged as if her betrayal meant nothing, when at the

time it had cut him to the bone. In the end, it didn't matter. She didn't matter. "She wanted a different life, a different lifestyle."

"Sounds like you dodged a bullet."

And that's when he knew. Meg mattered. What she thought of him mattered. What she thought about everything mattered. She was the opposite of Melinda—strong and generous, providing for her niece and her family while her dreams withered and died. "You're absolutely right, but in her defense—not that she deserves one—have you given any thought to who you'd be without the store?"

She drew her lips into a thoughtful frown.

Bryan relented, rubbing his thumb along her shoulder, a gentle touch to soothe the sting of his question. "It's not easy to separate ourselves from our jobs."

She stared at the glass in her hand, her voice tissue-paper soft. "I don't know who I'd be without the store. I'm afraid if I can't get a handle on Amanda's part of the business, I'm going to find out."

Bryan wrestled his conscience. Dustin had told him things about the store—things he was duty bound not to repeat. But Meg looked so sad, and she'd cracked the door open enough to flirt with danger and ask for mercy later. "Don't be mad."

She leaned away and cocked her head as if bracing for bad news. "Mad about what?"

"Dustin told me you're worried about making ends meet. He said your program is giving you fits."

Thirty-One

The break music ended, and Dustin returned to the stage. Meg didn't register a word of his banter meant to loosen up the crowd. She couldn't take her eyes off Bryan, stroking his eyebrow with a pained look on his face. His you're-killing-me swallow sent his Adam's apple bobbing.

Meg dropped her head, pulling on the hem of her skirt. She wanted to be mad. Mad was an easier emotion to handle than the embarrassment coloring her cheeks. "He shouldn't have told you."

"Don't be mad at Dustin. I ask him every day how you're doing. He told me you were worried, and it just kinda went from there." He placed his hand on her knee. "I'm sorry if that makes you uncomfortable."

"Of course it make me uncomfortable." Almost as uncomfortable as his hand on her leg, warm and wide and distracting. "How would you feel if people were talking about your personal business behind your back?"

"I'd be hurt." He squeezed her knee. The petty part of her wanted to make a scene by shoving his hand away instead of taking comfort from his touch. "We care about you, Meg. What worries you, worries me."

She stared at him, a tight knot fisting her belly. "You barely know me."

His brows winged upward. "We both know that's not true." He dropped his hand and glanced away only to angle his body closer, talk into her ear over the sound of Dustin's song. "Look, I know I'm not responsible for what happened to your sister, but my brother was with her when she died. Corey didn't leave behind a business or any other obligations to juggle. I donated most of his stuff to charity. But you're left to raise your niece and run your business alone. That's a huge burden."

Everything he said was true, but only one needed defending. "Raising Lily isn't a burden."

"That's not … I said that wrong. What I mean is raising a child is a massive responsibility on top of running the store by yourself."

The pity in his eyes was like a mirror to her soul and the reflection wasn't pretty. How many times had she yearned for someone—anyone other than Eva and Barb—to notice the load she carried alone? "It's a lot but I'm handling it."

"You are. But needing a hand doesn't make you weak."

Admit a weakness? If she admitted one, she was afraid she'd admit them all and scare him away.

"Dustin told me Amanda handled all the back-office work."

She flicked her eyes to Dustin, his eyes closed, singing away on the stage. Her musical volunteer was going to get an earful for spreading her private business around town. If he told Bryan, who else had he told? Was everyone on the island laughing at her and waiting for the store to fail?

"Amanda did the books and paid the taxes and did all the stuff that really matters when running a business. I'm learning as I go." She gripped the edge of the bar and bristled like a dog on alert. "Just because I'm afraid of messing up something important doesn't mean I'm running the business into the ground."

"I never said that. Dustin never implied anything close to that." He tilted his head and studied her face.

Could he see the panic bubbling just under the surface? Could he tell she wanted to hop off the stool and run away from his eyes that picked her clean?

"Let me help you, Meg. I'm a math guy—a teacher, for goodness' sake. And I'm here all summer."

He'd already helped her by clearing the inventory so she could spend more time with the books. That she'd spent more time daydreaming about his gorgeous brown eyes and heart-stopping kisses than learning the program wasn't on him. "Just because our siblings died together doesn't mean you owe me. I'm not going to monopolize your time because you feel some warped sense of responsibility."

He straightened, the pity in his eyes turning fierce, and leaned in close. He didn't angle his mouth to her ear but looked her straight in the eyes. "Let me be crystal clear. You're the strongest, most fascinating, most amazing woman I've ever met. Wanting to spend time with you and help you out of a jam has absolutely nothing to do with duty."

He couldn't have shocked her more if he'd stabbed her in the stomach, the stomach he left fluttery and fazed. The steel in his voice, the absolute certainty, had Meg squirming in her seat. The last thing she intended was to bring what had been simmering between them all night to a boil.

He must have seen the surprise on her face because he reached up and tucked a lock of hair behind her ear, the corner of his mouth lifting into a cocky grin. "Besides," he said, his tone teasing and light. "What else am I going to do? Work on my tan?"

Meg let out a shaky breath. "You don't tan," she said, her voice snarky and low and revealing way too much about how he affected her. "You burn."

"Exactly. Don't be stubborn, Meg. Whether you want it or not, you need my help—if only to give you confidence you can do it yourself. Isn't that your goal?"

He sure sounded like a teacher now with his I-know-what's-best tone and trust-me head nod. But spending time with Bryan, trying to ignore or pretend she didn't feel the pull between them— was an impossible task. "A Day's Wait is more than just a retail store. It's my parents' legacy. It's where they chose to put down roots and watch them grow. It's where Amanda found her footing after becoming a single mom. It's the only consistent thing in Lily's life."

"The store has history and memories." Bryan followed his acknowledgment with a brief nod. "But it's not the only consistent thing in Lily's life. *You're* the most consistent thing in Lily's life."

Meg snorted and reached for her drink. If he kept looking at her like that, like she'd saved Lily from a burning building instead of being the only fallback in the family, she would do something stupid and kiss him. Meg was nobody's heroine, stumbling through life, grumbly and nervous about the business side of their family business. "Besides me."

"Don't." His harsh, sandpaper tone had the straw slipping from her mouth. "Don't dismiss yourself like that. You just told me what the store meant to your parents and your sister. What does it mean to you?"

The breath stuttered from her too-tight lungs. Bryan did more than notice her—he had x-ray vision—and used it to strip her bare. "The store is our home."

It was the answer he'd been waiting for by the way his shoulders relaxed, and he pulled back a fraction of space. "And when the roof of your home leaks, do you patch it yourself?" He didn't wait for her to answer. "You call a roofer. You call a plumber when the pipes burst and a repairman when the air is broken."

"I never said anything was broken."

"Of course, you didn't. You're too hardheaded for that."

She huffed an exasperated breath. It was a special kind of torture for someone to see her and call her out after being tiptoed around for months. "You can't insult me into letting you help."

"You're right." His gaze turned wicked and dropped to her mouth. Seconds passed. The music faded to a low hum. He leaned closer, taking back the space he'd yielded, and licked his lips. His eyes flicked to hers.

Snagged in his stare, unspeakably aroused, Meg's breath clogged her lungs.

In slow, torturous beats, Bryan closed the distance between them, pressing his lips to hers. The kiss was quick, just a swipe of mouth to mouth.

"You did that on purpose." Her raspy, graveled-over voice told him as much as her slow to lift lids.

"Maybe." He used his finger to push the hair from her face, laid his hand on her neck, his thumb resting where her pulse pounded beneath her skin. "I've wanted to kiss you all night."

"You can't ... people will think ..."

"No one's watching, Meg." His voice had turned to velvet, warming her like the stroke of his tongue. "No one cares. Everyone is focused on Dustin."

Not everyone. She saw Tim standing in the corner of the bar stacking glasses and eyeing them intently.

"Let me help you. I want to help." He picked her hand up where it had gone limp in her lap, laced his fingers with hers. "What have you got to lose?"

What didn't she have to lose? Admitting she couldn't keep the store afloat had already dented her pride, and opening her books meant losing control and left her vulnerable. Not to mention that hanging out with him would leave her more confused and unstable at a time when Lily needed her to be strong. But depending on him, spending time huddled close at her computer, the biggest risk was to her heart.

Thirty-Two

Bryan had pushed Meg too far. She'd gone quiet, pulling her hand from his, turning away from him, pretending to be enthralled with Dustin's music. Dustin played good music. Good enough to know that if Meg were truly listening, she wouldn't have been sitting there with a scowl on her face deep enough to act as a don't-talk-to-me-shield.

Bryan got the message loud and clear. He closed the tab when Dustin announced his last song and waited for Meg to look his way, say something—anything—to salvage what had been an enjoyable evening. He planned to walk her to her car and hopefully give her something else to think about other than his offer to swoop in and make all her problems disappear.

He needed to take a good look in the mirror and analyze the God complex he'd recently discovered lurking in his psyche. He was a people pleaser by nature, but Meg's reaction to his multiple offers of help had him stepping back and looking at himself with a critical eye.

To Bryan's way of thinking, Meg had more than earned a break or two in life. But was Bryan's constant need to help and Meg's needing help a distinction without a difference? Help was help was help—or was it?

Meg scooted off the stool and stood, angling away from him, looping her purse over her shoulder, and sparing him a fleeting glance. "I should probably get going."

Much to Bryan's disappointment, Dustin's final song, a gritty rendition of Coldplay's "Fix You" hadn't melted Meg's frosty manner or made her any more inclined to accept anything he'd offered. Resigned, he lifted his hand to her back and ushered her through the crowd to the exit. Once outside the bar and on the sidewalk, her silence screamed louder than the worry thrashing around his head.

He thrust his hands into his pockets and scrounged for something to say. "Thanks for coming with me tonight."

She kept her pace as brisk as her voice. "Thanks for inviting us. And for dinner."

"You're welcome. I'd like to do it again—take you and Lily out sometime. Maybe Sunday after our lesson?"

She took four sidewalk-eating steps before mumbling a response that left him grumpier than before. "I'm not sure that's a good idea."

"You don't think we'll work up an appetite on the water?"

Meg stopped at the corner and faced Bryan for the first time since leaving the bar. "You're surfing this Sunday?"

The way she said it, that emphasis on *this*, as if seeing him so soon wasn't a pleasant idea, made his heart slink to his shoes.

"Lily said Sunday mornings work best because the store doesn't open until noon and there was no way you'd let her go without you coming along as a chaperone."

Her lips twitched and then settled back into a frown. "She's right about that."

"She suggested we start with paddle boarding since I've never done it." Baby steps, she'd called it. Even Lily knew not to jump in with both feet before testing the water. His face tingled and street noise grated on his nerves. How many ways could he screw up with Meg?

"Where?" she asked. "I don't … we sold our paddleboards."

"They rent them at the public beach access where Corey used to work. I figured we'd go there unless you know of a better place."

Mentioning his brother only irritated her more. Her face tightened and she flinched when a passing teenager brushed her elbow. "No. That's … fine."

Nothing about her or the end of what should have been a nice evening together was fine. But since he'd already ruined the night, he may as well ask the question that had scraped his subconscious since making plans with Lily. "Do you think us being in the water together is a good idea considering what happened to her mom and my brother?"

Meg inhaled, her eyes scanning the crowd. "I talked about that with the guys who run the surfing camp before I signed her up. I trusted them and she did fine." She shrugged and her eyes landed back on his. "I don't think she'll have any issues, but if she does, I'll be right there—and so will you. We live on an island. It's not like I can keep her out of the water."

If Meg had any idea how many parents Bryan knew who let their kids do whatever they wanted only to get them out from under their feet, she'd have cut herself a break. If he thought she'd take it to heart, he'd have told her about the two-parent families of kids he taught who gave no thought to what was best for their kids. "So, what do you think? Paddleboarding and breakfast on Sunday before the store opens?"

"Geez, you're persistent." She huffed a breath, fluttering the hair in her face. "Does anyone ever say no to you?"

"All the time." He spied a group walking toward them, chins lowered, eyes on their phones and tugged Meg out of the way.

As soon as they'd passed, Bryan followed her toward the back of her building to her car. The security light on the corner of the building, while a hotspot for bugs, didn't provide much security beyond a halo of light. Shadows lurked among the cars and motorcycles cluttering the lot.

Meg stopped by her sedan and fumbled with her keys, dropping them by the driver's side door. Bryan bent and picked them up, held them out to her while watching her face. Meg was either too angry or too nervous to look him in the eyes.

He went with instinct and stepped closer, close enough so her back was against the car, close enough that when she lifted her head, he felt her breath tickle his face. The salty-sweet smell of her had longing pooling in his mouth.

She grasped the keys, tried to tug them from his hand but he held tight.

"Meg. Look at me."

She lifted her lids. In her eyes he saw nerves and the first light of resignation. She could tell him no and push him away, but she was only delaying the inevitable. What was building between them was bigger than any excuse she could've come up with to keep them apart.

He gripped her chin, his thumb grazing her plump bottom lip. "Spend time with me, Meg. I want to know you better."

Her eyes pinged between his. "To what end, Bryan?"

"To this end." He lowered his head and captured her lips with his. Go slow, he told himself as he swooped back for more. Go easy. Don't scare her away. But when she fisted his shirt and pressed their bodies together, moaning into his mouth, his tether snapped.

His hands roamed. Her face, her hair, her shoulders softer than the shadows where they stood. There was fire in her fingers, igniting his skin, making him throb. She arched against him, hiking her leg around his waist, sending his hands lower to align their bodies and ease the pounding ache in his groin.

Bryan had never been prone to public displays of affection much less a full-on make out session within spitting distance of anyone wandering by. When a honking horn brought sanity front and center, he pulled away millimeter by millimeter. Grateful she'd parked in a darkly lit corner that somewhat hid them from onlookers, he ran his lips from her collarbone to her ear, drunk on her scent and the sweet taste of her skin.

Meg panted, her forehead pressed against his chest. "You have to stop doing that." She lifted her head and shook the hair from her face. Her lips were swollen and her eyes dazed.

He had to stop himself from going back for more. "Doing what?"

"Kissing me like that. I run a business on this island. People talk." She shoved him back. "I can't do this. I can't act like some half-drunk tourist out for a cheap hook up."

He stepped back enough to let her breathe, but not far enough to let her leave. "Then come home with me, Meg. Spend time with me." He wouldn't, he couldn't, walk away from her now.

She looked up at him with big, doubtful eyes and snorted a stinging laugh. "You tempt me, Bryan. You know you do. But I'm not going to start something with you that has absolutely no hope of going anywhere. I've done that before and it didn't end well."

She'd felt this tug-of-war, live-or-die passion before? He found the idea impossible. "When?"

"It doesn't matter."

"If you're going to judge me by someone else, I deserve to know what I'm up against."

She stared at him for two beats before the emotion trickled out of her voice. "He was a musician here for the summer. After an intense couple of weeks, I agreed to follow him to Chicago where he'd make music and I'd go to art school."

Bryan clenched his teeth so tight his jaw ached. "What happened?"

Her eyelid twitched. "My mom's diagnosis."

"He didn't stay?"

"I didn't ask." She lifted her chin and posed the words like a dare. "He didn't offer."

Poor, sweet, innocent Meg. Always the one to sacrifice. Always the one to suffer. Bryan cupped her cheek and said something he didn't quite believe. "We don't have to become lovers, Meg."

"We can't. You're only here for the summer. I have sole custody of Lily and the store, not to mention my mom and dad and everything they're going through. I don't have the time nor the interest in a summer fling."

Did she really think that's all he wanted? Did she believe him a fly by night fool? "I'm not interested in a summer fling."

Meg lowered her chin and the leery look she gave him labeled him a liar. "What are you interested in?"

He said the only thing that was true. "You. I'm drawn to you, Meg, like I've never been drawn to anyone." He ran a frustrated hand through his hair. "Why can't we take things one day at a time?"

"Because that's how I get hurt. And I've been hurt enough."

She had been hurt—too much, by too many. If he thought he could walk away, he would do it to spare them both. "I don't intend to hurt you."

Her wry smile was like a knife to the gut. "Your intentions won't matter when the summer's over and you're gone. It's best for both of us if we agree to being just friends."

He wanted to argue. Shake her until she agreed. Kiss her greedily until she changed her mind. But she was right. His trademark optimism leaked away, puddling at his feet, as useless as wishing on the stars twinkling overhead. Saddled and cinched with resignation, he stepped back and let her go.

Bryan avoided the bar and went straight up to the apartment. He wasn't in the mood to celebrate with Dustin after Meg's banishment to the friend zone. He kicked the door shut and threw himself onto the couch, only to stare at the ceiling and lick his wounds.

He'd been dumped before. It wasn't possible to be a single man at the age of thirty who hadn't been rejected. But Meg's dismissal hurt worse than most. It didn't make sense to feel so heartsick after only a few kisses, but there was no other way to explain the gnawing ache at the center of his gut.

He pushed himself to standing, his pent-up frustration spurring him to prowl the perimeter of the room. He wanted to run to the beach and exhaust the adrenaline surging through his veins. Howl and curse at the moon. Buy a six pack and drink himself into a body-numbing stupor. None of that would change the fact that Meg had to look out for herself and her niece and protect her heart.

It only made him admire her more.

He went into the bedroom and scowled at the neatly made bed. It felt like a million years ago when he'd whistled while straightening his room, in hopes of bringing Meg home for the night. He'd told himself it was better to be prepared than wind up embarrassed, but the tidy room mocked him and made him feel a hundred times worse.

Bryan kicked his shoes off and put them away out of habit, eyeing the remaining boxes of Corey's things where they sat in the corner. The bitterness he felt toward his brother—the same bitterness that had dwindled with every day Bryan spent mooning after Meg, snapped back to life. His brother was the reason he'd met Meg. His brother could take the blame for Bryan's mood. He hefted the largest box onto the bed and opened the flaps, determined to find the answers he'd come to unearth.

Lost in paper scraps, bar receipts, and the minutia of Corey's life, Bryan startled when Dustin cleared his throat from the entrance to Bryan's bedroom. "This seems like an odd time to be going through that stuff."

Bryan tossed a wad of notes into a trash pile he'd made on the bed. "I've got nothing better to do."

"I thought when Eva and Barb took Lily with them, this would be your big night. I was prepared to see a sock tied on the doorknob and to sleep in the bar."

Bryan grunted, flipping through the pages of a water-damaged paperback. "I don't know what I expected. She made it clear from the start she's not interested."

"That's not what I saw." Dustin folded his arms. "What happened?"

"Meg's a pragmatist. While her sister was willing to run off with my good-for-nothing brother, Meg's too smart—too cautious—to do the same."

"You realize you just called yourself good for nothing?"

"I'm calling myself a fool for falling for someone I can't have. Now or ever."

"Come on, man." Dustin pushed away from the door jam and eased closer to the bed. "Don't give up so soon."

"I'm not giving up. I'm just ..." Moping like a kid denied candy. Feeling like ten-year-old Bryan who could never find his way out of Corey's too-big shadow. "It's not fair. I finally find a woman who intrigues me on every level, and she won't let me try."

Dustin sat on the bed, disrupting Bryan's neat little piles. "I get it. I've got a wife who won't let me try. Welcome to my personal torture."

"I'm sorry." *Stupid, stupid, stupid* to complain to Dustin, especially after the night he'd had on stage. He tossed a pair of sunglasses into the maybe pile and smiled at Dustin. "You slayed tonight, D. I'm proud of you."

"Thanks." Dustin shrugged like it was no big deal, but the stain on his cheeks said otherwise. "It was fun. Tim asked me back whenever I want."

"That's awesome, man." They bumped knuckles the way they had when they were kids. Back when life was simple, and they could shrug off a girl's rejection because they had their best bud by their side. "You should do it, perform at Westies, as often as you can. It's good to see you smiling again."

"It feels good to smile." Dustin's grin dissolved as he stared at the callouses on his hands. "I want to call Tegan and tell her how good it felt to be on stage making music. She wants me to be happy. I finally found something that did the trick."

"Then call her. She'll be happy for you. You know she will."

He sighed, long and deep, like he'd already made up his mind. "I want to, but I can't. She sent me away. I won't be the first to reach out. If I can make it going on two weeks without her, I can wait a bit longer."

Bryan ached for Dustin, for himself, for the unfairness of it all. Why did relationships turn into gamesmanship instead of grown men and women talking it out? But while Dustin could benefit from communication with his wife, Meg had laid it out for Bryan, closing the door on a romance. He wasn't feeling any better than Dustin. "How long are you going to wait?"

"As long as I have to. As long as I can. Tonight was a big step for me. I don't have to tell you how lost I've been, how much this separation has blown my confidence. I'm glad you pushed me into doing it. I don't think I'd have done it on my own."

"All you needed was a nudge." Bryan found a checkbook underneath an old knee brace. He picked it up and scanned the information.

"What are you scowling at?" Dustin asked.

"I'm not sure." That nervous, weighed-down feeling he used to get whenever Corey called settled low in his gut. "I closed Corey's accounts, but I don't recognize this bank." He flipped through the registry, noted the entries. The ground shifted, and that weight bore down on him like a freight train on his chest. He should have known.

"What's wrong?"

Bryan could barely lift his eyes. "I think I know how Corey supported himself."

Bryan barely slept, the past and present whirling through his mind like a weathervane in a storm. Meg's rejection and Corey's deceit a two-sided sword that split him in half. No matter how many times he flipped the angles or stepped back to see the bigger picture, nothing changed.

At first light, he fixed his coffee and went back into the bedroom so as not to wake Dustin. This conversation needed to be private. He watched the clock and waited until he knew she'd be awake and most likely alone before dialing her number. She answered on the second ring.

"Hey, sweetie."

"Mom." Bryan purposely modulated his tone. What good would it do to expose her to the full force of his disappointment or to raise his voice and yell? "How ya doing?"

"I'm … okay." Was that grief he heard—or guilt? "It's good to hear your voice."

"Sorry it's been a while since I called."

"I know you're busy."

His mom wasn't going to make this easy, and she wasn't going to come clean. Bryan wondered if she'd forgotten about the payments or if she'd been waiting and worried he'd uncover the truth. "I found the checkbook, Mom. I know you were sending Corey money."

The pause on her end stretched to a hair's breadth from breaking. She finally choked, her voice like a whispered prayer. "Please don't tell your dad. Please."

"Why, Mom?"

"He was my son."

The defiance in her voice shocked him, had him spouting a rebuke. "So am I, and he'd have bled me dry without thinking twice."

She said nothing, all but confirming she agreed—and would have approved.

"We talked about cutting him off. I came to you and Dad, told you what happened, explained my decision. You agreed I was only making it worse by giving him money. You said it was time for him to stand or fail on his own."

"Your father said it was time. I never agreed."

"You didn't disagree."

"You don't understand." Her voice went rusty-knife dull. "You won't understand until you have a child." She twisted that rusty knife and kicked it for good measure.

"I don't have a child, but I'm your child too." Her second born, her second favorite. "And you knew how hard it was for me to cut him off and then you went behind my back and gave him money."

"When your child asks for help, you help. I love you, Bryan, but I don't owe you an explanation. I did it, and I won't apologize."

"But you won't tell Dad."

"He's a proud man. If he knew I was helping Corey he would think less of your brother, and he'd be angry with me."

What about me? Bryan wanted to shout into the phone. Even doing the right thing was never enough to measure up to her favorite son. He heard Meg's car pass outside and tortured himself by walking to the window and watching her taillights disappear into the lot. She was as out of reach to him as the peace he thought he'd find in the Keys.

"Well, I don't know what to say." He rubbed his throbbing

temple. "Thanks for making me the bad guy."

His mom's sigh sounded like surrender. "You're not the bad guy, Bryan. You tried to help him, and it didn't work out. You made the best decision for you, and I made the only decision I could live with. You don't have to agree. I only ask that you try and understand."

He didn't understand. Not even a little. "If Dad asks, I'm not going to lie."

"You do what you have to do."

In the end, it wouldn't matter. Corey was gone and nothing would bring him back.

Thirty-Three

Hovering above the horizon, the sun promised a day of soaring temperatures, sticky air, and sun-kissed skin. All morning Meg tried but failed to match Lily's excitement. Smelling of coconut sunscreen and bouncing on her toes, Lily ran down the stairs and waited for Meg to unlock the car so they could meet Bryan at the beach.

Bryan. Just the thought of him left Meg jumpy and weak. For days she'd questioned her decision to put a halt to their budding romance. It was hard to concentrate on the priorities that mattered when all Lily did was talk about Bryan and Dustin and how much she couldn't wait to teach Bryan to paddleboard.

The girl needed a father figure in her life almost as much as Meg needed a man. As excited as Lily was about seeing Bryan, Meg felt the opposite. Nervous to the point of nausea, she'd spent too much time picking out a bathing suit. No matter how much Meg wanted to wait on the shore and watch Lily and Bryan interact from a distance, the day's forecast argued otherwise. With temperatures climbing into the nineties, there was no patch of shade or ocean breeze strong enough to keep her cool on land.

She found a parking spot at the public beach where they planned to meet, and she and Lily got out of the car. Meg scanned the lot for Bryan's truck but didn't see it. She took a calming breath and followed Lily up the steps.

Bryan stood wearing swim trunks and a t-shirt by three paddleboards. "Good morning," he said as they approached. "Ready to hit the water?"

He was all smiles for Lily and barely spared Meg a glance.

"I am," Lily said, struggling to grab her board with her beach bag in hand.

"Let me get that." Bryan leaned the board against his leg and looked at Meg for the first time. "I'll be back for yours."

"You didn't have to rent me a board."

"You're going to roast sitting on the beach. Besides"— Bryan gave her a friendly wink—"how can you chaperone from the shore?"

Meg was the one who'd shoved him into the friend zone, so why was she the one whose heart sank at his good-natured gesture? Look at me, his wink projected. Being nice. Respecting your wishes. Being friendly and fun without pushing for more.

The last few days, she'd done little but obsess about her decision to cut Bryan off. She'd told him about Zander, but after doing a deep dive, the situations didn't compare. Meg had jumped headfirst into a romance with Zander without any thoughts of the future. Once he realized she wasn't coming with him, their relationship fizzled as quickly as it had started.

With Bryan, she thought of nothing but the future and the inevitable end to their connection. But he was still around, respecting her wishes, helping her and Lily, even though she'd cut him off at the knees. Their attraction felt fated and real, deeper than looks, based on more than proximity and an odd connection to their shared past. But still impossible to pursue.

"Come on, Aunt Meg. It'll be fun."

Meg and Amanda had grown up boarding around the island's inlets, finding passages through the mangroves, their eyes glued to the fascinating underwater world, but she hadn't boarded in years. Doing so without her sister felt like another kind of betrayal. "I don't know."

"Think about it while I carry these down." Bryan kicked off his flip-flops and pulled the shirt from his back, then hefted the boards in each hand. "I'll be right back."

Lily grabbed the paddles and life vests and jogged after Bryan.

Meg stood rooted in place, her mouth watering, her eyes locked on Bryan's rippling back and shoulder muscles like a sponge soaking up water. She expelled a shaky breath. Not wanting a replay when he returned for hers, she picked up her board. She lagged, letting Lily take the lead with Bryan.

Lily took over at the shoreline, zipping her life vest and wading into the water where she instructed Bryan on how to get onto the board. He copied her, walking to the side of the board, and kneeling in the center. Lily handed him the paddle and showed him how to stand up.

Meg watched from the beach line, admiration lightening her mood. Taking orders from a child wasn't something most men took in stride—at least not the men she'd been around.

The sun beat down from a cloudless sky and the water lapped

at her ankles. It was too hot to stand on the sand and watch. With a resigned sigh, she crossed her arms and pulled her shirt up and off, tossing it aside where she'd set their towels.

Bryan glanced over his shoulder and did a double take. The board wobbled under his feet.

"Keep your eyes on the horizon," Lily scolded.

He arched his eyebrows at Meg, stared at her for one long lusty beat, before turning back to Lily.

Meg quickly unbuttoned her shorts and shimmied them over her hips while his attention was diverted. But she saw him adjust his position, a slight shift of the board, to keep Meg in his sights. This … whatever they were doing … felt like playing with fire. Playing with emotions. The morning promised to be slow-motion torture, every move feeding a thirst that could never be quenched.

Meg stopped brooding and put her life vest on and took her time getting into the water so as not to disturb Lily's lesson. Standing in knee-high water, she watched Lily talk Bryan through the best way to hold the paddle and how to stroke. They moved out over the break line into deeper but still shallow water, Bryan's attention on Lily and her patient instruction.

Lily relished his interest, laughing, and goofing around like a normal twelve-year-old. Bryan was a good guy, showing up on a Sunday morning, renting them boards, letting Lily teach him a skill he could've easily mastered on his own.

Seeing them together did funny things to Meg's heart. Until Lily's questions about Deke, she hadn't realized how much the girl craved a father. Which was silly considering how much Meg missed her own.

The breeze diminished and the heat became unbearable. Sweat glistened on Lily's nut-brown skin. She set her paddle on the board and eased into the water, dunking her head beneath the crystal blue surface. Bryan copied her moves off the board and floated on his back, dipping his head in the too-shallow water. Lily showed him how to get back on the board and Bryan heaved himself into the kneeling position.

Lily looked back at the shore, called to Meg, and waved her over. Meg paddled nearby, keeping her distance in case Bryan fell. "You're doing great," she said to Bryan.

"Thanks." He shook the water from his hair. "I've got a good teacher."

But Lily didn't hear Bryan's compliment, her attention snagged behind them on the beach. Meg turned and spotted a group of boys and girls on the beach playing spike ball. "Do you know them?"

"They're from my surfing camp." Lily's voice sounded disinterested, but Meg saw a flicker of interest in her eyes when one of the boys waved at Lily.

"Do you want to go say hi?"

Lily seemed torn, chewing her lip, her gaze shifting between Bryan and the kids. "No, that's okay. I'm teaching Bryan."

"It's okay, Lily." Bryan made a smooth transition from kneeling to sitting with his legs dangling on either side of the board. "Go say hi to your friends. I think I've got the hang of it now. And Meg will keep me company."

Lily flashed Meg an anxious, can-I-go look.

"Go," Meg said. "Remember to secure the board and the paddle."

Her quick grin was as blinding as the glare from the sun. "I will." She paddled for shore at a steady, brisk pace.

Meg sat down, mirroring Bryan's position, and watched Lily tug the board onto the sand and join her friends.

"You worried?" Bryan asked.

"No." Meg sighed, dragged her gaze from the shore. "It's good. She needs time with kids her own age."

"But?" Bryan prodded, a gentle teasing in his tone.

Talking about Lily wasn't against their just-friends rules. And he wanted to help. "It's the boys. They notice her. She has no idea, but it scares me."

"Your niece is a beautiful girl."

"She looks like her mother." But the shy, standoffish way she approached the group was nothing like Amanda. "Boys loved Amanda. She drew them without even trying—and she loved the attention."

Bryan swished his legs in the water. "I wish I could tell you different, but you probably should be scared. Teenage boys are the worst."

Meg glanced back at Lily, now fully immersed in the group, and stomach acid lurched up her throat. "Thanks for the pep talk." Melting under the sun and the worry clawing up her throat, Meg twisted and lowered into the water, leaning back to submerge her head.

When she stood upright, her toes sinking in the sand, Bryan watched her with an intensity that made her neck tingle. "Do you want my advice?"

Meg nodded, draping her arms over the board.

"Don't let your guard down. Listen to your gut. All guys—even the nice, quiet ones—want the same thing. Lily is innocent. You want to keep her that way as long as you can."

Worry for Lily—and herself—made her voice a sarcastic snarl. "Are you speaking from experience or as a teacher?"

"Both."

Annoyed with herself and the situation and his too-calm demeanor, she grabbed the board and tugged herself up. "Is this how it's going to be now that we're friends? You drop the pleasantries and tell me the truth?"

Bryan didn't flinch or frown at her nasty tone, so ungrateful and mean. He gave her a regretful smile, the kind of smile that pinched her heart in two. "We are friends, Meg. And I'll always tell you the truth. Men are pigs. But some of us understand when no means no."

There was no censure in his tone, nothing to stop her from feeling foolish and small for taking the regret and fear out on him. Shame rolled up her chest, inflaming her cheeks. "I'm sorry. You didn't deserve that."

"I'm sorry I scared you."

She dragged her eyes to Lily, too ashamed to see the disappointment on his face. "I need to be told the truth, especially when it's not what I want to hear."

"You're a good parent, Meg. Good parents know when to press and when to let up. Good parents also ask for help. Find people you trust and ask their advice, but don't discount your instincts. You know Lily better than anyone."

I trust you, she wanted to say. *I want to trust you with my heart.* Because she couldn't say the words, she stared at her toes and said nothing at all.

Bryan stood in one graceful motion. "Why don't we move closer to shore? Keep an eye on the kids."

Meg paddled next to Bryan, and they moved side by side toward the beach. When he was gone there would be no one to offer advice or offer to help. She'd be a fool to turn him down by either measure. She swallowed her pride and her reflex to resist his help. "If your offer still stands, I could use your help with the books."

Bryan's stroke stuttered but his expression stayed neutral. "I'm happy to help."

Thirty-Four

Bryan came to the store at Meg's request, on a slow-cruise Tuesday when Lily was at camp. He stepped inside and caught her unaware, running the vacuum at the back of the store, her hair held high in a ponytail that showcased her long, slender neck. Hunger and heartache clobbered his stomach with a one-two punch.

Being around her was a special kind of torture. Now that he'd discovered how Corey afforded to live his life on the island and take trips with beautiful locals, Bryan's purpose for staying was clear. He'd fulfill his commitment to Tim, and help Meg as much as she'd let him before returning home to mourn what was with his brother and what could have been with Meg.

He eyed the muscles of her toned legs. Not for the first time, the memory of her in that skimpy, black bikini floated to the forefront of his mind and had him cursing the unfairness of the situation.

She was the most beautiful woman he'd ever known—inside and out—and she was completely out of reach.

He watched her, the brisk movements and total focus. Meg ran the vacuum the way she ran her life—with purpose and an edge of frenzy. She cut the machine and the poppy soundtrack she preferred took over with some guy singing of strawberry kisses and wanting it all. *Get in line, pal.* She turned his way and gasped, clutching her chest when she saw him. "You scared me."

"Sorry."

"No, no. It's fine." She fluttered her hand to the carpet. "I broke a snow globe, and the glitter made a mess."

He fisted his hands in his pockets to keep from touching her, to stop himself from trying to quiet all that pent up energy. "Need some help?"

"With this, no. With the books …" She shrugged and tried her hand at a smile. "Unfortunately, yes."

"I'm ready when you are."

She looped the cord around the ancient machine and pushed it to the storeroom, tucking it between a break in the shelving. He followed her back and waited for her to lead.

She seemed nervous, pushing the stray strands of hair away from her face, her movements jerky and unsure. She motioned to the desk. "Have a seat."

He pulled the chair from the second desk over beside hers, his shoulders tensed at the nerves projecting off Meg. He kept his tone light and friendly. "So, tell me what's not making sense."

Her long bangs fluttered as she sighed. "It's all confusing, but the app we use to synch with our accounting software doesn't seem to be calculating the taxes correctly. I know something is off, but I can't figure out what."

"Okay." He studied the screen. "What's the name of the app you're using?"

She told him and he googled the app, clicked on links, and scrolled through reviews. "Looks like others have been having the same issue."

"Oh." Her shoulders hunched, and she chewed her thumbnail. "What do I do?"

"Let's do a search for other integration apps and see what's out there." He used her keypad and searched for apps, clicking on those with the best reviews. He pointed at the screen. "There's—"

Meg grumbled when she heard the doorbells, and a customer entered the store. She stood. "I'll be right back."

Bryan tormented himself by watching the sway of her backside before digging into the task, identifying apps, reading the reviews. He found one that seemed to make the most sense for her needs.

She returned a few minutes later, wearing the same watchful expression she'd had when they started. "What'd you find?"

"I think you should download this one. It has over seven hundred reviews and a four-point-nine rating."

She leaned over his shoulder, her scent like a freshly washed blanket, and he gritted his teeth. "I can't afford another monthly payment for something that may not work."

"There's a free two-week trial. That should give us time to figure out if it works the way it says it should." Her eyes fluttered when he said, "us." He pretended he didn't notice.

"Okay. Is it just for taxes?"

"It should do everything the other app does. Hopefully better." He patted the seat next to his like a creepy Santa Claus playing nice for the kids. "Come take a look. You need to put in your password."

He walked her through the integration and started importing

her data, hyperaware of every move she made. The nervous way she tucked her hands between her knees and the adorable way she squinted at the screen, chewing the color from her lips. Whenever Meg left the room to see to a customer, Bryan would get up to pace, stretching his neck and cracking his knuckles—anything to recharge the focus it took for him to willfully ignore the energy pulsing between them.

He glanced at his watch, his stiff muscles crying for relief. "Play around with it, run some reports, let me know what you think." He stood and stretched his back.

"You're leaving?" she asked.

"I'm working at three and I need to run some errands before my shift." Or run a few miles in the sweltering heat—anything to take the edge off and drain his mind. "I'll stop by tomorrow and check on your progress." He swallowed a smile as she pouted at the screen. "What's wrong?"

"Play around with it?" She blinked up at him, her horror-stricken eyes like bullets to his heart. "Do you know who you're talking to?"

"Yes." He couldn't help it, he bopped her on the nose. "I'm talking to the owner of this store. You won't lose anything. If the app doesn't work the way you want it to, the other app is still functioning. And there's a lot more we can try."

Her shoulders slumped and she stared at the computer. "I kinda thought your offer of help meant you'd fix it for me."

She was unbearably cute sitting there begging to be coddled. He'd like to coddle her—in more ways than one—but like his students, she'd be worse off in the end. "You know the saying, 'Give a man a fish, and you feed him for a day. Teach a man to fish, and you feed him for a lifetime?'"

Meg scowled up at him, her expression not unlike like the petulant kids in his algebra class. "I bet your students really hate you sometimes."

"I bet you're right." But not as much as he'd hate himself for leaving her helpless.

Days later, Meg looked up from checking out a customer to find Eva loitering at the counter. As she wrapped a candle holder in bubble wrap and decorative tissue, she'd have bet all the money in her bank account Eva had come to snoop for details about Bryan. He'd been by three days in a row to check on Meg—three days too many to evade the prying eyes of her nosy neighbor.

"You're off your game," Meg said to Eva as the customer exited the store. "I expected to see you sooner."

Eva placed her palm, fingers outstretched, against her heart as if deeply offended. "I don't know what you're talking about." Her outrage as fake as the jewelry on her finger.

"He's helping with the books."

"Is that all he's helping you with?"

She was going to die of mortification right there on the spot. "Eva, stop. You sound like Lily. She sang the k-i-s-s-i-n-g song so many times last night I ended up singing it in the shower."

"And how are his kisses?"

Meg sniffed, lifting her chin in the air, and straightened the paper on the counter. "There haven't been any." The sulky sound of her voice grated. So much for playing it cool.

"Why in heavens not?"

"Why do you think? He's going home at the end of the summer."

"And?"

"What do you mean 'and'? Isn't that enough?"

"I don't know." She pointed at Meg's face, her rhinestone ring glittering in the overhead light. "Is it? And be honest with me *and* with yourself."

Her don't-mess-with-me tone took the fight out of Meg. She slumped against the counter, scrubbed her hands through her hair. "No, it's not. He's just so perfect." She tried to ignore the whine in her voice. "He's nice and good looking, and he's so great with Lily. He listens to her—really listens—and not just for show."

"I can see why you're keeping your distance," Eva said, her voice sopping in sarcasm. "Sounds like a real horror show."

"Eva …" Meg gripped the counter. "I'm trying to be smart."

"You are smart. Smart enough to recognize a catch when you see one. That man has it bad, even without any kisses. Why not do you both a favor and give him some?"

"I'm going to get my heart broken." Her quiet response and emotionless tone brooked no argument.

Eva patted Meg's hands like she was soothing an injured dog. "Do you think even if he stayed there's any guarantee you won't?"

"No." She sighed, long and deep, as confused as she'd ever been. Being around Bryan and pretending not to care was exhausting. "I'm scared, Eva. I'm falling for him. I put the brakes on anything physical, but being around him feels like tempting fate."

"So, push the gas and see what happens. Why not enjoy him while he's around?"

"It'll be that much harder when he leaves."

"You don't think he's falling too?"

Meg straightened and shook her head. "I don't know, but it doesn't matter. I'd never ask him to stay."

"Maybe he'll want you to ask. Maybe you won't need to ask."

Maybe, maybe, maybe. "And maybe I'll win the lottery and find a cure for Alzheimer's."

Eva spared Meg a pitying stare. "Honey, I know why you're careful. I get it, I really do. But if there's one thing this old life has taught me, it's that tomorrow is not guaranteed. All we have is today. So, deal with today. Do you want the man in your life today?"

Anything close to a denial would have been a lie. "Yes."

"Do you think your dad would give back any time he spent with your mom if he knew how she'd end up?"

Talk of her parents was like a slap to the face. "No. Of course not."

"Then there's your answer." She squeezed Meg's hand. "Enjoy today. Tomorrow will take care of itself."

Thirty-Five

Bryan stopped by A Day's Wait every day. To check Meg's progress. To be near her. To torture himself with her smiles and her gratitude. One night she relented and let him take her and Lily for dinner at one of his favorite waterfront dives. They ate fried shrimp and fried fish sandwiches while Lily prattled on about her days spent at outdoor adventure camp learning archery and how to care for the animals on the property.

Every day he woke with anticipation of seeing them again. Every night he went to sleep with Meg on his mind and Lily's laugh echoing in his ears. He was getting attached. Like a drug eating away at his organs, even though he knew it wasn't good for him, he simply couldn't stop.

He went by the store early Friday evening after his shift at the bar. Meg had made good progress with the app, running reports, and keeping him updated. She was smarter than she gave herself credit for. She also had more balls in the air than he felt comfortable with her handling on her own.

"Hey there." Meg came out of the back of the store carrying a box in her arms.

Bryan hustled over and took it from her, surprised by the weight. "Where to?"

"That table by the wall, please."

He set the box down and turned to face her, prepared to scold her for not using the hand truck when he stopped short. Something was different. Something was off.

Instead of wearing her usual shorts, top, and tennis shoes, Meg wore a black romper with slinky straps that left her shoulders and upper chest exposed. Her flip-flopped toes were painted a fire engine red, and she'd done something with makeup that made her eyes look impossibly large, impossibly green. He swallowed the shocking jolt of lust pooling in his mouth.

"Thank you." She tucked her hair behind her ear and gave him a shy smile.

He could smell her perfume in the air, something spicy and elusive. "You're welcome." He cleared the yearning from his voice. "How's it going?"

She shrugged one shoulder and angled her chin, a saucy grin on her lips. "It's going."

Bryan forgot what he'd asked. Forgot what day it was. Forgot his name and most of the alphabet. For someone who wanted him in the friend zone, Meg was acting like a woman on the prowl. Confused and more than a little suspicious, he stepped back. "Do you … ah … have plans?"

A wrinkle formed between her brows. "Why?"

"I don't know. You look …" He waved his hand up and down in front of her. "… fancy."

"Oh, this?" She looked down at herself, a blush coloring her cheeks. "It's old and it's Friday and I thought, what the heck."

What the heck was right. What the heck was she doing to him, standing there like his fantasy come to life? And what the heck was he supposed to say now? "Uh … have you had any more time to play around with the app?"

Good one, Bryan. Way to kill the vibe.

"A little." She pulled her bottom lip between her teeth, drawing his eyes to her mouth.

His body temperature notched upward, and his lungs felt heavy and full. "Is it hot in here?"

"Maybe. Come on back and I'll turn on the fan."

Her skin beneath those itsy-bitsy straps glistened like his favorite butter pecan ice cream, tempting and rich. He shook his head and reined in his imagination. She was young. She was single. Just because she didn't want to go out with him didn't mean she never went out. He ground his molars. Did she have a date?

She circled the desk and leaned over to switch on the fan, giving him a generous view of her cleavage. Bryan clenched his jaw harder and looked away, unsure whether to advance or retreat. When she stood up and the fan's airflow brushed her hair back like a freaking model, all the blood rushed from his head. She had to know what she was doing to him. *Right?*

"Ummm," she purred, closing her eyes. "That feels amazing."

He was seconds away from embarrassing himself. "Got any reports?" His voice sounded weak and winded.

"Ah, yeah." She sat down and settled her hand over the mouse, her tongue flicking to the corner of her lips.

He joined her behind the screen, adjusting himself in the process.

"Here's the latest report. I'm no expert, but everything seems to be working the way it's supposed to." She waved her hand at the screen and then brushed his arm with her fingertips. He could have sworn he felt her squeeze his bicep.

"Good." He couldn't clear his throat enough to make his voice sound unaffected. "Do you think you're ready to delete the other app?"

"I don't know." She looked at him, her eyes as mesmerizing as an enchanted forest. "What do you think?"

He couldn't think at all, not with her gaze like that snake in the children's book—hypnotic and luring him under her spell. When her eyes lowered to his mouth and held, and she leaned infinitesimally closer, breath by seductive breath, his brain melted and leaked out his ears.

The world stopped moving as soon as her lips touched his and she made that noise in her throat whenever they kissed—part moan, part growl—and plunged her fingers into his hair.

Stunned and aroused beyond salvation, Bryan summoned herculean strength he didn't know he possessed to resist when everything inside of him cheered for him to take what she offered and plunder ahead—darn the consequences. But no matter how much he wanted her, no matter how thick his blood ran, no matter how many times he'd dreamed of this exact sequence of events— usually ending with him taking her on the desk—he wouldn't react. He couldn't.

Meg pulled away when he didn't respond, embarrassment pinking her cheeks. "I'm sorry. I ... I shouldn't have kissed you."

It took more time than a few beats for his brain to reengage. All he could manage was a strangled, "Why?"

She bit her lip hard. "I thought ... I thought you wanted me to."

He growled through clenched teeth, his chest filling with quick dry cement. "I do want to kiss you, Meg. More than anything. But you told me no."

"I ..." She swallowed, pushing the hair from her face with both hands. "I know. I sound like a lunatic, telling you no and then crawling all over you like a cat in heat." She shot to her feet and paced to the door before turning back to face him. "I can't stop thinking about you." Her voice and her shoulders lifted, her tone woeful and resigned. "I can't stop wanting you. Even knowing how this ends ..." She lifted her palms. "I can't stop. So, I thought maybe ... maybe we should just give in and get it over with. Get it out of our system."

He swallowed the mind-numbing shock. "Get it out of our system?" Did she really think making love would be an end and not the beginning of something bigger than them both?

"You know. Scratch the itch. Strike while the iron's hot. All the other stupid cliches that end with you and me in bed together."

His breath quickened and he couldn't grasp her theory when it kept rushing through so many holes. He sat frozen in the chair, trying to devise a response—in part waiting for her to laugh and say she was joking—but she just stood staring at him, her crossed her arms over her stomach as if holding it in place.

"I thought I could handle being around you." Her deadpan expression and needy tone twisted his gut. "But I'm weak and I'm needy and I might just explode if you don't put your hands on me soon."

She threw him a curve ball. Heck, she'd changed whole freaking game. If this was a test of his willpower, he was about to blow the lead. "I'm not—we're not—in your storeroom."

She laughed then, raspy and relieved, loosening the concrete in his chest. "Are you kidding? The walls are so thin I'd never do anything here."

Dear Lord. This was real. This was happening. "Where?"

"Anywhere." Her smile bloomed, reckless and free. "Your place. Mine."

"What about Lily?"

"She's sleeping at Eva and Barb's."

He stood unsteadily and closed the distance between them, gripping her arms in his hands. "Close the shop. Do it now. Do it now and let's go."

The knowing glint in her eye sent an arrow straight to his groin. He reached for her hand as she turned to go to the front of the store, wrapped his fingers around her wrist. "Meg, you need to know, as far as I'm concerned, there's no getting you out of my system. You're already there. And once you're all the way in, I won't be so easy to shake."

Thirty-Six

Meg turned her head away from the light slashing through her blinds. She stretched, her muscles protesting, and her knee hit something hard. Her eyes shot open, and she turned her head to the side. She was naked in bed with Bryan, his chiseled chest peeking out from under her soft sage sheet. He lay sprawled beside her, blissfully asleep. Blissfully beautiful.

Images from the night before played like an X-rated movie through her mind. The frantic drive across town to her apartment, shedding their clothes just inside the door, him lifting her and dropping her on top of the bed, staring at her with lust and something else in his eyes, something she couldn't name, something that sent a shocking thrill up her spine before he joined her and never let up.

After a couple of mind-blowing rounds, they ventured out of bed for food. Like gas to an empty race car, the frozen pizza and beer goosed their engines for a longer ride. They succumbed to exhaustion only a few hours before daybreak.

Even with her limited experience, Meg knew the man had skills. She had sore muscles and beard burn in interesting places to prove it—along with a healthy dose of embarrassment. She'd done things, said things, let him do things to her that she'd never imagined possible. If anyone from his school district had heard the naughty words he'd panted in her ear, she was pretty sure he'd lose his license. Or be in jail. Possibly both.

She was playing with fire. They both were. In the end, she'd be the one to get burned. But nothing in the tornado of emotions left to process was anything close to regret. She wanted him again, even now still sore from their last encounter. She lifted the sheet, looked her fill. He was the most beautiful man she'd ever seen, and he was hers for the taking.

Desire for him twisted her ribcage, melted her core. She angled herself above him, took him deep, watched his face as he began to stir, his body a step ahead.

His eyes opened to slits and he reached for her, her name like an answered prayer. "Meg."

She moved in liquid motion, watching him watching her. He'd called her beautiful more than once in the night. She'd never felt more beautiful than she did in this moment, drawing him up and out of sleep, taking everything he had to offer. And then taking more.

Sated, her muscles loose and tingly, Meg snuggled into the crook of his arm. "Good morning."

Bryan's deep, well-pleasured hum was the icing on her homemade cupcake. "Feel free to wake me like that whenever you want."

Meg rested her chin on his chest as everything they'd been running from the night before swam into focus. "Since we won't often have the chance to wake up together, I thought I should take advantage." Unfortunately for both, that wouldn't be much. "Bryan?"

He opened his eyes to slits, crooked his head like he was about to spout something about his recovery time, but he pulled up when he saw her face. "I hope you're not going to lie and say this will never happen again."

"I'm not going to lie."

"Good—"

"But …" She placed the pad of her finger on his lips, stopping his slide back to sleep. "We need to understand each other."

He played with the ends of her hair. "I think we understand each other just fine."

"We can't do this when Lily's home."

His hand stilled and his voice turned tap-water cold. "Lily's always home."

"Not always. I can ask favors, reach out to friends."

Bryan scowled and moved to sit up, dislodging the sheet.

Meg scrambled for the fabric, held it tight against her chest. She learned while eating pizza the night before he wouldn't even hear her if she sat naked on the bed.

Bryan leaned against her bed frame, his expression as sober as his tone. "I want to spend time with you, Meg. And I like Lily. I like hanging out with her. I'm not going to sneak around like this is something to hide." He cupped her cheek in his calloused palm, ran his thumb along her mouth. "We're good together—in and out of bed."

She couldn't deny it, so she didn't even try. "I have to put Lily's needs first."

"I'm not asking to you put my needs before Lily. I'm asking you to treat us like we're not some dirty secret." He ran a frustrated hand through his mass of wild hair, mussing it more. "We're grown, consenting adults. What we do together is no one's business."

In theory, sure. But watching Lily suffer because of her mother's personal business hardened Meg's resolve. "It'll be Lily's business. She lives here too."

"You think I don't know that?"

And he'd called her stubborn. She tried a different tack. "You're a teacher who works with teenagers. You know how they talk, how they judge. She's suffered enough with her mom dying while away with a man."

He blinked, and the pause before he answered told Meg she'd hit her mark. "I know kids talk." His expression soured into something like a pout. "I also know that if you treat this like a cheap affair, so will everyone else."

"There's a difference between treating this like a cheap affair and not throwing it in Lily's face."

"Do you really believe people won't talk about the bartender who sneaks into your bed when Lily is away?"

Meg wasn't looking for logic or an argument. She was looking for agreement. Why couldn't he just agree? "Stop twisting my words. I'm just saying—"

"It's complicated." He reached for her hand where she'd fisted the sheet and folded it into his. "You and I together has always been complicated. There is no easy answer and there can't be any hard and fast rules."

"I'm not setting rules."

"Good, because I'm the teacher. Leave the rules to me." He tugged her closer, set his lips at the base of her neck.

His charm wouldn't work. Not this time. Not with hers and Lily's reputations at stake. "I'm trying to be responsible."

"You're the most responsible woman I've ever known." He dragged his lips upwards, his tongue leading the charge. "No one who knows you thinks you'd jump into bed with someone without thinking it through first."

Her head fell backward, her eyes drifting closed. "I wasn't exactly thinking with my brain." Then or now.

"I like it when you don't think with your brain. If you were thinking with your brain, you never would have told me to …" He put his lips to her ear and repeated one of her more colorful demands.

Her forehead landed with a thud against his chest. "This feels like blackmail."

"It's not blackmail." Bryan cradled her face in his palms, lifting her face to his. "It's the beginning of something really, really good. For both of us."

For how long? The words were on the tip of her tongue, pressing against her clamped teeth, searching for escape.

He brought his lips to hers, drew her to him, drew the drawstring of her reasoning skills closed tight. She melted against him as if pulled by a force stronger than her willpower, stronger than her resolve to keep things light. He was exploiting her weakness, bending her to his will. And he was right. At the end of the day, nothing and no one would stop them from being together. Fatalist that she was, she simply couldn't resist.

He pulled back, a smug smile on his too-handsome face. "I told you I wouldn't be easy to shake and I'm not going to be easy to control. I want you in my life, Meg. You *and* Lily." He flung his legs over the side of the bed and picked up his boxers, pulling them on to her great relief. "I'm starving. I saw some eggs in your refrigerator last night and I make a mean omelet."

He rubbed his hands together and made for the kitchen leaving Meg to sigh in his wake. He could make a mean omelet, kiss her stupid, turn her body to mush in his hands. But at the end of the summer, no matter how good they were together, he'd be gone. She was already mourning his loss.

Bryan kissed Meg long and slow in the front seat of her car, over the whistling of her loose belt. She'd just given him the most incredible experience of his life. He was in too good a mood to mention he wanted a peek under the car's hood.

Meg pulled back first, but he snagged her bottom lip between his teeth, holding her captive. The taste of her was the sweetest candy on earth and he had a craving. When she set her hands on his chest and pushed, he figured he'd pushed his luck far enough.

"Get out," she said on a laugh. "I have to get to work."

"Okay, okay. I just needed a little to keep me going through the day."

"That'll have to do for a while." Her tone shifted low and quiet. "Lily's home tonight."

He felt the chill, ignored it, plowed ahead undeterred. "Saturday's date night. And Dustin's playing at the bar."

She cocked her head, and the air conditioner scattered the laundry-scented shampoo through the car. "Bringing a twelve-year-old to the bar on a Tuesday night was one thing. Taking her on a Saturday is not going to happen."

"Okay." He nodded, readjusting his plans. "How about I bring dinner? We can play cards or watch a movie."

"Bryan …" She stink-eyed the steering wheel.

He needed to mind his steps in the gap between pushing his luck and admitting defeat. "What's the problem?"

"I told her she could invite a camp friend over to watch a movie. It would be weird if you were there."

"You can't have a friend over too?"

Her hand on his face felt more than a little condescending. "Come on, I thought we talked about this."

She'd talked, he'd listened, they'd yet to agree. The clock was ticking, and he didn't have time to waste. "How am I supposed to court you if you won't let me come around?"

"You don't have to court me. I'm caught." She kissed him, light and sweet on the cheek, but that felt condescending too. "Give me a little time to work out the details. That's all I'm asking."

We don't have much time. He smothered the words and sighed instead. "Okay." He held his finger and thumb a fraction apart. "A little time. How about Sunday?"

She rolled her eyes. "You're relentless."

He was half-gone and frustrated and frighteningly close to showing his cards. Dealing with Meg was like playing poker and Bryan had never been good at holding his cards. "Think about it and let me know."

"I will." She pleased him by leaning over the console and giving him a quick kiss on the lips. "Now go. Do whatever you do when we're not together."

He didn't have to wonder how he'd spend their time apart. He'd think about her, come up with ways to see her again, and replay the more creative aspects of their time together on a continual loop in his head. "If you insist."

The sound of her car pulling away was like a taser attached to his eyeball. That belt needed to be replaced. He felt it all the way to his toes. He had to get his hands under her hood—and fast. But first, he needed to change out of his clothes from the day before.

The smell of stale coffee greeted Bryan as he opened the door.

Dustin came out of the bathroom wearing ratty shorts and holding one of Corey's paperbacks in his hand. He crossed his arms over his chest. "I was about to report you missing."

"I'm found, brother." He tried to smother the smug smile dying to break free. "Call off the search."

Dustin flashed his brows. He knew Bryan too well not to see his good mood and lazy swagger as anything other than what it was. "Son of a gun. You nailed the shopkeep."

"Hey." Bryan's tone was a warning shot, pointed and fierce. "Don't talk about Meg like that."

"She's not a shopkeep?"

"She's not some girl I nailed. I swear, you're less mature than my students." Restless and irritated, he turned into the kitchen to dump the coffee grinds and empty the pot.

It took more than a sharp tone to throw Dustin off his trail or to stop him from hulking like a shadow in the room. "You're awfully grumpy for someone who just got lucky."

Bryan ignored him and went into the bedroom to change his clothes.

"That good, huh?" Dustin leaned against the threshold in what Bryan had come to think of as his spot. "It's okay. I can tell it was good."

Could he tell Bryan wanted to be alone? He whipped the shirt from his back and tossed it into the full bin in the corner, considered throwing in a load in before work. He caught a whiff of Meg's soap, pictured her against the shower tiles, remembered her soapy hands on his skin, and felt marginally better.

"Those scratch marks on your back look fresh."

Bryan clamped his teeth and slipped his hands inside the waistband of his shorts. "You gonna do a body search or can I change my clothes?"

Dustin turned around but didn't leave. "Is there a hickey under all that scruff?" The laugh in his voice was unmistakable.

Bryan didn't answer. He was too busy lamenting having to share the apartment with a friend he'd known so long the line between appropriate and mind-your-own-business didn't exist.

"You're not going to tell me anything?"

"Nope."

Like a dog hankering after a bone, Dustin followed him into the den, sat across from him on the chair, and pointed the paperback at his face. "You don't just like this girl, do you?"

Bryan pinged Dustin with a no-duh stare and considered his options. While talking things out with Dustin might help Bryan, he'd be putting Meg's personal business in the crosshairs—and that didn't sit right.

Dustin stretched his legs and linked his fingers across his belly. "You need to be careful."

Being careful sounded a lot like Meg's earlier request to give her some time. Both suggestions grated on Bryan's keyed-up nerves. "Why?"

"For all intents and purposes, Meg's got a kid."

Bryan leaned back against the couch and flopped his hands in the air. "Why does everyone assume I've forgotten about Lily?"

"Lily makes this different. She adds a whole other level to whatever this thing is you've got going with Meg."

"A week ago, you told me not to give up hope."

"A week ago, I thought there was no hope. Meg didn't strike me as wishy-washy."

"She's not."

"So, what happened?" Dustin flashed his palm. "Not the details—I know you got laid—just the facts."

Bryan figured he could share the facts without infringing on Meg's privacy. "Meg suggested we get it out of our system."

Dustin's low, throaty laugh grated on Bryan's nerves. "She doesn't know you very well, does she?"

"What is that supposed to mean?"

"It means you're not the love 'em and leave 'em kind of guy. That was Corey. You're the long haul, til-death kind of guy. The guy who even now, sitting here throwing daggers at me with your eyes, is trying to figure out how to get Meg to move home with you. Tell me I'm wrong."

He wasn't wrong. Darn Dustin and their stupid lifelong friendship. "What's wrong with that? I mean, what's her future here all alone raising Lily and working her fingers to the bone?"

"The same future she had before you met her. Meg's not alone, Bryan. She's got friends—a lot of them. Eva and Barb are like doting grandmothers. Tim's said enough to know they look out for their own on the island. Meg's one of their own."

Tiny fingers tickled the base of Bryan's skull. "You talked to Tim about Meg?"

"He asked me what was going on with you two. I told him y'all were dancing around each other. I guess I'll have to revise my answer."

Tim's interest in Meg grated on Bryan's nerves even knowing it came from a good place. "I think you've said enough." Bryan settled his elbows on his knees and plowed his fingers through his hair. "If Tim asks about Meg again, tell him to come to me."

"I don't think he was trying to stir up trouble."

Bryan stood, shucking his hands onto his hips. "Then he shouldn't have any problem coming to the source."

"A word of advice." Dustin's normally affable voice held a subtle warning, stopping Bryan on his way to the bedroom to get his laundry. "If you want to keep the job that lets you stay near Meg, you may want to change your tone when talking to your boss."

His *temporary* boss. Everything about the island was temporary. His job, his life, his time. Everything but Meg.

Thirty-Seven

Meg couldn't wipe the smile from her face or disguise her better than average mood. Maybe better than ever. Repeated—and let's face it—stupendous sex was like adding color to her black and white life. She'd never felt so relaxed or so alive.

The way Bryan looked at her while whisking an omelet or peeling the clothes from her body, like he could see behind every single one of her insecurities straight to her soul, should have scared the wits out of her. Somehow it didn't. Somehow, *he* didn't.

After Zander, she'd cut herself off from even thinking about taking a chance with another man. It took someone like Bryan, someone who didn't yield and scoffed at her snubs to tear down her walls. And tear down he did.

No wonder her sister had gotten caught in the barnacle's sights. If he was anywhere as accomplished as his brother, she hadn't had a choice. Guilt tried and failed to wiggle its way in. Meg never would have met Bryan if Amanda hadn't passed away with his brother.

Or would she?

There was no way to guess what would have happened between Meg's sister and Bryan's brother if they'd lived and come home as planned. One or both could have gotten bored, and their relationship could have fizzled as quickly as it began. Or Amanda could have come home feeling like she'd found her other half.

Maybe Amanda could have changed the barnacle from the man Meg despised into a man she could respect. Maybe Meg and Bryan would have met at their wedding or a family gathering of some sort? Or maybe she was grasping at straws to justify her satisfaction at the hands of a man she never would have met if her sister hadn't died.

Thanks to fate or dumb luck or a combination of both, Meg and Bryan met and merged like two halves of the same whole. *No, no, no.* Meg grabbed her squeamish stomach. She couldn't think of Bryan as her other half. They'd had sex—really, really, good sex that released an amazing amount of pent-up tension in her overwrought body. For that alone she was grateful.

Lily appeared before her as if she'd materialized out of thin air, waving a hand in front of Meg's face. "Hello? Earth to Aunt Meg."

Meg startled and pasted on a smile. "Hi. You caught me daydreaming."

"Looked like you were talking to yourself."

Her Irish skin flared. "That too." Movement at the front of the store drew her eye. "Hey, Eva. Thanks for having Lily last night."

Lily pulled a plate from behind her back and presented it to Meg. "We made carrot cake from scratch. Eva said we had to save you a piece."

"Wow." Meg gawked at the three-tiered masterpiece. "That looks delicious."

"I never thought I'd like a cake made with carrots, but it's really good. Here," she shoved the paper plate with a huge piece in Meg's face. "Try it."

Meg pushed the edge of the plate away from her nose. "It's a little early for cake. Why don't you take this and put it in the fridge? I'll have it later."

Lily shrugged and headed toward the back.

Meg watched her walk, her suntanned skin, her gangly gait, and a wave of love for Lily nearly brought her to her knees. "I picked up that beading kit you were talking about the other day. It's on the desk."

Lily turned to flash her beaming face at Meg, and she raced to the back.

"Don't forget to the put the cake in the fridge." Meg shook her head at Eva. "Carrot cake, huh?"

"She's got a real knack for baking. Like her grandma." Eva patted her belly. "I used to gain ten pounds, thanks to your mother's Christmas cookies."

The bittersweet memory of her mom in the kitchen, flour dust dancing in the air, with cookies on every available surface, glittered like a hidden gem in her mind. "I miss those days so much. Seems like yesterday and a million years ago all at once."

"Yes, it does." So ..." Eva leaned against the counter, fluttered her lashes at Meg. "How was your evening?"

The topic change was expected, but no less annoying, if only for the blush she felt creeping up her neck. "It was great. Thanks for watching her."

"Great?" Eva angled her head and gave Meg a disbelieving stare. "That's not what your face says."

Despite her flaming cheeks, Meg tried to play it cool. "What does my face say?"

"It says Bryan is as good in bed as he is behind the bar."

"Eva!" Meg scanned the back for any sign of Lily. "Keep your voice down."

"Am I right?"

Meg lifted her chin in the air. "Yes, and that's all I'm going to say."

"I knew it." Eva's face fanned into a perceptive smile. "And he's nice to boot. When will you see him next?"

Meg glanced at the back once more. "He wanted to come over tonight and hang out with me and Lily, but she's got a friend from camp coming over, so I told him no."

"What? Why?"

"What do you mean, 'why'? I don't want to push this on Lily too soon."

"The man is only here for so long. You don't have a lot of time to drag your feet."

Eva could have been the devil on her shoulder who'd spent the better part of the morning battling the angel on the other. "That's exactly why I need to take my time. Eva, this is serious. I took your advice, and it was amazing. He's amazing. But if I spend a lot of time with him before he goes …"

"Then what?"

"You know what. I get hurt." What she wanted to say was she'd get hurt worse. Because even if Bryan left today, she'd be hurt. Way worse than she'd ever been hurt before. Zander's rejection was a pin prick compared to how she'd feel when Bryan eventually left. And Lily …

Eva sighed, shaking her head at Meg like she'd never been more disappointed. "Stop being such a fatalist. I swear, if your mother was here, she'd slap you silly."

"For being careful? I think she'd call me smart."

"Really? You think your mother, the woman who ditched a college scholarship and a comfortable life to run away with your father, would call you smart for blowing the chance at a once in a lifetime love?"

Her mother didn't need to be there. Eva's words were as harsh as a slap. "I never said anything about love."

"You didn't have to. I know you, Megan Holloway. I've known you since you were a snot-nosed kid trying every way you could think of to hide your soft and tender heart. You're not afraid to let Bryan in because he's already in. You're afraid of letting him go."

"Can you blame me? It's not like guys like him come around all the time." Or anytime. *Ever.*

Eva stared at her, and if pity were an evening gown, Eva wore it like a Broadway star. "You know what's worse than heartbreak?"

"Seeing it coming from a mile away and not being able to stop it?"

"Regret." Her gentle tone shook Meg to the core. "It'll eat you up inside—bones and all. Trust me on this one."

The door bells jangled and a group of women entered the store chattering between themselves. Eva straightened but didn't take her eyes off Meg. "I'd take heartbreak over regret any day of the week."

With Meg's refusal to see him, and nothing to keep him from crashing her place unannounced, Bryan offered to stay and work a double shift at Westies. The Saturday crowd shifted with the change from day to night. Lunch had been alive with tourists from all corners of the world needing food and drinks to fuel the rest of their day. Dinnertime and beyond was a mixture of locals and bed and breakfast guests looking for good food and live music along one of the Key's most iconic streets.

Bryan's mood was a lot like the weather. Hot and sweaty memories of the night before mixed with hot and steamy annoyance over his boss's prodding Dustin for information about their relationship. At the start of Bryan's second shift, a distracted Tim emerged from the kitchen with a box of liquor in his hands after being unusually absent from the bar for most of the day.

"Hey, man," Tim said when he spotted Bryan pouring a draft. "Why are you still here?"

He failed to find annoyance in Tim's voice. "I offered to stay, and Katie was more than happy to have a night off with her daughter."

Tim set the box on the ground. "You looking for extra tips?"

Bryan helped Tim empty the case. It was easy to feel annoyed from a distance. Up close and personal, it was harder to assign ill intent. Tim was a friend. "Dustin's playing, so I may as well make money while I listen."

"Guy's good." Tim inspected a bottle of gin. "Better than I thought he'd be. I've had more than a few people ask when he's playing again." He scanned the bar with a satisfied grin before placing the bottle on the shelf. "Place is filling up."

Pride and an awed sense of wonder inflated Bryan's chest. Dustin *was* good, and performing for others—getting him out of his own head—was healing. "He'll keep them entertained. I'm not sure what he's better at, the music or the commentary."

"He's an entertainer. Even the best musicians can't succeed with a live crowd without a personality to match. Your boy's got both."

Bryan placed his palm over his heart and made his voice sound choked up. "I'm so proud."

Tim shucked him on the shoulder and headed into the back. The smile dropped from Bryan's face. He had to find a way to bring Meg up without cutting Tim to the quick. His boss had been too nice to Bryan to let ill-feelings bubble over and burn a bridge.

It hadn't taken long for Bryan to realize the emotion swelling beneath the surface was envy. He was jealous of Tim's sly interest in Meg. Jealous of the time he'd have with her once Bryan was gone.

Meg was a beautiful woman, if not a little young for Tim. Maybe Tim planned to swoop in and rescue her and Lily from a lonely life on the island and Bryan had thwarted his plans. Tim was too nice a guy to do anything but stand back and wait for them to fizzle as soon as Bryan left for home. He unclenched his rigid jaw and forced a smile at the customers who approached the bar.

The chatter muted when Dustin appeared on stage, wearing khaki shorts and a t-shirt. After dragging a stool from the corner of the stage to the microphone, he folded himself over Tim's guitar and gave the audience an awe-shucks smile. He strummed some chords and tuned the guitar as he introduced himself and the song that was his opener.

The music and the steady stream of customers leveled Bryan's mood. Jealous or not, he'd had the night of his life with Meg. Whatever Tim's feelings were for Meg, Bryan's main competition wasn't with his boss. It was the lingering ghost of a past boyfriend fool enough to leave her when things got tough. Meg was better off without him.

Tim pitched in at the bar throughout the night between talking with friends and restocking supplies. Lost in his head and in the continuous flow of patrons, Bryan made drinks, pulled beers from the tap, and fielded questions about the night's musician.

Dustin's set list had improved from his debut performance. He'd worked to vary his songs by tempo and key, and style and rhythm. Jazzed by the crowd's enthusiastic response, Dustin played without stopping until he ran out of material and started taking requests.

The bar began to empty after one in the morning. Bryan, with two shifts on his feet, felt every hour in the small of his back.

Tim clutched his shoulder and squeezed. "You're dead on your feet. Go," he said. "I can handle the rest."

Bryan scanned the stragglers for Dustin, found him surrounded by a trio of starstruck women. Instinct warred with exhaustion. Instinct won. "Appreciate it. If you don't mind, I'll have a beer, stick around, keep an eye on the rockstar."

"He's on a leash?"

Bryan glared at Tim, wondered what he meant by that critical tone. "I told you about his marriage."

Tim spared him a half-lidded nod like he was halfway to baked. "Wife kicked him out."

"It's more like a mutual break." Bryan skirted the bar and slumped onto a stool. His feet wept in relief.

"You know his wife?" Tim asked.

"I've known them both since we were kids. Tegan's great. They're great together."

He poured a draft for Bryan with the perfect amount of foam and handed it over the bar. "If they're so great together, why is he here?"

The million-dollar question. "I think he needed to get out of town, get away from his life and figure things out." Bryan sipped and savored. There was nothing like a cold draft beer after a long, hot shift. "I try not to judge since I've never been married, but I know he loves her. And I'm not going to let him do something stupid just because he's feeling himself."

"From bartender to wing man." Tim tilted his head, gave Bryan a sympathetic stare. "You're a good friend."

Bryan's neck tingled. His jealous feelings felt petty and small. He sipped his beer, checked on Dustin. He seemed to be getting bored with the attention, reaching behind him to gather his guitar. When he unplugged the amp, a screeching sound not unlike Meg's belt soured the air.

"Hey," Bryan said to Tim. "Can you recommend a mechanic?"

"Having trouble with your truck?"

"Meg's car has a loose belt, a bum headlight, and God knows what else going on under the hood. I can replace the belt and the headlight, but I want to get the car checked from top to bottom."

Tim stilled, his gaze sharpening like a hawk on the hunt. "So, the rumors are true?"

Bryan kept his voice light, decided to play dumb. "What rumors?"

"You and Meg."

Bryan dipped his chin, flashed a look that was one part chummy and three parts nothing-to-see here. "We're …" Sleeping together, while true, sounded cheap and fleeting and would probably get under Tim's skin. Falling fast *was* true—at least for Bryan—but Tim wasn't going to be the first to hear about it. "… together."

Tim's nod was both vague and revealing. "I see."

Bryan couldn't ignore the censure in his tone. "You have a problem with that?"

"No." The way Tim extended the word and looked Bryan in the eye, he knew his denial was conditional. "As long as she doesn't get hurt."

"I would never hurt Meg."

"You still leaving at the end of the summer?"

His snappish comeback put Bryan in the hot seat. He didn't like it one bit. "More than likely."

"And how does Meg feel about that?"

Bryan took a breath and counted backward from five the way he did when dealing with an abrasive student. "You'll have to ask Meg about her feelings, but I think I need to ask about yours."

Tim flipped a rag over his shoulder and leaned against the counter, his expression carefully guarded. "Meg's a friend."

"Is that all she is?"

"That's it. She's a friend who's been through a lot—her parents gone, her sister dead." His eyes clouded and his voice dropped. "I lost some guys in the war who were like brothers, and I don't have to tell *you* what it's like to lose a brother. But Meg's fragile. I don't want to see her hurt so soon after losing Amanda."

Bryan disagreed with Tim's opinion. Meg had been through a lot, no question, but she was far from fragile. Meg would hate that label. "I'd rather cut off my arm than hurt Meg."

"Then don't. If your answer doesn't change from 'more than likely' to 'no', then leave her be. She's been through enough."

Bryan had little to no defense against a man who'd survived war and could probably kill him with his bare hands.

"And if you want to do something for Meg …" Tim picked up the rag and started wiping the bar with more force than before. "Fix her car, help her with the books, and leave her better than you found her. And find out where she stores the storm windows. There's a hurricane brewing in the Atlantic. Long range forecast says we could be in for a direct hit."

Thirty-Eight

Meg slept like the dead. After little to no sleep the night before, her body sore in places both shocking and unfamiliar, she hit the bed and never moved until the sun streamed through the cracks in her blinds. She inhaled, savoring the lingering smell of Bryan's scent on her sheets, and stretched. Even though she needed a solid, uninterrupted eight hours of sleep, she still felt the tiniest twinge of disappointment he hadn't tossed pebbles at her window like a lovesick fool.

If anyone was a lovesick fool it was the bleary-eyed woman staring back at her in the mirror, her hair in tangles, her stomach in knots. She brushed her teeth and wondered how she'd face the days after he left the island.

Deep inside she knew she'd pine for him, wonder what he was doing and who he was with. Images of his past girlfriends—the teacher and the teller—battling for his affection played through her mind and brought a scowl to her face. If she was jealous after one night, how jealous would she be after weeks of letting him share her bed and her life. She was too weak to keep him away much longer.

The smell of freshly brewed coffee wafted into her bedroom, had her waltzing into the kitchen wearing her tank top and sleep shorts in search of the source. She blinked at Bryan, shower fresh and pouring coffee into her *Coffee Before Talkie* mug, while Lily shoved a chocolate glazed donut into her mouth. "Wha ..."

"Good morning, sunshine." He gave her an appreciative up down and handed her the cup, pecking a kiss on her temple before nudging her toward the refrigerator. "I brought flavored creamer. It's in the fridge."

Her mind wouldn't engage. Not with him standing in her kitchen like a gorgeous illusion she'd conjured with her mind. "How ...?"

"I let him in." Lily sat at the table with a mouthful of donut, her lips smeared with chocolate.

Meg did as instructed, found the creamer in her refrigerator, and poured a splash in her cup. She turned, repeated the process with his freshly poured cup, and put the creamer back in the fridge. The hit of caffeine was like a jolt to her system, firing oxygen to her still-sleepy brain. She leaned against the counter, cradling the cup in her hands. "What are you doing here?"

"I found this great donut shop."

Oh, that grin of his combined with the stubble on his face did funny things to her heart. "And?"

Her mirrored her position, leaning against the counter on the opposite side of the sink. "Dustin's still sleeping."

The three of them in the kitchen sharing coffee and donuts

made her stomach feel inside out, an odd gut punch of missing Amanda and a base-level longing for physical connection. "How was his show last night?"

"It was great. He was relaxed and funny, and he worked on his play set, so the music just flowed." He angled his head at Lily. "The crowd ate him up the way your girl eats a donut." He winked at Lily licking chocolate from her fingers before looking back at Meg. Her stomach tumbled. "He's good and he's happy. I wish Tegan could see him on stage."

Meg set the cup down. With nothing in her hands, she was suddenly conscious of how she looked—braless and bedraggled and straight from bed. She reached for a powdered sugar donut and took a bite. "Are you thinking of calling her?"

Bryan twisted his lips, his finger tapping the cup in his hand. "I don't want to get in the middle of whatever's going on between them."

"But?"

"He said from the beginning she wanted him happy. The only time he's happy is when he's on stage. The rest of the time he's missing her like crazy. They've been together so long he doesn't know who he is without her."

Meg took the hit, felt the burn. She looked at Lily and they shared a knowing look. "We get it. That's how it feels with Amanda gone. We're still trying to figure out who we are without her."

Bryan looked at her like she'd kicked him in the balls, his face pinched and his shoulders slumped. "I'm sorry. I didn't mean to …"

"You didn't." Meg carried her mug to the table and took a seat next to Lily, desperate for a lighter mood. "Are you going to join us?"

He sat at their round table, a hulking presence in the cramped room, and draped his arm over the back of Meg's chair, fingering the ends of her hair. "What's on your schedule today?" he asked.

Meg ignored the feather-light brushes, intimate reminders of what they'd done in the dark. She'd wash her sheets before Lily caught his scent in her bedroom. "I've got laundry to do before going to the store, and Lily promised to start reading one of her summer books."

"They make you read?" Bryan shuddered for Lily's amusement. "In the summer?"

"Hey." Meg jabbed him with her foot under the table. "Aren't you a teacher?"

"Yeah, but I don't assign summer work. What kind of prison do you attend?"

"See?" The smile on Lily's face was huge, the likes of which Meg hadn't seen at this hour of the day in months. "He gets it."

Meg rolled her hand into a playful fist and shook it at Bryan. "He's gonna get it." She looked at Lily. "Why don't you go get your books? Mr. Smartypants can help you decide which one to read first."

Lily hopped up and disappeared inside her room. Meg blinked at Bryan, kept her voice playful and light. "How about a little support in the reading department?"

He leaned closer. "How about a proper good-morning kiss?" His smug smirk and husky tone lit a fire between her legs.

"Will you encourage her to read?"

"A kiss to pimp some reading? Sold." He let go of the back of her chair, wove his fingers through her hair, and aligned their mouths, watching her as he eased in slowly. The kiss was warm and tasted of vanilla, the perfect amount of pressure—not too light, not too demanding. Until he swiped his tongue inside her mouth, and the fire became a blaze. She forgot where she was—who she was—and gripped the collar of his shirt.

Bryan pulled away seconds before Lily breezed into the kitchen with two books held tightly to her chest, her head bobbing between Meg and Bryan, a suspicious look on her face.

Meg dropped her head, licking her lips to douse the flames from his kiss. Nothing could stop the embarrassment from coloring her cheeks.

Bryan rubbed his lips together, his smoldering gaze attached to Meg. He broke eye contact and smiled at Lily. "Whatcha got there, Lily-girl?"

Lily handed him the books. He examined the covers and flipped them over to read the back. "I'm a math and science guy, so I think this one about nature sounds cool."

Lily wrinkled her nose and tried to talk him into the other book, something about two girls trying to fit in at school, while Meg reminded herself to breathe. She watched the exchange, her blood flowing thick in her veins, and wondered how he could kiss her senseless and then change gears to carry on a conversation with Lily in a normal tone of voice like nothing had happened.

Lily decided to read Bryan's choice first, a major victory for him, by the grin on his face. Bryan stood, tucked the chair beneath the table, and looked at Meg for the first time since kissing her mute. "Walk me out?"

"Sure." She carried her cup to the sink, eyed her pajamas. "Give me a minute to change." She dressed quickly and avoided the mirror. He'd already seen her at her worst.

Bryan straightened when she exited her bedroom, opening the door and waving her ahead. He called to Lily on his way out, closing the door behind him.

His hand at the small of her back stoked the still-smoldering embers from his proper good-morning kiss. She stopped walking by his truck and turned to face him, braced for his proper goodbye.

He set his hands on her shoulders, eyeing her shorts and t-shirt. "I like the sexy pjs better."

"I'm sure you do." She surprised herself by leaning in and wrapping her arms around his waist and kissing the scruffy cleft in his chin. "This was a nice surprise."

"I wanted to see you." He dropped his hands to her waist, his fingers flexing before loosening his grip. A car in need of a muffler whizzed by on the road. "I missed you, Meg."

The knot in her stomach loosened before tightening at the look in his eyes. She was in so much trouble. "I missed you too."

Instead of the kiss she expected, he cleared his throat, and Meg stiffened at the strain in his voice. "I also wanted to ask about your storm windows."

She reared back, blinked up at him, the sun in her eyes. "My storm windows?"

Gone was the teasing tone he'd used with Lily. His expression soured like months old milk. "There's a tropical storm brewing in the Atlantic."

Relief and nostalgia mingled, flooded her veins. He sounded so much like her dad, always checking the weather, tracking the storms. "Bryan, it's hurricane season. There's always a storm in the Atlantic."

He gave her waist a squeeze. "The long-range forecast says we're right in its path."

"And when it gets closer, I'll start paying attention."

"Meg …" He packed a lot of frustration in that one little word. "How can you be so cavalier?"

"I'm not being cavalier—I'm being realistic. We go through this every summer. The last major hurricane hit in 2017."

"That was only five years ago."

"That was a lifetime ago. My parents were still on the island, my mom wasn't sick, and my sister was still alive." She shook her head, tried to shake the mocking from her voice. He hadn't been around then. He didn't know. "A lot has changed."

He mostly succeeded in hiding his impatience, but he couldn't hide the tension around his eyes or the pressure in his grip on her sides. "Did you evacuate?"

"We boarded the store and stayed with friends in Miami." Her parents always made evacuations seem like vacations. They did it, she knew, to lessen the worry, but it worked. Meg never dreaded hurricane season. It was just something they had to deal with like tourists and heatwaves. "Other than some minor flooding, we were fine."

"Tim's worried."

"Westies is at street level, so their flooding was worse. And Irma was his first storm. It spooked him."

"You didn't answer my question." He gave her a weak shake. "Where are your storm windows?"

She watched a car pull into the lot and turn in the opposite direction. "Behind the building in a storage unit."

"What else do you need to be prepared?"

"Nothing. I've got water-activated barriers in storage with the windows." She cupped his cheek, running her thumb over his face to soothe the tight lines around his mouth. She wouldn't tell him the worst part of the season would be when he'd be gone. "There's nothing to worry about."

His face told a different story, his eyes strained, his mouth in a thin line. She brushed her lips over his once, twice before his grip on her softened and he returned the kiss. He dropped his forehead to lean against hers. "I worry about you, Meg. You can't ask me not to."

"Then I won't ask. Thank you for breakfast."

"Next time an omelet?"

His meaning was crystal clear. "One of these days I may just let you."

"How about tomorrow?"

"How about I think about it?"

He gathered her close, close enough to feel his heartbeat thudding against her chest. "How about I give you something to think about?" He kissed her sinfully slow, deliberately tender. She was close enough to notice when other parts of him began to stir.

He took her deep, took her under. There was nothing she could do to stop the slow and steady drop. He'd overrule her with his passion and his logic, and she'd let him in and let him stay. The pull between them was just too strong.

When he gentled the kiss, she burrowed into his arms, inhaling his salty sweet skin. She was so far out of her depth she couldn't even see the bottom. But she knew what waited. No more kisses, no more surprise breakfasts, no more feeling like she had a partner.

And despite what Eva had promised, there'd be a mountain of regret. The question lingered just out of reach. Would she regret letting him in or letting him go?

Thirty-Nine

Bryan felt no guilt over pressuring Meg. Every day he made excuses to see her. Surprise breakfasts that occurred so regularly they became expected. Dinner invitations he gave her no chance to refuse. Lily was always on his side, urging Meg to agree. Harassed and exasperated, she eventually surrendered to him and her own desires.

It became their routine. They'd take turns cooking and doing the dishes, settling in after dinner to play games or to watch TV or to read. Lily would drift off to bed and Meg and Bryan would retreat to her room and make love.

In the beginning, they'd take their time exploring each other's bodies, learning what made them tick, what made them beg, what made them soar. As time passed and Bryan's deadline to leave got closer and closer, there was a frantic, almost desperate energy to their intimacy. One minute they were memorizing every dip and curve, the next they were wrestling for control.

They stopped trying to hide the fact that he stayed over when Lily told Meg him sneaking out of the apartment before dawn wasn't doing anything but waking her up early. Bryan and Meg never talked about him leaving. Bryan thought about the future. All. The. Time.

As July slipped into August, he saw Dustin less and less, breezing in and out of the apartment to shower and change clothes before and after work. Dustin didn't seem to mind or even notice. He worked on his music, worked for Meg when he got bored, and performed at Westies a couple nights a week.

On a muggy afternoon after his shift at the bar, Bryan found Dustin in his usual spot on the couch, strumming his guitar and jotting notes in a spiral notepad. His hands stilled when Bryan walked in.

"Hey, man," Bryan said. "Whatcha doing?"

"Just fooling around." He shrugged in a way that said it was more important than he let on. "Figured it wouldn't hurt to come up with something original."

"That's awesome." Bryan grabbed an apple from the counter and took a bite, peering over Dustin's shoulder at the gibberish on the paper. "I never could read music."

"You don't need to read music to enjoy it." He looked up at Bryan. "Haven't seen you in a while."

Bryan flashed a sorry-not-sorry grin. "Sorry about that."

"Don't apologize. At least one of us is getting some action." He gave the guitar one hard stroke. "I guess you and Meg are doing well?"

Depending on the metric, things were going well. Enjoying each other, yes, they were doing great. Keeping it light, they were failing miserably. *He* was failing miserably." "Yeah. She's ..." He couldn't put his panicked, wishy-washy feelings into words, settled for something inferior. "Amazing."

Dustin quit strumming and pinned Bryan with a guarded glare. "Does she know you're in love with her yet?"

Caught, Bryan rocked back on his heels. He walked on shaky legs and sat in the chair facing Dustin. "It's that obvious?"

"To me it is, but I've known you my whole life. I can't speak for Meg." He watched Bryan as he plucked something slow and mournful on the guitar, something that matched his melancholy tone. "You're not going home at the end of the summer, are you?"

Bryan leaned forward and rested his elbows on his knees. "Officially, I am. Between you and me, I'm probably not."

"So, make it official."

"I can't. Not yet."

"Why not?"

"I'm not sure how she feels."

Dustin shook his head and scoffed, his fingers seemingly playing of their own accord. "Unless you're spending the night somewhere other than with her, I'd say she feels the same."

"I think she does. My gut says she does. But we don't talk about the future."

"So, start talking."

Anytime they skirted close to the topic, Meg changed the subject. It wasn't just the elephant in the room, it was a parade of elephants in the room. "I've got to be smart. She won't believe I'm serious until I can prove it."

"Prove it how?"

Bryan stared at the apple in his hand, kept the nervous energy from his voice. "I've got an interview next week with the local high school. AP calculus teachers are in short supply. And they need a golf coach."

"Do you play golf?" Dustin asked in the same tone he'd have used to ask if Bryan rode bulls in the rodeo.

Bryan scratched the back of his neck. "I used to."

"When?"

"In college. I wasn't very good, but I can play. And if it helps me get the job …" He jerked a shoulder. "I'll figure it out."

"You'll get the job." Dustin nodded at Bryan, a somber smile on his face. "And then you can make it official. Good for you, man. Good for you."

Dustin's tone was at odds with his words and had Bryan questioning himself again. Leaving home, leaving his parents, his job and all he'd ever known. But all he had to do was think about Meg and Lily and he knew staying was the right thing to do—the only thing to do. Maybe if Bryan took a step forward, Dustin would too. "Any word from Tegan?"

"You'll love this." Dustin sneered and Bryan's stomach dropped like a weight in water. "She texted me about the trash."

"The trash?"

"Going on a month with no contact and she sends me this gem." He thumbed through the messages on his phone. "Hope you're well. How do we pay for trash pickup?"

Bryan looked at the apple, lost his appetite, and dropped his hand. "That was it?"

"Whoever said absence makes the heart grow fonder was lying through his teeth. Absence makes the wife go cold."

Bryan didn't know what it was, but it sure didn't sound like Tegan. Worry settled deep in his gut as he studied the circles beneath Dustin's listless eyes, the way the skin on his face seemed too heavy to lift into anything close to a smile. The irony of Bryan falling in love at the same time Dustin's marriage imploded wasn't lost on Bryan. "Honestly, you sound better than expected."

"What you hear is acceptance. It's over. My marriage is over." He jotted something on the paper and placed his hand back on the guitar. "I'm writing songs. Angry sad songs that are probably horrible, but it feels cathartic. I figured either I write about heartbreak, or I start fighting at the bar. Tim probably wouldn't take kindly to me wrecking the bar I sleep over every night."

"One insensitive text doesn't mean it's over."

"One insensitive text after weeks of no contact definitely means it's over." He gripped the guitar neck so hard the strings made a strangled noise. "I wish she'd just come clean and say it instead of dragging it out. I can't hide out down here forever."

Dustin's admission eased some of the tension in Bryan's neck. "Is that what you've been doing? Hiding out?"

"Where was I supposed to go when she kicked me out? A hotel? I couldn't stay there and go to work every day and act like everything was fine. Either way, I was a mess. I may as well be a mess in paradise and watch my best bud fall in love."

"Speaking of work …"

Dustin's sighed, the last gasp of a beached whale. "They keep asking when I'm coming back. I need to go back—I'm not making any money down here—but just the thought of it …"

"So stay," Bryan said. "You hate your job. You're finding your footing, making music, and making friends. If things go how I hope they'll go, I'll be here. This can be your fresh start."

Dustin started shaking his head before Bryan even finished. "There can't be a fresh start until I know where things stand with Tegan. I love her. Despite everything, I want us to be together."

"You sure about that?"

Dustin's eyes popped. "What?"

"You're angry."

"Of course I'm angry." He set the guitar down and shot to his feet. "She pushed me away with an ultimatum and doesn't have the guts to end it or even talk to me."

Bryan kept his voice and inflection calm. "Have you tried talking to her?"

The heat that rose during his outburst disappeared from his face. "You know I haven't."

"Quit playing games and call her. Tell her you love her. Ask what she wants. You can't live in limbo forever."

Dustin spun around and stalked to the window, stared out into the near dusk sun. When he turned around, his face was grim. "What about you?"

"What about me?"

"Tell Meg you love her. Ask her what she wants."

Bryan's face lit with shame at Dustin's serious stare. "I will."

"When?"

Bryan knew Dustin was deflecting and projecting, but that didn't make his questions any less pointed. "Soon. When I get the job—if I get the job. When the timing's right."

"Screw timing. If you love her, just do it. Don't overthink it, don't try and anticipate three or four steps ahead. Tell the girl you love her, and you want to be together. Limbo sucks, man. Trust me on this."

Forty

Meg looked out the store's front windows at the cloudless sky. She expected to see billowing rainclouds in the distance, dark, dismal clouds that foretold danger. Although the sky was clear, she'd seen the news, watched the radar, and felt the telltale tug in her gut. After a handful of false alarms, it was time to heed the hurricane warnings predicting a trajectory straight through the Keys.

She'd finally convinced Bryan to relax and stop panicking after every named storm hit the news. This time, if all the models were correct, the eye of this storm or one of its tightly wound bands would likely hit Key West with devastating results. She could no longer ignore what was staring her in the face. It was time to get the storm windows out of storage and familiarize herself with the flood barriers her dad had purchased after Irma.

She'd secure the store, pack her car, and with Lily by her

side, head north to see her mom and dad, passing the trip off as an overdue visit. Bryan would help her with the store. He'd help Eva and Barb and Tim and whoever else on the block needed assistance. They were a family on the island. For however long he stayed, Bryan was one of the family.

Some locals would stay and try to ride the storm out. Not only was riding out the storm a bad idea in general, but it set a horrible precedent on an impressionable young girl with the same daredevil tendencies as her mom.

Thinking of staying was useless. When he finally clued in, Bryan would never let her stay. He'd become protective of her and Lily; whether marking his territory or as a sign of his affection, everyone on the island knew he and Meg were an item. While it did her heart good to have a strong, attractive, caring man on her arm, it also meant when he left for home the whole town would know she'd been left behind. Again.

No use wasting time on what couldn't be undone. Meg had willingly let him into her bed, into her life, into her heart. She was in love for the first time ever. All the way in. The heart she'd fought so hard to protect was like Florida's barrier islands—in line for a direct hit. Everything she'd built—her independence, her confidence, her self-esteem—would be shattered and scattered in the wake of the storm. Just as predicted.

Eva popped her head inside the store when she spotted Meg. "I think it's time."

"I know," Meg said.

"Where's Bryan?"

"I don't know. Why?"

Eva looked at Meg like she'd lost her mind. "The storm windows are heavy."

"I'll call Bryan. It shouldn't take long."

"Hey," Eva placed her hand on Meg's arm. "They're wrong most of the time. We prepare for the worst and pray for the best. It's all we can do."

"I know." Meg tried out a smile. From the look on Eva's face, she'd failed miserably.

"What's really got you upset?"

"Nothing. I'm not upset. I just feel a little karmically challenged."

Eva quirked a brow. "Karmically challenged?"

"You know, I'm getting my feet under me with the store and with Lily and now this. It feels …"

"Too much?"

"Part of me thinks there's no way a hurricane will hit the island. And then part of me thinks, of course it's going to hit the island, because the hits just keep on coming."

"Mother Nature doesn't care if your luck's run bad. She just does her thing. There's no use questioning what we can't control."

Now there was sage advice. Too bad it was too late and not directed at the man who really had her worried. "You're right. I'm feeling sorry for myself and thinking of the hurricane as my own personal problem. I'm being selfish."

"You're allowed to be selfish occasionally. Now"—Eva nodded to the back of the store—"why don't you call that big, strong, man of yours and see if he can help us with the storm windows? He likes to feel useful."

Meg reached for her phone, thought of all the ways Bryan had been useful. Sinful, thoughtful, heart-melting ways. "That he does."

Her call went to voicemail. "He must be working or in the shower or something." He never avoided her calls—another reason he was too good to be true. "Let's take a peek in the storage area and see what we've got. I'm sure he'll call back."

Bryan exited the high school with mixed emotions. The campus was bigger than he'd expected. His research hadn't done it justice. The home of the Conchs was a sprawling collection of stucco buildings surrounded by palm trees and water. The interview went well, and the principal, a nice man in his fifties, seemed excited to add another man to the teaching staff.

Bryan had convinced himself switching schools was the right decision—the only decision he could make. While he loved his job, he loved Meg and Lily more. He just wasn't expecting the school tour and the interview to make the idea seem so, well … real.

Switching jobs, moving from Atlanta to Key West full time, was a big decision filled with lots of moving parts. Accepting the job he was offered meant quitting the job he had, breaking the contract he'd signed, and breaking his apartment lease—all without ever having even a hypothetical conversation with Meg about the possibility of taking their relationship to the next level.

His grand plan to sweep her off her feet with a job and a proposal suddenly felt like leaping off the peak of a mountain without a parachute. Blindfolded. With his hands tied behind his back.

Walking to his truck, he checked his phone. Two missed calls from Meg and no voicemail. He got in the truck and called her back. She answered on the second ring. "Hey. What's up? Sorry I missed your calls."

"That's okay. What are you doing right now?"

"Ahhh …" He pulled out of the high school, his mind as empty as the student parking lot. "Running errands. Why? What's wrong?"

"I could use your help with something. If you're not too busy."

He pulled out into traffic and punched the gas. "I'm never too busy to help. What's going on? Did you get a delivery or something?"

The pause and the measured way she'd asked him for help had the hair on the back of his neck standing at attention. "No." Her breathy sigh sounded like surrender. "Remember when I told you I'd let you know when to freak out about a storm?"

His heart took off at a gallop and he felt the thundering shockwaves in the lining of his stomach. "Yeah."

"It's time. There's a big one and all the models say it's coming our way."

He knew he shouldn't have stopped watching the news and keeping an eye on the weather. "How big?"

"They're predicting category four or five. It's slow moving, which means we've got time to prepare, but the longer it sits over warm water, the bigger and stronger it's going to get."

The people he cared about most in the world were sitting in harm's way. His doubts about the job, the future, and the progression of their relationship sharpened into a blinding drive to help. Like yanking the cord on a lawn mower, his adrenaline fired to life. "What do we do?"

"Secure the windows. Get everything off the floor. Pack the car and hit the road."

He peppered her with questions, one after the other. "Where to?"

"Lily and I will go to Orlando."

Lily and I? He absorbed the hit, pushed past. "Do you have a reservation?"

"Just made one at a hotel across the street from my dad."

He took a corner too fast, and his tires squealed. "Eva and Barb?"

"They'll go to Tampa with Barb's family."

"Tim?"

She paused, made a humming noise. "What do you think?"

"He wants to stay. Darn fool," he muttered. "Any chance I can change his mind?"

"You could try, but you'd be wasting your breath. Better to help him batten down the bar."

She sounded calm—too calm compared to the frantic way his hands gripped the wheel. "Are you okay?"

"Just focused on doing right now. I don't have time to freak out."

Admiration for her swelled in his chest. "I'm on my way." He hung up and dialed Dustin.

"Yo," Dustin answered on the first ring.

"Meet me at Meg's store."

"Hello to you too."

Bryan ignored Dustin's sarcasm. "Have you seen the news?"

"What's wrong?" His voice sharpened. "Is she okay?"

"She's fine. But there's a storm headed our way. They need our help."

"I'm there."

"I'm right behind you." He tossed the phone on the dash and scanned the bright blue sky. He'd do whatever it took to keep Meg and Lily safe.

Forty-One

Meg reached over the console and rubbed Lily's leg. "Lay your seat back and go to sleep."

Her eyes fluttered open. "I'm okay," Lily mumbled over a yawn.

"Go to sleep. You're making my neck hurt just watching your head bob."

Lily squinted out the darkened windshield. "Where are we?"

They'd been on the road for hours, a logjam of cars snaking north to safer ground. "Just above Miami."

"Where's Bryan?"

Meg flicked her eyes in the rearview and sipped her leaded soda. The caffeine added a layer of jitters beneath her tired exterior. "Right behind us."

It had taken two days to secure the storm windows at A Day's Wait and Blooming Glory, fortify their stock rooms, and set the barriers in place. After securing the store, Meg packed Lily's and her bags at the apartment, while Bryan and Dustin did the same after helping Tim lock down Westies.

True to his word, Tim refused to leave. "I survived the war. I'm not running scared from some silly storm."

Scared or not, staying was a bad idea. They'd all tried and failed to talk him out of it. Direct hit or not, they'd lose power and cell service. It would be days after the storm hit before anyone would hear from Tim. But no amount of persuading would change his mind.

The whole time they prepared to leave, Meg kept an eye on the storm with a pit of dread in her stomach. The track was freakishly similar to what Irma's had been. They'd skirted disaster with minimal damage before. Would they be lucky enough to do it again?

The normally six-and-a-half-hour drive took over ten with the evacuation traffic. With every mile north they traveled, Meg had more than enough time to obsess about the future—the uncertain future—and the man who'd worked his fingers to the bone helping her prepare to leave her home.

With only weeks left before he had to go home for work, Meg felt a bone-chilling certainty Bryan would see them settled in Orlando and make for home early. He'd be halfway there, and it didn't make sense for him to go back to the Keys when there might not be much left. His search for information about the barnacle seemed to have stalled out weeks ago, and there'd be less to find after dealing with the aftermath of a storm. It was probably best to end it now before she did something stupid and ask him to stay.

She'd gotten used to sleeping with Bryan. The way his arms would twitch just before he'd drift off for good. The steady rhythm of his heart beneath her fingers. Falling asleep in the cradle of his arms and waking with their limbs entwined.

How long would it take before she couldn't recall the details of his face? The feel of his stubbled chin? The wiry texture of his flyaway hair? The baby-soft skin of his back?

They pulled into the hotel at three in the morning, bleary-eyed and bone-tired from the long trip. Meg glanced at Lily, sound asleep in the passenger seat, and wondered how she would get her up to the hotel room.

Bryan met her as she stepped out of the car, stretching the ache in her lower back. He looked as tired as she felt, with heavy lids and dark circles above his five o'clock shadow. His hair looked as if he'd spent the better part of the drive running his fingers through the disheveled mass. "You okay?" he asked, rubbing his hands up and down her arms.

"Ready to crash." She indulged herself and snuggled into his arms, resting her cheek against his chest, inhaling his familiar scent.

He peeked into the car at Lily. "How long has she been asleep?"

"She finally conked out about an hour north of Miami."

He gave Meg a quick kiss on the lips. "Stay with her. Dustin and I will check us in. I'll carry her up to your room."

Meg nodded and watched him walk inside the lobby, his broad shoulders slumped with fatigue. She blinked away the tears that threatened. *Get it together. You knew it would end.*

Fifteen minutes later, Bryan carried Lily to their second-floor room and tucked her into the king bed. He went back down to the car to help Dustin carry up her suitcase and essentials from the car. As he was leaving for the rest of the night, she walked him to the door of her room, kissing his neck and snuggling into his outstretched arms.

"I can't thank you enough for all you've done for us."

"You don't have to thank me, baby."

Her breath hitched. He'd only ever used endearments when they were in bed. "I'm going to miss you tonight." She pressed her tongue between her teeth to keep anything else from escaping her lazy, sleep-starved lips.

He squeezed her tighter. "You're not the only one. The last time I shared a bed with Dustin, we were ten. I hope I don't try and spoon him, thinking he's you."

"Make a pillow barrier," she suggested.

"I doubt we'll have to. I'm so tired I probably won't even move." He held tight when she tried to pull away. "Meg, tomorrow, after you've seen your parents, we need to talk."

She swallowed past the lump in her throat, tried to keep her voice neutral. "I know."

He pulled back and cradled her face in his hands, lowering his mouth to hers, and kissed her like it was goodbye. In her heart, she knew it was.

Bryan blinked his eyes awake and stared at an unfamiliar ceiling. Reality came crashing down. He was in a hotel in Orlando. He turned his head to the side and saw Dustin, his hair a wild mess, breathing heavily into the pillow next to him.

Bryan pulled the covers back and closed himself in the bathroom, blinking against the stark white light and his reflection in the mirror. He looked like he'd been up half the night on a bender instead of driving in bumper-to-bumper traffic through central Florida. The whole ride when he wasn't talking sports or nonsense with Dustin, he'd thought of Meg and their future.

Admittedly, the storm had caught him off guard and derailed

his plans to talk to her about their next steps. What they'd find when they ventured back to the Keys added another layer of uncertainty to all that lie ahead. No matter what they found, he wanted a life with her—a life with her and Lily.

He simply couldn't imagine pulling up stakes and heading home to Atlanta without her and Lily by his side. Meg was home. No matter where they chose to settle, he intended to make that clear to her and to her family as soon as possible. Corey's sudden and unexpected death had taught him to grab onto happiness and never let go.

He showered and dressed and headed to the lobby for much-needed coffee. He made a cup for Meg and carried it up to her room, tapping lightly on the door. She answered with her hair and body wrapped in towels. The sight of her long legs and pink glistening skin woke him up more than the caffeine. "Good morning."

She held her fingertip to her lips and waved him inside the darkened room. "Lily's still sleeping."

He handed her the coffee.

"God bless you for this."

"How'd you sleep?" he asked.

"Good." She sipped and made a sexy humming sound that tickled his spine. "You?"

"Like the dead. What's your plan?"

"I talked to my dad. Visiting hours start at ten, so we're going to head over then. I'm just letting her sleep as long as possible."

Bryan smiled at Lily, her long limbs spread-eagle in the bed. "There's food in the lobby—waffles and yogurt and cereal. Want me to bring you something?"

"I'm good with coffee. I'll have Lily grab something on our way out."

He shifted his feet. "You want company?"

Her brows lifted in surprise, a look of sheer panic on her scrubbed clean face. "To see my parents? I …"

Too soon. He was pushing her too far, too fast. They had to talk first, then he could meet the parents. "It's okay. You haven't seen them in a long time. I don't want to intrude."

"I mean, I just never thought you'd want to—"

"Meg, they're your parents. Of course I want to meet them."

She stepped into the bathroom and waved him inside, closing the door behind him. The mirror was fogged from her shower, the air ripe with her lemon-scented shampoo. "They—my dad— he knows about my friend Bryan. He doesn't know you're Bryan Westfall."

"Oh." He couldn't blame her for not telling her parents about their connection. He hadn't exactly told his parents he and Meg were dating. "Right."

"It's not that I'm ashamed, I just didn't see the need to make the connection. I never actually thought you'd meet in person."

Ouch. "I get it. It's complicated to explain over the phone."

"Exactly. So …" She pulled the towel from her head, her auburn strands cascaded down her back, and she finger-brushed the hair from her face. "I'm not sure how long we'll be gone. What will you and Dustin do?"

"He's still asleep. You want me to wait for you to get some lunch?"

"No. Don't. I'm not sure how long we'll be able to stay, and I don't want you two waiting around for us. Have you seen any news on the storm?"

"It's skirting past Cuba now at category four. They're still projecting a direct hit in the Keys."

Dread and resignation settled on her face. "I can't believe Tim stayed."

"There was no talking him out of it. He's got a satellite phone and a weeks' worth of supplies."

"Is it raining here?"

"It just started as I was getting coffee in the lobby. It's going to get messy as the day goes on. You and Lily need to be careful."

"We will." She hung up the towel and wrapped her arms around his neck.

He tugged her closer and set his lips on her neck. He fought the urge to sink his teeth into her skin and mark her as his. "I need to talk to you, Meg. It's important."

She rested her forehead on his, a sad, almost fearful look on her face. "I'll call you when we get back."

Forty-Two

Bryan ate breakfast and monitored the storm. When he could no longer sit and watch the eye head straight for Key West, he hit the hotel gym for a grueling workout. After a shower and a check on the storm, he and Dustin played cards and went back and forth between the lobby and their room.

Most of the people in the hotel had evacuated from the islands that made up the Keys. Friendships were forged telling stories of what they faced after Irma and how they prepared for the hurricane headed straight for the homes and businesses they'd left behind. The TV never left the weather.

With no word from Meg as the day inched onward, Bryan felt empathy for Dustin and the weeks he'd gone without a peep from Tegan. He was losing his mind, wondering what Meg was doing, how far her mother had progressed into the black hole of Alzheimer's, and if Meg had told her dad about Bryan. Worry for her sat like a brick in his gut, weighing him down, yet making it impossible to sit still.

It was after five when Meg knocked on his door. He hopped up from the bed, yanked the door open, and enveloped her into his arms. She slumped against his chest as if she didn't have the energy to stand on her own any longer. Not wanting an audience, Bryan stepped into the hallway and let the door shut behind him.

He ran his hands up and down her back. "Where's Lily?"

Meg pulled away but didn't let go. Her tired eyes were puffy and red. "She stayed with my dad."

"How'd it go? How's your mom?"

She sighed, long and deep, and closed her eyes as she exhaled. "She's … she didn't know who we were." Her voice cracked as her eyes filled with tears. "She's like this empty shell. I had to get out of there."

Bryan pulled her back into his arms, kissed the top of her head. This was much of the reason he'd wanted to be with Meg today, to hold her up, to keep her steady. She'd faced it alone—by choice.

"I don't know how he watches her slip away." Her voice was like a frightened child's, shallow and small. "She's aged so much. They both have."

"Where's your key?"

She unzipped her purse and handed him the key card. He opened her door and led her to the bed. "Have you eaten?"

"We had lunch a couple hours ago." She toed off her shoes and sat, rubbing her stomach. "I'm not hungry."

"You're dead on your feet." He pulled the covers back and tossed her purse onto the table in the corner. "Lay down, baby."

She shook her head but there was no fight in her voice. "I can't. The storm. It's going to make a direct hit."

He reached for the remote, turned on the weather channel and lowered the volume. "Nothing you can do about it now." He shucked off his shoes and climbed onto the bed. "Come here. Lie back and rest."

"I can't." But she went to him willingly, curled into his side and rested her head on his chest.

He threaded his hands through her hair, massaging her scalp. Her eyes drifted closed.

"I have to go back and get Lily."

"Shhh." He lulled her to sleep. "You will. Just rest. I'll wake you."

"So tired," she mumbled before her breathing settled into a slow, steady rhythm.

He stayed as he was, holding her against him. The restlessness he'd felt throughout the day evaporated with her in his arms. He indulged himself by touching her face with feather-light swipes along her cheekbones and over her brows. She was so beautiful, so strong, and yet so vulnerable. He'd do anything to stop her from hurting.

She was fully asleep, exhaling gentle puffs of breath when her phone dinged an incoming text. Bryan extracted himself from underneath her, kissing her temple as he pulled away. Love for her surged through him with the force of the storm bearing down on the island she called home. He rubbed the ache in his chest and retrieved her phone from her purse. Her mother was getting agitated, and her dad wanted Meg to come get Lily.

Bryan texted a thumbs up emoji and stared at Meg, sound asleep on the bed. He could run across the street and get Lily and be back before she woke up. It would give him the opportunity to meet her dad and maybe build a bridge for the future he wanted with Meg and Lily. He needed the man's blessing. Of that, at least, he felt confident.

After scrawling a note to Meg, Bryan eased her door closed and then opened his door, nodding at Dustin laid out on the bed.

"Where's Meg?" Dustin asked.

"She's asleep. I'm going to run across to the facility and pick up Lily. If Meg wakes up, tell her I'll be right back."

Dustin motioned to the TV. "Storm's going to be close to a five when it makes landfall. A hundred and sixty mile-per-hour winds." The look he gave Bryan, the grim tone of his voice, reflected the fear they both felt for Tim and any others who'd stayed.

Bryan watched the radar loop, the storm swirling over summer-warmed seas. "There won't be anything he can do to save the bar against that kind of force."

"He made me feel like a wimp." Dustin ran his hands over his face like he was trying to wipe away the images he couldn't unsee. "I don't feel that way now. It hasn't even hit yet, and the pictures are brutal. Boats loose from their bindings, trees bending like straws in the wind."

"Pray for him. Pray for all of them." He jerked a thumb at the door. "I'll be right back."

Bryan jogged to his truck and started the engine, wiping the rain from his face and his hair. With the wipers on full blast against the driving rain, he made his way across the street to the sprawling facility. He parked under the awning and walked inside to the reception desk.

"My name's Bryan Westfall," he said to the girl behind the desk popping gum between her teeth. "I'm here to pick up Lily Holloway from her granddad, Steve Holloway."

"Oh." The girl's fingers flew over the keypad, and she scowled at the computer screen. "I don't see your name under the visitor's list."

"I'm doing a favor for Meg Holloway. She was here earlier with Lily."

"I see Meg's name and Lily's." She picked up a corded phone. "One second, please." She gave him the up-down with the phone to her ear. "Mr. Holloway? There's a Bryan Westfall here to pick up your granddaughter." She paused, repeated his name, and nodded before hanging up the phone. "He'll be right out."

Within moments, a tall, lanky man with salt and pepper hair extended his hand at Bryan. "Mr. Westfall. I assume you're the Bryan my girls keep talking about."

"I sure hope so." Bryan shook his hand, noted the same sunken, grief-tingedfeatures as his parents had. "It's a pleasure to meet you, sir."

"Steve." He motioned for Bryan to step away from the reception desk into the corner of the foyer. "You're Corey's brother."

His tone held neither question nor accusation. Bryan nodded, grateful he didn't have to make the connection. "I am."

"I'm sorry for your loss."

"Thank you, sir. I'm sorry for yours as well."

Steve studied Bryan openly over the bridge of his nose. "In light of what happened to Amanda, I have to ask your intentions toward Meg."

Bryan didn't hesitate or blink at Steve's boldness. He'd have asked the same in his position. "My intention is to marry her and be a father to Lily. If they'll have me."

Meg's dad rocked back on his heels, staring at Bryan while the crevice between his brows became a full-blown cavern. "That's a lot for any man to take on, much less a man grieving his brother. There's no room for guilt or obligations in a marriage."

"I can assure you, my feelings for Meg and your granddaughter have nothing to do with guilt or obligation. I love them. Meg's a strong, beautiful woman inside and out. She makes me a better man. She makes me want to be a better man for her and for Lily."

Steve stared, his expression guarded. As far as interviews went, Bryan had done better with the high school principal. "Is Meg aware of your intentions?"

He dropped his head, shame heating his neck. "No, sir. She thinks I'm going home to Atlanta in a few weeks."

"Are you?"

Bryan looked him in the eye, put all the conviction he felt into his words. "I'm not going anywhere without Meg and Lily."

Mr. Holloway said nothing, and his face gave nothing away. Bryan resisted the urge to squirm. "Meg might have something to say about moving to Atlanta."

"I'm not … that's not." Bryan stopped, sighed, kneaded the back of his neck. "I'm willing to relocate to the island for good."

Steve placed his hands inside the pockets of his loose khaki pants, narrowed his eyes at Bryan, rocked back on his heels once again. "If the forecast holds, there may not be anything left to relocate to."

The more her dad pushed, the more determined Bryan became to prove himself worthy. "Then I'll help her rebuild."

Wrong answer! Steve's body language screamed, his shoulders slumped and his expression sour. "Meg's never loved the island or the store the way her mother and sister and I did."

"It's her home."

Steve nodded as if conceding the point. "She's not prepared to lose her home, not after … everything."

"She's stronger than she thinks—than anyone thinks. And she and Lily won't be alone."

Her dad was unmoved by the conviction in his voice, staring at Bryan with a scowl on his face as if waiting for him to change his mind. "Life on the island isn't for everyone. Storms like this threaten every year. You can't live on Key West and not be prepared to lose everything with very little warning."

It was clear where Meg got her stubborn streak. "I'm prepared to lose everything but Meg and Lily. The rest is just … stuff."

"You say all the right things." Steve looked down at his tennis shoes before glaring back at Bryan. "When will you tell Meg of your plans?"

"I was about to when the storm hit." Bryan scrubbed his chin. He didn't need to explain Meg to her dad. He needed to explain he understood Meg. "Meg's cautious. I didn't want to scare her by broaching it too soon. Before she was ready to hear what's in my heart."

Steve gave a nod of approval, ran his tongue along his teeth. "And Lily? You're prepared to be a father to my granddaughter?"

Bryan chuckled, shaking his head. "I don't think anyone is ever prepared to be a father. Do you?"

Steve's lips twitched before stretching into a smile. "You've got that right." His smile bled into an earnest look of appeal. "If you make promises to Meg and Lily, you keep them. If you want them in your life, you must earn them. Every day of your life. The love of a good woman, for however long it lasts, is gold. You treat them like the treasures they are, and you'll have my blessing." He held out his hand.

The weight crushing Bryan's shoulders vaporized with Steve's firm handshake. "I will. I promise. Thank you, sir."

"Wait here and I'll get Lily."

Bryan watched him walk away with Meg's long stride. He

returned with Lily and a velvet pouch he shoved discreetly into Bryan's hand. "My granddaughter speaks very highly of you. When you're ready, you take this and ask Meg. It belongs to her mother."

Bryan shook his head. "I can't—"

"You can. It was Celia's grandmother's ring. Celia would want Meg to have it. Meg will know you have my blessing when she sees it."

Dumbfounded and profoundly moved, Bryan shook his head. "I ... I don't know what to say."

"Say you'll love them and care for them for the rest of your life."

He nodded, gripped Steve's hand, looked him in the eye. "You have my word."

Forty-Three

Meg woke alone in her darkened hotel room, blinking her eyes against the overly bright TV screen. Every part of her was tired. Her head, her muscles, her heart. The volume was too low to hear, but sound wasn't necessary. The images flashing on the screen told the story.

Trees snapped in two. Boats everywhere, some capsized, some beached, some loose and pounding against concrete docks. Debris littered the streets. Roofs lifted off structures. Abandoned cars floating in feet of water where streets used to be. All dark and grainy video. All before the eye had made landfall.

She reached for the remote on the nightstand and juked the volume only to have her nightmare confirmed. Her hometown would suffer a direct hit from a category five storm. Heavy with emotions she couldn't name, she fell back onto the bed and listened to the rain thrashing against the hotel window.

Where were the tears and the anger, ready to detonate like a bomb in her belly at the unfairness of it all? Instead of raging at the TV, at God, at the empty stillness of the room, Meg closed her eyes and imagined she was a fluffy pin cushion, waiting for the next needle to strike.

Where was Bryan? Why had he let her sleep so long? She had to get Lily and try to prepare her for the devastation she could barely believe herself. She sat up and looked around for her purse, spotting it on the table in the corner. She stood, draped the purse over her shoulder, tucked the room key inside, and went next door in search of Bryan.

Dustin answered, barefoot, dressed in lounge clothes, his hair sticking up in the back. "Hey," he said, waving her inside.

Meg stepped forward and the let the door close behind her. "Where's Bryan?"

"He went to get Lily. He'll be right back."

There it was—the next pin to pierce, jolting her out of her numb stupor. Dumbfounded and working toward angry, she fisted her hands at her sides. "What? Why didn't he wake me?"

"I don't know." Dustin sat on the end of the bed. "He said you were sleeping."

"He was supposed to wake me."

"What's the big deal?"

Meg struggled to get enough air into her lungs. "My dad's not going to let Lily go with a stranger."

"Hey." Dustin stood and faced Meg. "I'm sure he was trying to do you a favor. And he's not exactly a stranger. Your dad knows about Bryan. *Right*?"

Embarrassment added another layer of humiliation to the irritation flickering beneath her skin. Her gaze bounced from the bed to the chair in the corner to the ugly curtains on the window, anywhere but at Dustin. "Kind of."

"*Kind of?*" He gaped at her, a mixture of shock and disappointment in the angry set of his mouth. He dropped his chin to his chest, chuckling humorlessly. "You two deserve each other."

"What's that supposed to mean?"

"It means wake up, Meg. I know you're tired and worried about what's going on at home, but open your eyes."

She'd never heard him use that tone with her before, so bitter and shrill. "What are you talking about?"

"I'm talking about Bryan. The man you're sleeping with. The man who worked his butt off helping you and everyone you love get prepared for this storm. The man who drove half the night to get you to safety and who's been pacing the halls of this hotel while you were with your parents. Are you seriously telling me you never mentioned him to your family?"

Shame coated her stomach and shook her voice. "You don't know my situation. You can't understand the pressure my dad is under right now."

"I know your mom has Alzheimer's. I know your sister died. I also know there's a huge storm about to take out your home and everything he built from the ground up. I'm just guessing, but I bet he'd feel pretty good knowing his daughter and granddaughter are being looked after by a stand-up guy like Bryan. I bet he'd love to meet the man who, in his absence, has made sure you're out of harm's way."

"He knows about Bryan." The defensiveness of her tone sounded like rage. "He just doesn't know who he is or that we're anything more than friends."

Dustin narrowed his eyes at her, a mocking smile on his upturned lips. "So, your dad's stupid?"

Meg would have been less offended if he'd slapped her. "How dare you."

"Forgive me for being blunt, but as someone who's watched this whole situation come together over the last month, I think you need a reality check." He pointed at her face. "You're scared. You're going to blow the best thing you'll ever find if you keep reacting out of fear."

That it was true didn't matter. All that mattered was defending the festering, bubbling vulnerability he'd uncovered. "You don't know me, Dustin. You don't know anything about me."

"Maybe not. But I know Bryan. I know that man would rather die than see anything happen to you or Lily. And I'm going to tell you something that doesn't even need to be said. He's. Not. Corey."

"You think I'd have let him anywhere near Lily if I thought he was anything like his brother?"

"So, what's the problem?"

"He's leaving." The words erupted like tinder struck with a match and extinguished just as quickly.

Dustin only shook his head at her with pity in his eyes. "I guess your dad's not the only one who's stupid."

They were both under stress, tired and worried and waiting for news. Meg always wondered what it would be like to have a brother. Dustin's brutal, in-your-face rudeness was what she'd envisioned. "I don't expect you to understand. It's complicated."

"Everything worth having is complicated. *Life* is complicated."

"What do you want me to do?" Drained and unbearably tired, she scrubbed her hands over her face. "I'm barely hanging on right now."

He stared at her for so long and with such open curiosity, she began to squirm. "Honestly," he said, his voice a calm contrast to the storm raging outside. "I want you to fight for him."

"Fight for him?" It was her turn to use that mocking, know-it-all laugh. "Are you kidding me right now? *You're* going to lecture *me* about fighting for love?"

Her dig didn't even make a dent. "I've never been more serious or more qualified to offer advice. Fight for what you want, Meg—not for what you think is best for Lily or what you think is best for Bryan—but what *you* want. Dig deep and fight like hell. If he leaves ..." Dustin shrugged, but there was nothing casual about the gesture. "At least you tried."

Fighting for what she wanted felt like spitting in the wind. "I'm tired of fighting. I've been fighting—for Lily, for the store—and just when things start to feel a little under control, here comes a monster storm to knock me back and make me feel like a fool for trying. I'm not going to have a home to go back to. Bryan has a job and a family who need him. I won't be another burden for him to manage."

Dustin sat on the bed and looked her in the eye, licking his lips like he had a secret he was dying to tell. "Ask Bryan where he was when you called him about the storm."

"What?"

"Where did he tell you he was?"

"I ..." She rubbed the tension headache building behind her eye. "I don't remember."

"Think, Meg. What did he say?"

Her call to him felt like a million years ago. "I think he said he was running errands."

Dustin flashed an I-told-you-so smirk. "He lied."

"Why would he lie?" And what rabbit hole was Dustin leading her down?

"Ask him where he was."

THE LAST LAP

It sounded like a dangerous dare from a guy who knew too much and had nothing left to lose. "What difference does it make?"

"Trust me. His answer will make all the difference."

Forty-Four

Bryan pulled under the hotel awning and put the truck into park. He glanced at Lily struggling to unhook her seatbelt with the food bags in her lap. "Hang on a second and let me call Dustin."

"I can get it," she insisted.

"I know you can get it." He hit the call button. "But he needs to come down to eat anyway." Dustin answered immediately. "Hey. Lily and I have food in the lobby. Come on down."

"On my way," Dustin said and hung up.

Bryan unhooked her seatbelt and pointed out the windshield to the lobby next to the reception desk. "There are tables and chairs where they had breakfast set up this morning. I'll get the drinks and meet you inside." He got out of the truck, skirted the hood, and opened her door. She hopped out with the two bags fisted by her sides.

Dustin met them at the hotel entrance. "Hey, squirt." He

rustled Lily's hair. Bryan motioned him over and opened the back door. "I got a case of water."

"Good thinking." Dustin grabbed the water and led Lily inside the building.

Bryan headed back into the driving rain, parking along the side of the building. Without the umbrella he'd left for Meg, he had to make a run for the door, splashing through puddles and ducking beneath the steady flow of water streaming off the awning.

Like a dog who'd played in the rain, he closed his eyes and shook the water from his head. When he turned to walk inside, he found Meg standing outside the hotel doors. The look on her face, a mixture of dread and annoyance, had Bryan fingering the pouch in his pocket. "Hey."

"You should have woken me to get Lily."

"You were sound asleep. It's no big deal." But her voice and the stiff set of her shoulders said otherwise. Instead of closing the distance between them, he stayed where he stood, dripping onto the sidewalk. "I would have said it was worth it, but you don't look like you feel any better." He wrung the rain from his t-shirt. "We got food if you're hungry."

"What did you say to my dad?"

He ignored the accusation in her voice. "About what?"

"Come on, Bryan. Did you tell him we were a couple?"

All the helpless frustration he felt during the day watching the storm inch toward the Keys, waiting for Meg to return without any word from her, landed on his shoulders like a backpack stuffed with bricks. Did she have to sound so horrorstruck by the idea of her dad knowing they were together? "I didn't have to, Meg."

"Did you tell him who you are? Who your brother was?"

For someone who constantly underestimated herself, she

seemed more than willing to underestimate everyone else as well. "I didn't have to tell him that either. Your mom's sick, Meg. Not your dad."

Her haughty expression was more Palm Beach than Key West. "You think this is funny?"

There wasn't anything funny about the way she stared at him, her lips twisted and trembling with anger as if he'd committed the ultimate sin. But to Meg's way of thinking, he had. She exposed parts of her life to him on her timetable, and he'd broken one of her cardinal rules by pushing through her barriers without asking. Considering everything they'd been through and the ring that sat like lead in his pocket, tap dancing around the truth felt dishonest and cruel. "No. I think your dad is a really nice man."

She chewed her bottom lip and stared at him like she was wrestling with demons. "Where were you the other day when I called you about the storm?"

He could hardly hear her over the rain thrashing the metal overhang. "What?"

"You said you were running errands, but you didn't answer your phone. Where were you?"

He didn't want to open his heart to her when she was angry, and he was tired, and she'd put him on the defensive. "Why are you asking me this now? And why are you so upset? Did your dad call? Is it your mom?"

"I haven't heard from my dad since I left."

"Is it Tim? Has he made contact?"

She folded her arms across her chest, her mouth set in the same stubborn line as her father's. "Answer the question, Bryan. Where were you?"

There was no way she'd connected the dots on her own. "What did Dustin tell you?"

"Why won't you answer the question?"

She was on a roll, determined to push him over the brink. He was frazzled enough and irritated enough to let her. He stepped closer. "I don't think you're ready to hear the answer."

"Ready or not, I'm asking. And I'm going to keep asking until you answer." Those long, elegant fingers he'd admired pattering away on her keyboard and making lazy circles on his chest, tapped impatiently against her arms. "Where were you?"

Bryan looked through the window at Dustin pulling food out of the bag for Lily, talking to the family from Marathon with the scared kids and the husband who smoked too much. His best friend had planted this seed in Meg's garden instead of dealing with his own failing marriage. Bryan looked back at Meg and shrugged with a you-asked-for-this indifference he didn't feel. "I was at the high school."

Her fingers stilled. "What high school?"

"Your alma mater. Home of the Conchs."

She wasn't prepared for his answer by the way her fingers dug into her skin. "Why?"

He pinged her with a self-righteous smirk she'd more than earned. "Job interview."

"What job?"

"A math teacher job." He softened his voice when she jolted at his frustrated tone. "I'm a math teacher, Meg."

She was pale and fragile as glass, her voice barely a whisper. "You have a job. In Atlanta. Where you live."

"Which is why I'm looking for a new job." He stepped closer. "Where you live." Closer still. "Because home is where you are, Meg." He reached for her, smoothing his hands against her goose-flesh arms. "You're my home now—you and Lily."

Her lips quivered and her eyes filled with tears. "I can't ask you to move."

It was past time to empty his heart and deal with the consequences. "You didn't ask, and I know you well enough not to expect you to. I love you, Meg. I want to make a life with you and Lily. I want us to be a family."

She slumped against him, dropping her forehead to his chest. He would have let go and fished the ring from his shorts, but he wasn't sure she wouldn't fall over if he did.

"No one's ever loved me enough to stay."

Her choked whisper was his undoing. He cupped her cheeks and lifted her face to his. "I put off the trip to the Keys because I feared what I'd find out about Corey. Turns out I found you. I love you, Meg. I'm so desperately in love with you."

She gripped his wrists, her green eyes swimming. "I love you too. So much it scares me. But, Bryan. We may not have a home to go back to."

Hearing the words, seeing the truth on her tearstained face, made everything inside of him settle. Their future was still unsure, but he finally had the pieces. All that was left was to link them together. "Then we'll go back and rebuild. Or start over somewhere new. Closer to your parents. Closer to mine. Anywhere you and Lily want to go."

She did a very un-Meg like thing and jumped into his arms, wrapping her legs around his waist, and sealing her mouth to his in full view of the hotel. He took the kiss deeper, claiming what he could finally call his own. When they pulled apart and Meg set her feet on the ground, Dustin and Lily and a crowd had formed at the window, clapping and whistling. Meg ducked her head into this chest and groaned.

Bryan had already won the prize and given the group a show, so he had nothing to lose by pulling the pouch from his shorts and lowering to one knee in front of an astonished Meg. "May as well give them their money's worth."

"Wha—Bryan." She cupped her hand over her mouth.

He drew the ring out, held it up to her. "Your dad knows we're a couple and he approves. I wasn't planning to do this here without talking to Lily first, but life's short and plans have a way of getting thrown off course. So, what do you say? Will you marry me, Meg?"

"Are you sure?"

"Absolutely. You're my home, Meg. I found my home."

She lowered herself to the ground, so they were eye to eye. His Meg, his partner, his equal. "You think I'm stupid?" she asked, her eyes brimming with fresh tears. "Yes, I'll marry you."

He slipped the ring on her trembling finger and gathered her into his arms.

She pulled back, staring at the ring on her finger. "I wish my sister was here to see this, to meet you."

Bryan pushed the hair from her face and wiped the tears from her cheeks. "She's here, baby. They both are. And I think they approve."

Epilogue

One Year Later

Meg watched through the screen door as Lily jogged next door. Their new neighbor had a daughter Lily's age, a rambunctious yellow Labrador, *and* a trampoline in her back yard. In the days since they'd moved to the small South Georgia town they now called home, she and Lily had become fast friends.

Everything about their lives was different since the storm destroyed *A Day's Wait* and a large portion of the island where Meg grew up. Leaving behind the familiar was the hardest part, besides facing the reality of what was left—a flooded, uninhabitable building that would have taken the better part of a year to rebuild. But Tim was safe and unharmed, and Eva and Barb, in nearly the same situation as Meg, decided to relocate to Tampa to be closer to family.

Guilt threatened to overshadow the blessings of the past year. Guilt for leaving her friends and neighbors in their time of need.

Guilt for all the times she'd wished to run, to pick up and leave the island, the store, and her suffocating life behind. Thanks to the hurricane, she'd gotten her wish in spades. So many memories. So much history. All of it gone.

Even if her dad hadn't needed the insurance money to pay for her mom's continued care, the logistics of them staying were too complicated. Meg didn't have a job and the damage to the high school where Bryan would have worked was extensive. Bryan had a job in Atlanta, and it only made sense for them to relocate there until they figured out their next move. Uprooting Lily to a city where they knew no one added another layer of guilt. Starting over again was hard.

Looking around at the house full of boxes, she knew this time that starting over meant putting down roots and making a home. Meg wandered into the extra bedroom Bryan insisted she use as a studio until he had time to transform the storage building in the backyard to the artist's retreat he envisioned when they bought the fixer-upper house. The man had plans galore. She grabbed the scissors she used as box cutters and started unpacking her supplies.

"I thought I'd find you in here." Bryan leaned against the threshold, twisting the simple gold band on his finger.

She fingered the matching band on her own. "Thought I'd empty the boxes, try and make a plan for the space."

"Temporary plan. I cleaned out the storage building. I want you to come take a look."

"What do you think?" she asked.

"It's got potential." He pushed off the door jam, angled his head. "Where's Lil?"

"She went next door to play on Christina's trampoline."

His gaze zoomed to hers, his brows lifting suggestively. "A quiet house. How about we take a break, take advantage?"

She eyed his shorts and t-shirt smudged with dirt, shook her head. "Not until you shower."

He looked down at himself and up at her and started around the boxes. "Shower sex. I like the way you think, Mrs. Westfall."

Meg still wasn't used to her new last name, but she was getting there. "I'm not dirty."

"Honey ..." He pulled her into his arms, set his lips at the base of her neck. "We both know that's not true."

Bryan had proved himself a worthy and patient partner, putting up with her mood swings and sadness and lingering doubts—not to mention the teenage drama that came from his step-niece who was in every respect his daughter.

"Dad!" The shrieking call came from the front of the house, jarring Meg and then making her melt. Lily's shout, while frantic, was streaked with joy.

Bryan jerked back, pulled his hands from beneath Meg's shirt, blinked his unfocused eyes. "In here."

Lily appeared from the hallway, breathless and sweaty. "There's a huge spider on Christina's trampoline. I told her my dad would get it."

Not long after the wedding, Lily asked if she could call Bryan "Dad." He took his new title seriously. Watching her bloom under his love and attention was worth the growing pains of their new life as a family. Bryan Westfall had been worth the wait—for both Lily and Meg.

"How huge is huge?" he asked, an uneasy edge in his voice.

She cupped hands into the shape of an orange. "It's big."

"Ugh. I hate spiders," he whispered to Meg.

She laughed and patted his butt. "Go save the day, Super Dad. I'll meet you out back at the storage shed."

Meg went out the back door and spotted the pile of junk beside the storage building. Making that place habitable seemed an impossible task. But if anyone could do it, he could. Him and his endless plans.

The morning breeze fluttering her hair held a hint of pine from the nearby stand of trees, so different from the salty air of the Keys and the city air of Atlanta. Meg had loved the trees and hills of Atlanta. The colors and textures, along with Bryan's insistence, had coaxed her into painting again. But the culture of the city, so fast paced and frenzied, was too different for Meg and Lily to find their footing and truly feel at home.

Moving from Atlanta was a joint decision, but not everyone had been on board. Dustin grumbled as only Dustin could. He let up when they said he had dibs on their guest room.

Bryan's parents had welcomed Meg and Lily into their family with cautious optimism. Meg had come to like them if only for the way they treated Lily as their own. By the time the school year was over, having them around with their constant talk of Corey (she finally started saying his name) added another tangle to their time in Atlanta.

Her heart did a funny little whop-bop, watching Lily give her hero a hug for fixing the spider problem. Bryan had fixed more than the spider problem—he'd made them a family. Their life was messy and loud and complicated and so, so sweet it moved her to tears. She blinked those tears away as her husband walked back into their yard and joined her by the building.

"I know it's ugly," he said as he approached, a concerned look on his face. She must not have blinked the tears away fast enough. "Just hear me out."

"Just hear me out" had become his catch phrase. "Just hear me out," he'd said to Meg when Lily had gone quiet when they first moved to Atlanta, spending too much time alone in her room. It wasn't long before he'd talked her into the therapy that brought her back week by week.

He also suggested getting Lily involved in athletics. "Just hear me out," he'd said, going on and on about how much he and his brother enjoyed the camaraderie of team sports. Pretty soon they spent their weekends at the park working with Lily, and with Bryan's gentle coaching and Meg's constant praise, Lily played her first season of soccer. She was already signed up for a fall league in their new hometown and Bryan had volunteered to serve as assistant coach.

"Just hear me out," he'd said to Meg when he first approached her about relocating to a small city in the southern part of the state, nowhere near anyone they knew. Without any signs of regret, he'd said goodbye to his hometown, accepted a teaching job halfway between his parents and Meg's, and they'd bought a house and planned to put down roots. Those roots were shallow until they unpacked all their belongings and turned their house into a home.

He guided her inside, pointed at the roof. "Imagine skylights and bigger windows along the back and side to bring in the light." He motioned to the corner of the darkly lit building. "You can set your easel up there." He turned and waved his arm at the opposite end. "I'll build you some storage shelves along this wall for all your paints and supplies." He flashed his heart-stopping smile. "What do you think?"

"I think it'll be perfect. I think you're perfect." She stepped into him, into the place she felt loved and safe and free. "But what's the rush? With all the unpacking we have left to do, I didn't think you'd tackle this until later."

He set his lips below her ear and nipped her lobe. "I've got some plans for that spare room. Just hear me out. I'll tell you in the shower."

Of course he had plans. The man could hardly sit still. "We're going to *talk* in the shower?"

"Among other things." He pulled her out of the building, linked their fingers, and walked back toward the house.

Meg glanced over her shoulder at the trampoline, listened to the happy squeals.

"I fixed the lock on the bathroom door," he said, his voice as impatient as his stride. "And Christina's mom is making them pancakes." He looked into her eyes and saw all the love she felt reflected back at her. "Trust me."

That was the thing about love—the thing about Bryan. She trusted him more than anyone. He knew her heart. He saw her soul. And when tragedy struck, he'd protected everything she cared about. She trusted him enough to share the secret she'd only recently discovered. "I've got some news that might throw a wrench in your plans."

"Oh, yeah?"

She stopped him in the yard under the shade of the big live oak tree, the first thing she planned to paint, and whispered in his ear, "I'm pregnant."

About the Author

Christy Hayes is a USA Today Bestselling author. She grew up along the eastern seaboard and received two degrees from the University of Georgia. An avid reader, she writes romance and women's fiction. Christy and her husband have two grown children and live with a houseful of dogs in the foothills of north Georgia.

Connect with Christy Hayes online at
www.christyhayes.com

If you enjoyed *The Last Lap*, please leave a review at your point of purchase location. Reviews are the best way to hug the author!

CPSIA information can be obtained
at www.ICGtesting.com
Printed in the USA
BVHW030831090223
658199BV00006B/60

9 781625 720283